RITA MAE BROWN
& SNEAKY PIE BROWN

Sour Puss

A MRS. MURPHY
MYSTERY

THE *NEW YORK TIMES* BESTSELLING SERIES

It Takes a Cat to Write the *Purr-fect* Mystery

Don't miss
Mrs. Murphy's newest
adventure in

THE *NEW YORK TIMES* BESTSELLING SERIES

RITA MAE
BROWN
& SNEAKY PIE BROWN

Puss 'n
Cahoots

A MRS. MURPHY
MYSTERY

It Takes a Cat to Write the *Purr-fect* Mystery

Now available in hardcover
from Bantam Books

BANTAM BOOKS

ISBN 978-0-553-58681-7

US $7.50 /$9.99 CAN

50750

WHISKER OF EVIL

"A page-turner ... A welcome sign of early spring is the latest sprightly Mrs. Murphy mystery. ... There's plenty of fresh material to keep readers entertained. For one thing, the mystery is a real puzzler, with some subtle clues and credible false leads. ... [They] have done it again. Give them a toast with a sprig of catnip." —*Winston-Salem Journal*

"Rita Mae Brown and Sneaky Pie Brown fans will gladly settle in for a good long read and a well-spun yarn while Harry and her cronies get to the bottom of the mystery. ... The series is worthy of attention."
—*Times-Record News*

"Another winsome tale of endearing talking animals and fallible, occasionally homicidal humans." —*Publishers Weekly*

"The gang from Crozet, Virginia, is back in a book that really advances the lives of the characters. ... Readers of this series will be interested in the developments, and will anxiously be awaiting the next installment, as is this reader."
—*Deadly Pleasures*

"An intriguing new adventure ... suspenseful ... Brown comes into her own here; never has she seemed more comfortable with her characters." —*Booklist*

"Another fabulous tale ... wonderful ... The book is delightful and vastly entertaining with a tightly created mystery."
—*Old Book Barn Gazette*

"Undoubtedly one of the best books of the Mrs. Murphy series ... a satisfying read." —*Alabama Times Daily*

THE TAIL OF THE TIP-OFF

BOOKS BY RITA MAE BROWN
WITH SNEAKY PIE BROWN

Wish You Were Here
Rest in Pieces
Murder at Monticello
Pay Dirt
Murder, She Meowed
Murder on the Prowl
Cat on the Scent
*Sneaky Pie's Cookbook for
    Mystery Lovers*

Pawing Through the Past
Claws and Effect
Catch as Cat Can
The Tail of the Tip-Off
Whisker of Evil
Cat's Eyewitness
Sour Puss

BOOKS BY RITA MAE BROWN

*The Hand That Cradles
    the Rock*
*Songs to a Handsome
    Woman*
The Plain Brown Rapper
Rubyfruit Jungle
In Her Day
Six of One
Southern Discomfort
Sudden Death
High Hearts
*Starting from Scratch: A
    Different Kind of
    Writers' Manual*

Bingo
Venus Envy
*Dolley: A Novel of Dolley
    Madison in Love and War*
Riding Shotgun
*Rita Will: Memoir of a
    Literary Rabble-Rouser*
Loose Lips
Outfoxed
Hotspur
Full Cry
The Hunt Ball
The Hounds and the Fury

Sour Puss

RITA MAE BROWN
& SNEAKY PIE BROWN

ILLUSTRATIONS BY MICHAEL GELLATLY

BANTAM BOOKS NEW YORK • TORONTO • LONDON • SYDNEY • AUCKLAND

SOUR PUSS
A Bantam Book

PUBLISHING HISTORY
Bantam hardcover edition published March 2006
Bantam mass market edition / March 2007

Published by
Bantam Dell
A Division of Random House, Inc.
New York, New York

This is a work of fiction. Names, characters, places, and incidents either
are the product of the author's imagination or are used fictitiously.
Any resemblance to actual persons, living or dead, events,
or locales is entirely coincidental.

Library of Congress Catalog Card Number: 2005053595

Bantam Books and the rooster colophon are registered trademarks
of Random House, Inc.

ISBN-13: 978-0-553-58681-7

Printed in the United States of America
Published simultaneously in Canada

www.bantamdell.com

OPM 10 9 8 7 6 5 4 3 2 1

Dedicated to
Patricia Kluge and Bill Moses

Their many acts of generosity
go unheralded in keeping
with their sensitivity and kindness.

Acknowledgments

Ruth Dalsky dumped a cartonload of technical information concerning diseases and pests that attack grapes. It's the only time in my life I have regretted not taking organic chemistry in college. She proved a whirlwind of research as well as a cherished friend.

Lynn Stevenson, my neighbor, trooped herself out to local vineyards. She also made numerous phone calls for specific information to vintners. She was in her element because she and her husband, Gib, appreciate fine wine, but also Lynn isn't happy unless she's learning something or doing something productive. God forbid she sit idle. Nor would she take a penny for her considerable efforts. Kay Pfaltz, an expert in these matters, put together a carton of reds and whites for Lynn. Well, Lynn thought that was too much, so she wrote a check to the hunt club for my foxhounds. Lynn, you really are worth the money/wine! (And you're an original.)

Kristin Moses of Kluge Estate Winery and Vineyard helped Lynn in her efforts, as did David King of King Vineyards. Veritas Vineyards and White Hall Vineyards also answered questions. Those who go from the vine to the bottle, every step of this arduous process, are so happy to share their knowledge. Truly, it is a great passion.

Kaiser Bill, retired polo pony, feels strongly that Lynn Stevenson would not have been able to perform her wonders without his contributions. That horse lives like a king thanks to "Mom" Lynn.

One of the most unique experiences in preparing for this novel was visiting Chellowe, an estate founded in the early 1700s, near what is now Route 15, in Buckingham County, Virginia. Owned by Mr. and Mrs. Gene Dixon, this extraordinary place is being restored using all the original methods and, in most cases, materials. It has been years in the doing and will be some years yet before completion. Chellowe was the site of the first grant in the Old Dominion to create a vinery. Its original owner, Mr. Bollin, was also a poet. Perhaps the wine induced the Muses.

Mr. Lucius Bracey, Jr., provided prompt answers to my question about the disposition of bail money. In over thirty years, Lucius has always come through.

Should you become interested in any of the above-mentioned vineyards, some are occasionally open to the public, others are open year-round.

You can find out more about them and other Virginia vineyards if you go to:

www.virginiawineguide.com

I should confess here that I don't drink wine. I don't drink, period. I'm not an alcoholic who must avoid spirits. I never learned to like the taste, and as a youth, being varsity, I never wanted to risk getting on the bad side of Coach, which drinking would do.

However, I was born to farming and farm now, so studying the methods of cultivating the various types of grape, the necessary soil, sun and altitude conditions, provoked intense admiration for those people running vineyards. Farming is not for weakhearts anyway, but operating a vineyard is unbelievably intense in both labor, intelligence involved, and cold, hard cash. Next time you drink a good vintage, say a prayer for the person out there in the fields who started it all.

Ever and Always,
R.M.B.

Cast of Characters

Mary Minor Haristeen, "Harry"—Curious, hardworking, logical, she's almost forty. Having left her secure job at the Crozet post office, she's starting a new career in nursery stock.

Fair Haristeen—An equine veterinarian specializing in reproduction, he's finally won back his ex-wife. He's honest, extremely handsome, and, in many ways, more emotionally mature than Harry.

Susan Tucker—As Harry's best friend, she knows all her faults and loves her despite or maybe even because of them. These two were cradle friends and have been through a lot together.

Ned Tucker—Susan's husband serves in the state legislature, having been elected last November. He's learning the ropes and is in Richmond more than Susan likes, but she'll adjust.

Olivia Craycroft, "BoomBoom"—She's drop-dead gorgeous, another cradle friend of Harry's, although they've been enemies as well as friends. She's a good businesswoman, running a cement plant, and is now becoming fascinated with Harry's return to farming.

Alicia Palmer—A big movie star in the seventies and eighties, she came home last year, free at last to be herself. It took her a year just to detox from Hollywood.

Miranda Hogendobber—Harry's former work partner at the post office, in her late sixties. She's very religious but has moved away from the more-radical elements of her Church of the Holy Light. She will work with Harry once the crops come up, but for some of this volume she has been visiting her sister in Greenville, South Carolina.

Marilyn Sanburne, "Big Mim"—Fabulously wealthy, often imperious, very bright, she rules Crozet with an iron hand in a velvet glove. She has a good heart, if you can stand being bossed around.

Marilyn Sanburne, Jr., "Little Mim"—She's become her own person, at last, moving out of her mother's shadow. Becoming vice-mayor of Crozet (Republican) was her turning point.

Jim Sanburne—Husband to Big Mim, father of Little Mim, he is the mayor of Crozet and a Democrat. This certainly makes for interesting family discussions.

Deputy Cynthia Cooper—Observant, intelligent, loves law enforcement, she's respected in the community. She's a good partner for her boss.

Sheriff Rick Shaw—He tries not to become cynical. Cooper is good for him even as his Camel cigarettes are not. He's surrendered all hope of quitting. There are times when he could throttle Harry because she gets in the way.

Rev. Herbert C. Jones—Warm, wise, and observant, he is on call not only to members of his congregation at St. Luke's but to anyone who needs help. He practices Christianity and sidesteps dogma.

Rollie Barnes—Aggressive, driven, needlessly competitive, he's made a bundle in the stock market, "retired" to Crozet, and is starting a vineyard, Spring Hill.

Chauntal Barnes—Much younger than Rollie, she possesses the sensitivity and tact her husband lacks.

Arch Saunders—Passionate about making wine, he studied at Virginia Tech, taught for two years, then took a job in Napa Valley to learn as much as he could. The chance to develop his own wine with Rollie's resources brought him back to Virginia. He had an affair with Harry when she was first divorced.

Toby Pittman—Another brilliant graduate of Tech, he started Rockland Vineyards, a success. He's beyond competitive and probably mentally ill. But he is damned smart.

Hy Maudant—A middle-aged Frenchman who started White Vineyards. He brings insouciance as well as the depth of French knowledge of the all-important grape to his work. Toby flat-out hates him. Hy is quite shrewd about money.

Professor Vincent Forland—Diminutive, ready to lecture at the drop of a hat, he taught both Arch and Toby. Like many academics, he's so good in his field and pretty useless outside of it.

The Really Important Characters

Mrs. Murphy—Harry's tiger cat watches everything and everybody. She's smart but more critical, given the messes her human gets into. Mrs. Murphy is level-headed and a quick thinker.

Pewter—Harry's gray cat. She has a bit of a weight problem and does not appreciate being reminded of same. She goes along with Mrs. Murphy, often grumbling, because she lives in fear of missing something.

Tee Tucker—The bravest corgi in the universe. She puts up with Pewter's complaining. She and Mrs. Murphy make a good team. She does love Pewter too, if only Pewter would shut up.

Owen—Tucker's brother is Susan's dog. He possesses all the corgi qualities of brains, sweetness, stamina, and the willingness to herd anything.

Flatface—The great horned owl, female, lives in the cupola of Harry's barn. She slightly disdains the groundlings but recognizes they are her family, damaged though they are. Life without wings must be dreadful.

Simon—A possum who never saw anything shiny he didn't like. He takes anything broken or left out. He's timid, but he likes to show his treasures to the other animals.

Matilda—An old, huge blacksnake, she doesn't much like anyone but she tolerates them. Her comings and goings are determined by the temperature, and the chatter of the warm-blooded creatures can be irritating. Like Flatface and the cats, she is death to vermin and, therefore, highly useful on a farm.

Jed—Toby's donkey doesn't have much between those two long ears. Jed may be the only creature Toby loves and trusts.

The Horrid Blue Jay—Devious, beautiful, likes to shout in that most unmelodic voice of his, he lives to torment the cats. He also drops stones on other birds' eggs. He's an all-around bad actor.

Harry's hunters and broodmares—As it's spring, they're turned out, so they're not part of the story this time. The foals are healthy and happy. Mrs. Murphy especially likes horses. Pewter would like them better if they ate tuna or even chicken, because they often drop some of their food. She's not lowering herself to eat hay or crimped oats.

Sour Puss

"Mary Minor, wilt thou have this man to be thy wedded husband, to live together after God's ordinance, in the holy estate of Matrimony? Wilt thou love him, comfort him, honor and keep him in sickness and in health; and, forsaking all others, keep thee only to him, so long as ye both shall live?"

"I will," Harry answered in a clear voice.

The Reverend Herbert Jones, in his sonorous tone, then asked, "Who giveth this woman to be married to this man?"

Susan Tucker, next to Harry, said, "I do."

Fair, smiling, repeated what he had memorized. "I, Pharamond Haristeen, take thee, Mary Minor, to be my wedded wife, to have and to hold from this day forward, for better, for worse, for richer, for poorer, in sickness and in health, to love and to cherish, till death us do part, according to God's holy ordinance; and thereto I plight thee my troth."

Perched on the balcony ledge, Mrs. Murphy, Harry's tiger cat, and Pewter, the roly-poly gray cat, observed intently. Tucker, the corgi, sat on a bench next to Mildred, the organist.

"Finally," the dog sighed.

"They're right for each other." Mrs. Murphy had cat's intuition about such matters.

"They tried it once, the second time should be the charm." Pewter wished the ceremony would speed along, because she was eager to attend the reception. The extravagance of foods thrilled her far more than contemplating human rituals.

"If you think the farm runs along like a top now, you just wait until Fair puts his back into it. He's strong as an ox." Tucker had always loved the six-foot-five-inch veterinarian. The feeling was mutual.

"Does this mean we won't be sleeping on the bed? I mean, do we have to put up with their thrashing around and all that moaning and groaning?" Pewter cherished sleep almost as much as food.

"Why would it be any different now, Pewts? Flop on the end of the bed and when they're done then go up and sleep on the pillow," Mrs. Murphy replied.

"Well, if they're married maybe they'll be doing it more, you know?" Pewter considered human physical intimacy an irritation. Then she giggled. *"Or less."*

"Won't be any different, except he'll be more relaxed. He's worked so hard to win her back. He'll be happy. Harry really is his great passion." Mrs. Murphy watched as Herb blessed the rings.

"Is Fair her great passion?" Pewter cocked her head.

Neither Mrs. Murphy nor Tucker said anything. After long thought, Tucker finally responded, *"That's a hard question to answer."*

"*See, I don't think he is, even if she is marrying him,*" Pewter blurted out. "*Look at Miranda and Tracy. He's loony about her and she swoons every time she looks at him. I mean, BoomBoom and Alicia, besotted with each other. Cow eyes, you know. But I never see that in Harry.*"

"*Too rational.*" Tucker understood Pewter's point.

"*Oh, we've all seen Harry toss reason to the winds. Not often, granted, but she can lose her temper or let her curiosity get the better of her. Judgment flies right out the window.*" Mrs. Murphy, too, pondered Pewter's observation. "*She loves him. She wouldn't be standing there in that pretty dress if she didn't love him. She's,*" Mrs. Murphy paused, "*diffident. Our dear mother gets more excited about ideas, about building a shed or planting redbud clover than she does about people. She likes people well enough and, like I said, she truly loves Fair, but her passions aren't about people. But he knows that. He knows just what he's getting.*"

"*Guess so. They've known each other since before kindergarten.*" Tucker noticed Miranda wiping her eyes with a Belgian lace handkerchief. She also saw Paul de Silva holding Tazio Chappars's hand. He obviously was wildly in love with the young, talented architect. Alicia and BoomBoom didn't hold hands, but she saw Alicia give BoomBoom a handkerchief, as the Junoesque blonde was crying, too.

"*Funny, BoomBoom crying, since everyone blamed her for the breakup of Harry's marriage even though they were separated,*" Tucker remarked.

"*No one can seduce a man who doesn't want to be seduced. Fair was wrong and he paid penance. I say we forget the whole thing. Harry finally has.*" Mrs. Murphy was glad that Harry and BoomBoom had reclaimed a friendship out of painful circumstances.

"*Guess BoomBoom and Alicia can't get married, huh?*"

Pewter twitched her tail, massive boredom setting in along with a grumbling stomach.

"*They can, sort of, but the state doesn't recognize it.*" Tucker shifted her weight on the bench, which made Mildred Potter, the organist, pat her on the head.

"*Why do people get married? We don't. It's such an expense, a big public display, and it costs a bloody fortune. Can't they just pair off and be done with it? Think of all the chicken and salmon and tuna and catnip you could buy with that money.*" Pewter honed in on her passion.

"*This wedding isn't that expensive, because it's a remarriage.*" Tucker was getting hungry herself.

"*Ha. The reception is going to cost about six thousand dollars. Probably more once the bar bill comes in. That's a lot of tuna,*" Pewter said.

"*There's more than tuna at stake for humans. Marriage establishes paternity so a man isn't putting a nickel in another man's meter.*" Mrs. Murphy laughed. "*'Course, now with DNA, paternity can be established in ways that don't please all men. You play, you pay. They can no longer claim the baby isn't theirs.*" She paused. "*The whole marriage thing is so ingrained in society that they can't really do without it. Doesn't even matter if they have children. It's something you've got to do.*"

"*Like death and taxes.*" Pewter giggled.

"*Aren't you glad you don't have to go through all this rigmarole?*" Tucker sighed. "*I'm happy Harry is marrying Fair, but it is exhausting.*"

"*Who wants to be human? If there is reincarnation I'm coming back as myself.*" Pewter puffed out her gray chest.

"*My, my, don't we think a lot of ourselves.*" Mrs. Murphy slyly batted at Pewter.

"*Oh, and you'd like to come back as a caterpillar?*" Pewter sassed.

Mrs. Murphy lashed out, a real whack.

Pewter struck back.

"Hey, hey, you two!" Mildred cautioned them, because it would be a long tumble down into the congregation.

Just as Herb uttered, "Those whom God hath joined together let no man put asunder," the people gathered below were treated to a hissing fit of such volume that a few heads tilted upward. Harry cast her eyes to behold the spectacle of Pewter giving Mrs. Murphy such a swat that the tiger cat slipped over the side of the balcony, hanging on by her claws.

"Dear God," she sighed.

"Little pagans," Herb whispered, which made Fair laugh.

With heroic effort, Mrs. Murphy hoisted herself up onto the balcony railing. Pewter shot off the railing, hit the organist's bench with all fours, endured a reprimand from Mildred and a yap from Tucker as she leapt onto the keys, which produced a mass of discordant notes throughout lovely St. Luke's Lutheran Church.

She then soared off the organ as Mrs. Murphy, in hot pursuit, gained on her. Up to the last row of the balcony, down to the exit, thundering down the carpeted stairs, Pewter skidded across the highly polished vestibule floor, knocking over the lectern with the red leather visitor's book opened. The book hit the floor. Mrs. Murphy left a few claw marks as she scrambled over the book. Pewter then turned a ninety-degree angle, bolting down the center aisle of the church.

BoomBoom reached out to grab her, but Pewter eluded the bejeweled hand, as did Mrs. Murphy. The two crazed felines headed straight for the nuptial pair.

Tucker had sense enough not to stop either cat. She watched with fascination, as did Mildred.

"You're a good doggy," Mildred crooned between her laughs.

"*Yes, I am.*"

"*I will kill you. I will kill you on Harry's wedding day!*" Mrs. Murphy shouted.

"*Gotta catch me first.*" Pewter, realizing she was the center of attention, was loving the limelight, quite oblivious to the discipline that might follow.

Herb bravely continued, and as he was pronouncing Fair and Harry husband and wife he rolled his eyes skyward, imploring the Lord not only to bless those two humans but to bless the two cats in quite a different way.

Pewter ducked under Harry's train. Mrs. Murphy wiggled right under. Pewter then emerged from the back of Harry's train with such force that Fair held on to her as Herb ended the ceremony with "...that in the world to come ye may have life everlasting. Amen."

Before Fair kissed his bride, they both watched Pewter land on the altar. She crouched behind the large gold cross. Mrs. Murphy landed on the altar, as well, the two towering floral displays on either side of the cross swaying unpredictably. The cats fought each other on either side of the cross.

Fair whispered, "Honey, let me kiss you before they wreck the place."

He kissed her and she kissed back, and when they broke the kiss, they just laughed until the tears came to their eyes. By now everyone was mesmerized, and it was dawning on Pewter that as much as she adored all these eyes upon her there might be hell to pay.

"*She started it!*" Pewter bellowed.

"*I did not, you fat fat water rat!*" Mrs. Murphy aimed a precise blow across the top of the cross.

Rushing in from the back to the side of the altar were Herb's cats, Elocution, Cazenovia, and Lucy Fur.

"What are you doing?" Cazenovia called to the warring kitties.

"You'd better stop or there will be blue murder," Lucy Fur, a sensible type, admonished.

"I'll kill her for sure!" Mrs. Murphy, livid, agreed to the murder rap.

The three church cats positioned themselves in front of the altar.

Elocution very sweetly pleaded, *"If you don't stop, Poppy will get awfully upset. Come on."* She loved Herb.

Mrs. Murphy, her back to the congregation, turned to look down at the three cats. Then she looked at all the people. She'd forgotten about them.

"Holy shit!" She leapt down.

"See, not only did she start it, she's a blasphemer." Pewter rejoiced in this moment.

With three strides of his long legs, Fair walked up and scooped Mrs. Murphy, ears flat against her head, into his arms.

"Pewter, you get out from behind the cross," Fair commanded.

Harry lifted her train, joining her husband. "Pewter, come on now. We'll forgive you if you come off the altar. Remember, forgiveness is Christian."

"Do it." Cazenovia added to Harry's plea.

Pewter slunk out from behind the cross. *"I am innocent."*

"That's what they all say." Fair laughed as though he understood Pewter's meow.

Bride and groom, each carrying an extremely naughty cat, walked down the center aisle as Mildred hit the keys.

Miranda, the lead singer in the choir of the charismatic

Church of the Holy Light, said as the bride and groom walked by, "My delight is in the Lord; because He hath heard the voice of my prayer."

"Happy that they're finally married, honeybun?" Tracy held her hand.

"Yes, but my prayer was those two bad cats would get caught," Miranda replied.

The reception, held at the farm, exceeded everyone's expectations for a perfect April day. Small tables set up under the trees each had a lovely spring-flower arrangement. The food was truly superb, and Patricia Kluge and Bill Moses supplied all the wines from their Kluge Estate Vineyard. Over two hundred guests came to celebrate this glorious day. Even Mrs. Murphy and Pewter were forgiven as Harry fed them bits of turkey, ham, roast pork, and salmon.

She said to Fair, "No one will forget our wedding day."

He'd just given Tucker a whole sweet potato as people toasted the bride and groom. "I know I won't."

It was all seemingly perfect.

2

The heaven-sent warmth and sunshine of Sunday, April 16, Harry and Fair's wedding day, evaporated on April 17 as a cold front swept down from Canada, bringing glowering skies, a drop in temperature, and cool showers.

T. S. Eliot wrote, "April is the cruelest month." It is doubtful he had agriculture in mind when he penned that immortal line, the beginning to one of the most famous poems in English letters, but any farmer in Virginia can tell you he was right.

A sixty-eight-degree day can be followed by a blizzard. This Monday, while not blizzard weather, proved cold enough for scarf, gloves, Barbour coat, and Thinsulate-lined work boots, all of which Harry wore as she checked the mares and foals. The mares, bequeathed to her and Fair by a friend who died quite young, unexpectedly, each delivered beautiful foals. Harry could never have afforded the stud fees. She marveled at how correct the three fillies and one colt were as they nuzzled up to their respective mothers.

Most couples marry in June; October is the second-most popular month, and the Christmas season is also popular. Since Harry worked the farm and Fair, a vet, specialized in equine reproduction, April was the best choice. The crush of delivering foals at two in the morning abated for him; the press of farm chores remained relatively light.

Harry walked the paddock fence lines. So many horse injuries are fence-related. Checking the fences every day was part of her routine. The health of her animals came first.

Tucker trotted behind Harry. Mrs. Murphy and Pewter stayed in the barn, the excuse being that the mouse population had mushroomed out of control. The reality was that Pewter didn't like cold and Mrs. Murphy wanted a good gossip with Simon, the possum living in the hayloft.

Also living in the hayloft was Flatface, a great horned owl, and Matilda, a huge slumbering blacksnake.

In Pewter's defense, she did perch on the tack trunk in the heated tack room, peering down at the cleverly hidden mouse hole behind the trunk. Her whiskers swept forward in anticipation of seeing a mouse snout appear. So far, the mice, smelling her, elected to stay put.

In the hayloft, Simon, a kleptomaniac, displayed his latest treasure for Mrs. Murphy.

"Doesn't it sparkle?" He proudly pushed forward a little clear tube of iridescent sunscreen.

"Where'd you find that?"

"In the old bucket full of the natural sponges."

"Hmm, Harry must have dropped it last summer. She rarely uses sunscreen. She should but, well, she gets busy and forgets those things."

"How was the wedding?"

Mrs. Murphy declined to relate her participation in the ceremony. *"Harry was a beautiful bride. Just seeing her in a dress was worth the trip, and Fair wore a morning suit, which makes him more handsome, if that's possible."*

"He is a handsome fellow. How come they didn't take a honeymoon?"

"Ha," Mrs. Murphy laughed. *"Harry told Fair that every day with him was a honeymoon, besides which they'd been married before so why not just press on? I think they'll take a little vacation midsummer. Anyway, Simon, it was pretty good. I'm surprised you didn't come out for the party yesterday. Lots of little tidbits on the grass."*

"Too many people. And so many people are afraid of possums. They think I'm ugly."

"Nah," Mrs. Murphy lied. She thought Simon looked as he should.

"Well, is there anything left out there?"

"With Tucker and Pewter on patrol?" She laughed.

"Pipe down!" came a stentorian voice from the cupola.

"Sorry, Flatface."

The huge owl ruffled her feathers, looked down. *"Chatterers. I never met two creatures who could run their big flannel mouths like you two. I had a busy night."*

"Okay." Simon didn't want to get on the bad side of his frightening roommate.

"If she had little owlets, she'd be nicer," Mrs. Murphy whispered, her lustrous green eyes bright.

Simon whispered back, *"If she had owlets, then we'd have the daddy to deal with, too. They raise them together, you know. One owl is bad enough. At least she's a great horned owl and she sings so beautifully."*

"True." Mrs. Murphy admired Flatface's melodic deep voice, a dark alto.

"Think Harry's happy?"

"Yes. She's struggled so long over these years, you know, just making ends meet, and now she has his help, they've bought Blair's two hundred thirty acres, and those pastures are really good, plus she's reviving the old Alverta peach orchard. Rev. Jones bought the house and ten acres, so it worked out. Blair's farm was the Jones home place, remember? Harry and Susan are timbering Susan's land, the old Bland Wade tract. She gets a commission for that, and the girls have started their sunflower business. They're going to start a small tree nursery, too."

"What about the grapes?"

"Well," Mrs. Murphy lowered her voice as she realized she had raised her level to a normal tone, *"she's put in a quarter acre of Petit Manseng. A white kind. It will take about three years to really produce. She's being cautious. Too cautious, I think."*

With all the preparations for the wedding, Mrs. Murphy and Simon hadn't had a good jaw in weeks.

Simon remarked, *"Will be pretty easy to grow."*

"You know last fall when Harry was in such a crisis over what to do after leaving the P.O.—"

Before Mrs. Murphy could finish, a bloodcurdling scream of triumph wafted out the animal door of the closed tack room.

Simon, not the bravest fellow, shrank back into his nest in the hay bales. *"A dragon!"*

"A gray one." Mrs. Murphy, the bravest of all tiger cats, leapt to the edge of the hayloft, then backed down the ladder fastened flat to the wall. She burst through the animal door to behold Pewter, mouse between her paws.

"Triumph!" Pewter, mouth wide open, eyes wild, bellowed.

"Brute!" The mouse wasn't going down without a fight.

"Pewter, how'd you do it?"

"She cheated, she lied!" the little mouse, Martha, accused the cat in whose front paws she was securely imprisoned.

"Bull!" Pewter drew her up to eye level.

"You haven't kept the bargain," Mrs. Murphy reminded the mouse. *"So she's within her rights to snap your neck."*

"We are keeping the bargain!" Martha defended herself.

"Then why is there so much noise back there and why do I see you all running around?" Mrs. Murphy coolly surveyed the back of the tack trunk.

Many little noses were poking out of the rather grand entrance to their living quarters.

"Sugar high," Martha stubbornly replied.

"Oh, come on, there isn't that much candy left in here," Pewter said disbelievingly.

"You're right. It's the food from the wedding reception. First, remember all the preparations? And then goodies were left behind after the reception and dinner; do you have any idea how much we've eaten? That's why you nabbed me, Pewter, I can't hardly move."

"It's true, it's true," came the chorus from behind the trunk.

"Well." Mrs. Murphy considered the evidence.

The cats heard a conference. Within a minute, ten little mice came out from behind the tack trunk, led by Arthur, Martha's spouse.

"See," Arthur, robust, pointed to his stomach. *"Icing from the wedding cake. We're so full of sugar that if Pewter ate Martha, she'd be on a sugar high, too, and as I recall, cats don't like sugar."*

"True." Mrs. Murphy inclined her head toward Pewter.

"I didn't say I was going to eat her. I said I was going to break her neck. Crack!" Pewter gleefully threatened.

"Pewter, I think they're telling the truth."

Simon peeped through the animal door, the flap comically resting on his head. *"No bloodshed. Please."*

"Oh, Simon, for Christ's sake." Pewter, disgusted, let Martha go.

Contrary to expectation, Martha didn't scamper off. Instead, she lifted her small paw, the black claws glistening as she was a well-groomed mouse, and she patted Pewter's paw. *"We would never break our contract with you and Mrs. Murphy. It's a good deal, and we mice respect a good deal."*

"Yes!" the other mice agreed.

"All right." Pewter, terrifically pleased that both Mrs. Murphy and Simon had witnessed her prowess, was now magnanimous.

As the mice returned to their home, the cats and Simon heard Harry come into the barn just as the phone rang.

She hurried into the tack room and picked up the receiver. "Hello."

"Harry, I'm a mother." BoomBoom Craycroft laughed. "Keepsake delivered a mule."

"No!"

"Your husband has just delivered a mule. You know, I had hoped when Keepsake jumped her paddock last year that she had run over to Smallwood Farm and gotten bred by that son of Castle Magic, but, no, as I feared, she visited the donkey two farms down the road. Oh, well."

"Mules are pretty smart."

"I know. They can jump, too, so I'm going to work with my little fella and one fine day he'll be in the hunt field. Don't you think it will give Big Mim fits?" BoomBoom mentioned the Queen of Crozet, a superior rider, passionate foxhunter, and breeder of winning steeplechase horses. She was also rich as Croesus.

Mim could be imperious.

"She'll get over it." Harry liked the sexagenarian and especially liked Mim's Aunt Tally, who was closing in on one hundred.

The Urquharts, Mim's family, lived forever, it seemed.

"Is Alicia there?"

"No, she's coming over for dinner. She'll see him then."

"Name?"

"I'm going to call him Burly since he's the color of bright burly tobacco leaf. Burl, for short."

"Good name. Names are important, you know. I wonder about women named Candy or Tiffany. It's hard to imagine calling a woman in her eighties Candy. 'Course, it will be some time before the Candys and Tiffanys of the world achieve eighty."

"You come on over and see Burly when you can. Oh, almost forgot, I ordered Italian sunflower seed. You should have it in a few days. Thought you might try a few different varieties."

"Great."

After Harry hung up, she sang and whistled to herself. Most barns have radios blaring, but Harry loved silence, broken occasionally by her singing. She only turned on the radio for news or, more important, weather. Truth be told, popular music gave Harry a terrific headache, whether it was from the 1920s or current.

That evening, when she and Fair ate their first quiet supper as renewed husband and wife, they caught up on the day's events.

"He's a perfect specimen." Fair smiled as he related Burly's entrance into the world. "He's truly a little beauty."

"I'll swing by tomorrow."

The two cats and dog, having eaten, snuggled in the

sheepskin bed in the kitchen. Tucker didn't mind cuddling with the cats, but she had heard quite enough about Martha and the largesse of Pewter.

Fair, paper opened to his right as he drank a cup of hot green tea, peered more closely. "This ought to be exciting."

"What, honey?"

He handed her the paper, opened to the state section, pointing to a column with a photo.

Harry read aloud, "Professor Vincent Forland, a Virginia Tech world expert on various fungi, especially black rot, Guignardia bidwellii, a fungus devastating to winegrowers, will join a panel on agriterrorism." She paused. "Poor fellow, looks like a worm with glasses."

"You should see all the material I get concerning safety procedures in veterinary bacteriological laboratories. The other panel member is an expert on anthrax. Let's go." He took the paper back as she handed it to him. He again checked the photo. "Forland does kind of look like a worm with glasses."

3

As luck would have it, Fair got to meet Professor Forland before the evening presentation. He'd been at Kluge Estate to check on a mare, and Patricia Kluge and her husband, Bill Moses, asked him to please stay for the small luncheon that would include the professor and a few local vineyard owners.

Leaning forward across the mint-green tablecloth, Professor Forland held the guests at the informal luncheon spellbound. "We have knowledge that mycotoxins have been used in warfare and are probably being used now. Substantiating the information proves difficult, as there is much at stake politically."

"What? Arousing the nation, you mean?" Hy Maudant, a transplanted Frenchman, asked, his English enlivened by a seductive accent.

"Not just the United States, but verifying chemical-warfare attacks calls an entire complex of international relations into play. There are those who will deny that Iraq used them and those who simply sit the fence. Naturally when all is resolved the fence-sitter wants the best deal on oil and wants to rebuild Iraq." Bill Moses wasn't cynical, just realistic.

"But did Saddam use mycotoxins?" Toby Pittman, a former student of Professor Forland's, now proprietor of Rockland Vineyards, asked earnestly.

"I believe he did." The diminutive professor pushed his thick glasses further up on his nose, as they had a habit of slipping down. "On January nineteenth, 1991, during the Persian Gulf War, I believe an Iraqi aircraft penetrated our defenses and sprayed aflatoxin over Seabees and the Twenty-fourth Naval Mobile Construction Battalion near the port of Al Jubayl in Saudi Arabia."

As an undergraduate at Virginia Tech, Toby displayed such brilliance that he secured a teaching fellowship as a graduate student. His thesis adviser was Professor Forland.

After completing his Ph.D., Toby assumed he would start as a lecturer to undergraduates. His classmate, Arch Saunders, not as gifted as Toby in Toby's estimation, also was awarded his Ph.D.

When no offer to stay on at Tech was forthcoming, Toby approached his adviser, who told him, truthfully, there was a budget crunch. What Professor Forland didn't tell him was that after working closely with Toby for three years, he felt the young man lacked mental stability.

When Toby found out, a few days after he'd packed up, that Arch Saunders was offered the position, he was beside himself. Two years later, Arch left to work at a large vineyard in Napa Valley. Somehow, that seemed like another slap in the face to Toby. Arch repudiated what he, himself, wanted.

Out on his own, Toby worked like a dog to make a success of his vineyard. He often wondered what his life would have been like if he'd been given the job at Tech along with a regular paycheck.

"I'll spare you the denials and the subsequent explanations by our government." Professor Forland tenaciously kept on his subject. "Perhaps what threw off authorities about this event, what led to denials, was the fact that our intelligence people were still back in the mustard gas or anthrax stage of chemical warfare. How could they admit they hadn't kept pace with what Saddam was really doing, which was developing various toxic substances in dizzying array?" Professor Forland shrugged, then continued. "But the fact remains that fungal toxins are easier to produce than anyone can contemplate without feeling deeply depressed."

"How easy?" Rollie Barnes, rich and aggressive, had been invited to the small gathering because of his large plans for Spring Hill Vineyards. He betrayed his nervousness by cracking his knuckles under the table.

Accompanying Rollie was his newly hired vineyard manager and partner, Arch Saunders. It seemed to Toby that Arch had come back from California to taunt him.

Fair was polite to Arch and vice versa, but neither man warmed to the other. When Harry and Fair divorced, she'd enjoyed a brief affair with the outgoing, good-looking Arch. He fell hard. She didn't.

Arch burned gas driving back and forth from Blacksburg to Crozet. When Harry broke off the affair, he resigned his position and burned more gas hauling to California. He flourished there, learning even more about soil, grapes, sunshine, and rain and how they combine to form magic in a glass. Arch steered clear of entanglements, which may have been a good thing since he had so much to soak up.

He had returned to Crozet only two weeks ago.

"A bright student of chemistry, of agriculture, could figure this out. Now, figuring it out means you have to assemble the laboratory to produce the mycotoxins. Still, the knowledge is well within the grasp of a good student." Professor Forland's bushy eyebrows darted upward. "The trichothecene mycotoxins are fungal toxins. The molds attack corn, barley, rye, oats, millet, even straw and hay. If a bright soul had access to lab equipment or the money and determination to build his or her own lab, he could distill the trichothecene mycotoxins from the mold. A lethal dose for humans need only be from three to thirty-five milligrams, depending on the severity of the toxin. For instance, T-2 is the most potent. A ridiculously low dose would kill someone. Unfortunately not without prolonged agony."

"Has this happened?" Fair thought it revolting that so much of human intelligence was harnessed to produce pain instead of alleviating it.

"Yes, I think so. You can't lock up knowledge. It's been tried over the centuries and, sooner or later, it leaks out." Professor Forland leaned back in his chair as dessert was served. "Can I prove other nations have used chemical attacks in the last twenty years? Not conclusively. Do I believe Saddam deployed them when he was in power; do I believe the former Soviet Union used chemical warfare in Chechnya? I do." The professor compressed his thin lips until they disappeared.

Toby Pittman spoke up, eager to shine, especially with Arch present. "There was a case in 1944 when thirty percent of the population of the Orenburg district near Siberia came down with sickness because they ate tainted food. It wasn't chemical warfare, just moldy grain. I think it was alimentary toxic aleukia, or ATA."

Professor Forland smiled indulgently at Toby. "I commend you for remembering after all these years."

Hy Maudant, no fan of the intense Toby, nor the more congenial Arch for that matter, piped up, "Ah, well, I can see you covered a lot of ground in your classes."

"Well, I did, and as you have occasionally asked for my monographs, Mr. Maudant," Professor Forland pointed his finger good-naturedly at Hy, "you know that we study fungi and insects as part of our preparation to go to war for the health of the grape."

"Which brings us back to our original table talk, the health of the grape." Bill genially prodded them, although he, too, was fascinated with this discussion about chemical warfare.

"Before we get back to that, Professor, how many countries have developed chemical warfare using fungus?" Rollie found himself morbidly curious.

"Obviously Iraq, but really they benefitted from the work of the former Soviet Union, work that began in the 1930s. It's reasonable and will someday be proven beyond contest that any client state of the Soviet Union's had access to the substances, and even to the scientists who produced them. That means that the communist forces in Vietnam, Laos, and Cambodia as well as Afghanistan used them on insurgents. It will all come out in the wash, as they say, but the victims remain victims, and the dead remain safely dead."

"What about us?" Fair raised a skeptical eyebrow.

"Meaning?" Rollie was wary of Fair because he was blond and handsome; Rollie was neither.

Arch prudently kept quiet, letting Rollie talk. He glanced once at his old classmate Toby when Toby rolled his eyes. Toby thought Rollie a perfect ass and Arch a fool for going into business with him.

"What have we developed?" Fair replied. "I doubt we've been twiddling our thumbs."

"We are advanced in these matters, but exercising restraint. That's the policy." Professor Forland sounded unconvincing.

"Meaning we haven't sprayed Al-Wherever with mycotoxins?" Fair thought about the animals who suffered for these killing agents and devoutly wished the leaders who could be so cruel to man and beast were sprayed themselves.

"No, we have exercised restraint," Professor Forland repeated.

"I find that hard to believe. It seems that if men have a toy, a weapon, sooner or later they have to use it." Patricia, who had quietly taken all this in, spoke at last.

"History would support your thesis." The professor smiled amiably at his hostess.

"Is there no vaccination against these bioweapons?" Bill asked.

"No vaccination exists against mycotoxins. There is a vaccination for anthrax and for botulism toxin but none for these mycotoxins." Professor Forland reached for wine, the Pinot Gris with a seven percent Riesling, a product of Hy's vineyards. He tasted the liquid, smiling broadly. "Fortunately, our grapes are not used for any such nefarious purposes."

"But couldn't it be done? Couldn't some of the fungi that attack grapes be used for chemical warfare?" Fair wondered.

"Yes. Any fungus could potentially have a lethal application if reduced to its most potent form, but the molds that attack the grain crops are available, the technology has been around for decades. There's no need to besmirch our beautiful grapes, our thriving viticulture, with such a dreadful misuse of our knowledge."

"Having said that, Professor, what is the health of our vines?" Bill was determined to bring them back on course.

"So far so good." The professor held up his glass, nodding his head toward Hy. "Very good, I might add."

"A modest effort." Hy smiled. "I'll be most interested in your opinion," he swept his eyes over the others, soliciting their opinions, too, "of my estate mix—that's what Fiona and I call it." He mentioned his wife, whom he loved deeply without feeling the need to be faithful. "We age it in French oak. It's my baby." He inhaled deeply, then smiled again at Patricia. "You've had success with your Simply Red."

"Cabernet Sauvignon, Merlot, and Cabernet Franc." Bill happily supplied the information.

"We thought about using casks from Hungary but decided against it." Patricia exhaustively researched the different properties of oak, even hickory, from around the world.

Arch listened pensively, then said, "I was down in North Carolina last week visiting an old friend who sticks to Concord grapes"—this made the others smile, since they considered the Concord lowly—"and he swears the sharpshooter is becoming cold-resistant."

"We'll see about that!" Professor Forland's mouth snapped shut at the mention of the insect pest. "That would be like the bubonic plague to grapes." He frowned. "In the thirties, the sharpshooter destroyed the vines of entire states. A very nasty customer."

Toby, happy to contradict Arch, however, said slightingly, "It can't happen. It would have to mutate."

"Or be genetically altered." Professor Forland stared into his wineglass. "That would take a twisted genius."

"Let's not yell before we're bitten, gentlemen." Bill interjected a note of color. "I fear late frosts more than the bugs."

"Indeed," Hy replied.

Patricia lifted the mood. "You know, I was reading the other day about resveratrol, which is an antioxidant that helps prevent heart attacks and cancer, too. Red wine is the best medicine. Pinot Noir contains 5.01 milligrams per liter. We should market our wines using this information. Think of it as a little medical pizzazz."

"Ah." Hy liked this. "What about Beaujolais?"

"It's got 3.55 milligrams per liter," Patricia quickly replied.

"You read carefully." Professor Forland was impressed. "Cabernet Sauvignon from Chile contains 1.56 milligrams of resveratrol per liter, yet Cabernet Sauvignon from California contains only .99 milligrams per liter. The medley—the magic of soil, sun, temperature, elevation, drainage, and the skill of the vintner—can never be quantified."

"But we can taste it," Arch added.

"Indeed." Hy sounded self-satisfied.

"To the vine." The professor toasted them all.

4

"...delivery." Professor Sidney Jenkins finished his remarks concerning bacteriological agents via cattle.

He followed Professor Forland, who listened with great interest. "If I might ask a question before the audience does. You've detailed how bacteria and viruses can be developed in labs and even how they can be delivered. But what do you think are the chances our cattle will be infected?"

Inclining his balding dome, the fortyish Professor Jenkins said, "Highly unlikely. Terrorists can strike more fear and disruption into our system if they aim directly for humans."

Rita Nicolas, former head of the Virginia Angus Association, raised her hand and was recognized. "While I agree, Professor Jenkins, infecting even a few thousand beef cattle would create a negative economic climate for cattlemen immediately."

"Yes, and that is one of their goals—not just to harm

cattlemen, but to bleed us dry, if you will." Professor Jenkins nodded.

The audience, standing room only, contained soybean farmers, cattlemen, poultry farmers, and other interested parties. Local doctors and nurses had also turned out in large numbers.

All the large vineyards were represented: Kluge Estate, White Hall Vineyards, Prince Michel Vineyards, Veritas Vineyards, King Family, Mountain Cove, Rockland Vineyards, White Vineyards, Spring Hill, and many others.

Dr. Donald Richardson, a leading breeder of polled Herefords, a gorgeous type of cattle bred without horns, asked, "Are there protocols in place should an outbreak occur in cattle?"

"Yes, Dr. Richardson," Professor Jenkins acknowledged the dermatologist with whom he'd spent many an interesting time at various polled Hereford conferences and auctions, "the problem is, we really won't know how effective they are until we are under siege."

"What are the chances of grapes being tainted?" a tiny woman asked Professor Forland.

"I would think terrorists would be much more successful if they destroyed hops," he replied.

This drew a laugh from the audience, since beer drinkers far outnumbered wine drinkers nationally.

Arch Saunders, a slight potbelly growing on his tall frame, stood up and said, "Professor Forland, you've discussed fungus and virus as agents. Are there other ways to kill crops, any crops, outside those you mentioned?"

Professor Forland pushed his large black-framed glasses to the bridge of his short nose. "There are. I hasten to add, they are not my expertise, but a casual knowledge leads me to believe that our enemies have access to Agent Orange, and to various other types of defoliants. As Professor Jenkins has reminded us, it's not access to these substances that's the real issue. Face it, they have them. The real issue is, can they deliver these agents where they will create the most harm? Unlike Professor Jenkins, I think they can. Let me modify that. I think they can create chaos to vegetation, to crops. Perhaps it is more difficult to infect or kill enough stock. Certainly Professor Jenkins would know far better than I, but in terms of, say, corn, it's not that impossible or even unthinkable if you have determined, well-trained people. We've been concentrating on mycotoxin contaminants, but let's reflect on our own history: the boll weevil." He paused as his audience sat utterly silent. "Insects are easy to disperse, they reproduce at a rapid rate, therefore they spread at a rapid rate."

Hy Maudant quickly spoke. "Indeed, Professor, but each insect has an Achilles heel. As you know, the sharpshooter," he cited the terrible pest to grapes grown south of Virginia, "can't endure frost. So South Carolina can't grow the type of grapes we can here in Virginia. We're safe. Any insect that would be unleashed could be stopped fairly quickly once you identified the vulnerability."

"Correct." Professor Forland pursed his lips. "Unless, monsieur," he acknowledged Hy's origins, to the delight of the audience, "the insect has been genetically altered."

"Can't do it," Toby Pittman called out.

Professor Forland replied, "If not today then in some not-too-distant tomorrow."

"We do know that insects as well as viruses become adaptive." Professor Jenkins addressed the issue. "Look at how the protein shell of the AIDS virus mutates. And a more virulent AIDS strain developed, possibly in response to the drugs. It's one of the reasons, to date, that no effective vaccine has been developed. All that can be done now is to try to limit the virus once a human is infected."

"What are you saying exactly?" Big Mim wanted it in plain English, although she was capable of understanding what they were saying. She also knew many people would be embarrassed to ask for that. She was above embarrassment.

"I'm saying it is possible to create a supervirus. It is possible to create a bacteria resistant to conventional treatments. It is also possible to develop a superinsect." Professor Jenkins ran his hand over his dome.

"Has it been done?" Fair finally spoke.

"Nature is already doing it," Professor Jenkins flatly stated.

Emily Schilling, who specialized in exotic breeds of chickens, raised her hand, was acknowledged, and said only two words, "Avian influenza."

Professor Jenkins audibly exhaled. "H5N1. Julie Gerberding, Director of the U.S. Centers for Disease Control and Prevention in Atlanta, said in 2005 that there is a real risk of avian influenza—bird flu—transforming into a global threat comparable to the great influenza epidemic of 1918, which killed between twenty and forty million people."

The whole audience gasped as one.

Professor Forland added, "I believe Shigeru Ome, the World Health Organization regional director, was even more dolorous in his pronouncements. And if we know anything about virii, we know H5N1 will evolve, as well. There may well be H5N2s, etc."

Professor Jenkins nodded in agreement. "Rural southeast Asia lacks the means to halt the potential threat. It's spread by poultry traders and unfortunately has been found in wild birds in China.

"Consider these two factors quite apart from the social disorganization caused by wars, tidal waves, the Khmer Rouge, etc. The first factor is that chickens are used as currency in Cambodia for many rural people. The second factor is it's one of their few affordable sources of protein. The third and most disturbing factor is that chickens die when infected with H5N1. Waterfowl do not. Ducks calmly go about their business, seemingly uninfected, but they spread the virus through their droppings."

Jim Sanburne, mayor of Crozet, asked, "Then what triggers an epidemic?"

Both Professor Jenkins and Professor Forland simultaneously answered, "Opportunity."

The two men looked at each other, smiled, then Professor Jenkins elaborated. "To date, the people who have died from H5N1 have handled infected or dead chickens or have handled human corpses. Within a few days of contact, the person develops a fever, coughs violently. They die in about ten days, and the percentage of those who die once infected is a very high seventy-two percent."

Another collective gasp in the room prompted Professor Forland to soothingly amend Professor Jenkins's statements. "But the virus doesn't easily spread from birds to humans or humans to humans. You must have direct physical contact."

"True," Professor Jenkins said, then added more gloom. "But each time H5N1 finds a human host it has an opportunity to evolve into a more communicable form."

"Is there a vaccine?" Big Mim inquired sensibly.

"The French have manufactured a vaccine. Sanofi-Aventis SA is the company responsible. We are testing it here. The British are stockpiling Tamiflu. It's proven effective.

"Obviously, tracking human cases is a top priority, but

the areas where the outbreaks have occurred make that extremely difficult," Professor Jenkins finished.

"Could terrorists harness H5N1?" Fair asked.

"If it evolves into a more communicable disease, I think they could. The delivery would be easy. Send infected people into major cities before those people show signs of the disease. That gives them maybe a two-day window." Professor Jenkins folded his hands together.

"That's monstrous!" Hy blurted out. "They would deliberately infect a man or woman and deliver them to Paris or London or New York?!"

"Hy," Professor Forland calmly replied, "they flew stolen commercial airliners into the Pentagon and the Twin Towers. They've killed people in London's subway and on a bus, as well. The terrorists considered themselves holy suicides. Why would human time bombs, if you will permit the description, be any different? They would willingly die of the Asian bird flu."

"So we'd better stockpile flu shots, too." Jim thought of his responsibility to Crozet.

"Remember the last flu-shot shortage in 2004?" Harry felt as uneasy as everyone else.

"Yes," Professor Forland grimly replied.

Professor Jenkins shifted in his seat. "Let us remember that biological warfare has been with us since siege warfare. Besiegers would toss decayed corpses over the town walls in the hopes of spreading contagion or fouling the water supply."

"And let us not forget that Lord Amherst, for whom Amherst College is named, gave blankets to the Native Americans that carried the smallpox virus for which they had no resistance." Professor Forland shook his head in resigned disgust. "Smallpox and anthrax are always a danger."

"You're saying terrorists could break in to labs and use our own developments against us the same way they used commercial airplanes." Harry cut right to it.

"It is possible," Professor Jenkins conceded, "but why break in to our labs when they can use their own? They have them."

Professor Forland quickly interjected, "Our labs currently investigating such possibilities enjoy security. The problem is if some doctor or technician goes off on their own, a Unabomber of agriculture. That person could cause considerable distress, because we don't think of one of our own behaving in such a fashion."

"He's right. Our attention, thanks to the media, is focused on Muslim terrorists, on bombs, radiation, anthrax. Those are immediately understandable and, I guess, exciting in a way. Agriculture is only exciting if you're a farmer. Let's face it, city dwellers wouldn't know a boll weevil if they saw it, and most of them couldn't tell the difference between tent caterpillars and a yellow swallowtail-butterfly caterpillar. We aren't on their radar screen, but they all demand cheap food," Pittman sarcastically said.

"Which makes it more dangerous, because they aren't prepared," Aunt Tally piped up, her voice still strong and clear.

"Well—yes," Professor Jenkins agreed. "Many of you remember when Dutch Elm disease swept the East Coast. People in big cities saw the trees die but it didn't register, in any way at all, that this would compromise oxygen. Think of it, that many trees dying in that short a time span means there is less photosynthesis. Less oxygen is being produced. Therefore pollution in the big cities becomes more pronounced. These basics do not occur to people who work in buildings where the windows don't open." He said this with a half smile, but it was obvious the ignorance distressed him. "Nor did they replenish their trees. While industry and cars cause pollution, removing trees exacerbates the problem."

"Do either of you think we are more in danger from an American crackpot than a true terrorist?" Tracy Raz, an ex-Army ex-CIA man, asked.

"Who knows?" Professor Jenkins threw up his hands.

"I'll take that on." Professor Forland became animated. "We are in far more danger from foreign terrorists than homegrown. Number one, they are highly trained, motivated by political and religious concerns, and well funded. An American may be highly trained, they may have some hideous motivation that makes perfect sense to them. To date we've suffered a few isolated crackpots. It's not inconceivable that sometime in the future an extreme religious or political organization could fund such activity. Right now that appears unlikely. But I think it's much harder to guard against a well-organized group with an expressed purpose."

The discussion rolled on. Jim Sanburne could add up the time spent in meetings, conferences, and lectures in years. He'd been mayor of Crozet since 1964. He leaned over and whispered to his daughter, "Never seen anything like this."

A glow of enthusiasm lit Little Mim's face. "Isn't it wonderful to see people so involved?"

"Sooner or later even the laziest son of a bitch wakes up when the Yankee soldier tramps through his potato patch." Jim chuckled low.

"Daddy." She pinched his arm.

Blair Bainbridge, born and raised in the North, leaned past his fiancée, looked at his soon-to-be father-in-law, and whispered, "Who won the war?"

"No one. The North thinks they won, but it was the worst thing that ever happened to this country."

"Killed the nascent wine industry in the South," Hy Maudant, a keen student of wine history worldwide, turned and whispered from his seat in front of the Sanburne clan.

"If you were an agriterrorist, what crop would you attack?" Jim shrewdly asked the Frenchman.

"Wheat."

"Ah." Jim nodded.

"And you?" Hy asked.

"Since you took wheat, I'll take corn." Jim smiled genially.

The panel didn't really break up as much as those who worried about the babysitters reluctantly left for home.

Not until ten-thirty was the auditorium cleared.

Driving home in her truck, Harry and Fair reviewed the evening.

"Aren't you glad that horses aren't on the list of terrorist targets?" Fair draped his arm around Harry's broad shoulders.

"I'll sleep better at night."

"You sleep better at night because I'm next to you." He laughed.

"You know, honey, that really is the truth. There's nothing like falling asleep with your strong arms around me to make me feel safe."

"Likewise, when you're on the outside, I mean," he said.

"Really? You feel safe in my arms?"

"Of course I do, sugar. Love isn't just a way to open your heart, it's armor against the world." Fair squeezed her shoulder.

"I never thought of that. I am strong, though," she bragged.

"Yes, you are."

Aunt Tally's taillights glowed up ahead. She was being

driven in her car by Blair and Little Mim. As her farm was two miles down the road from Harry and Fair's, they often passed or followed each other on the secondary state road.

"Bet she's chewing their ears off."

"The last thing to die on Aunt Tally will be her mouth," Fair laconically said.

Harry laughed, adding, "Actually, I do feel reassured that horses aren't a target."

"Terrorists won't bother using horses. Horses stay awake at night thinking of ways to hurt themselves."

A moment passed, then Harry, who knew what he said was only too true, smiled. "Baby, you'll never be out of work."

5

"...disappointed." Susan Tucker, Harry's best friend, exhaled, as the cats and Tucker and Owen, Susan's corgi, trotted after them as they walked down the steep path on the mountainside of the Bland Wade tract.

"What did Ned want?" Harry inquired as to Ned's preferred committee appointments since he had been sworn in as the state senator for District 7.

"He wanted Ways and Means. Since the whole legislature is controlled by the Republicans, he feels he is being pushed into the backwaters."

"He'll make the most of it. Ned's smart," Harry continued. "Susan, agriculture is the third largest industry in the state of Virginia. It brings in 2.4 billion dollars, and guess what? One billion of that is thanks to the horse industry. And the profits from the horse industry would double if the damned legislature really fostered racing, in all its forms. We make that money despite Richmond. Ned ought to be happy he's on such a committee."

"That's what I said. He says he knows nothing about agriculture, which is exactly why they stuck him on the committee."

"I can be his practitioner expert." Harry smiled broadly.

She was right. She'd been born on the farm on which she lived. She'd farmed all her life, with the exception of four years at Smith College, where she majored in art history. She figured it would be the only time in her life when she didn't have to be ruthlessly practical. Her father appreciated her attitude. Her mother did not.

Eventually, Mrs. Minor accepted Harry's "frivolity"—her view of Harry's major. She thought one should study what might produce income.

What Mrs. Minor failed to comprehend was that Harry, for the first time in her life, was removed from the South, far from blood ties and the close-knit Crozet community, and thrown into a world of bright, competitive women. On the weekends she could spend time with bright, competitive men from Amherst, Yale, Dartmouth, Colgate, Cornell, and the odd Harvard man or two. She discovered, once everyone got over her soft Virginia accent, that she could hold her own. The four years in cold Massachusetts helped forge her belief in her own intellect, her powers of judgment. Figuring out emotions proved more difficult than mastering complex material. Perhaps that's true for many people, not just Harry.

Susan, on the other hand, possessed formidable emotional radar. They joked with each other that together they made one genius.

The cold snap that had set in on Monday continued. The two friends, hands jammed in their pockets, hiked toward the tough little Jeep Wrangler that Ned had bought his wife to mollify her during his long absences. Susan needed something rugged to tend to the Bland Wade tract her great-uncle had willed to her, since there were only disused farm roads on the 1,500-acre property.

This extraordinary piece of land wrapped all the way from Tally Urquhart's Rose Hill Farm to behind Harry's farm. The two friends had gone almost to the top of the last ridge before the Blue Ridge Mountains to check a stand of black walnuts, hickories, locusts, and pin oaks. Scattered throughout the tract were Virginia pines.

"We should thin the pines. The old Virginia pine doesn't live much longer than twenty-five or thirty years, and then it just falls down and rots." Susan, though not a timber person, had been reading like mad on the subject of timber management.

"One bolt of lightning will take care of the pines," Pewter remarked as she tagged along, feeling the cold air's sharpness.

"Nature's clear-cutting," Tucker agreed.

"Hasn't happened for a long time around here. We've had so much rain these last years," remarked Owen, who, like all the animals, registered the weather's every nuance.

"Hey." Tucker stopped, putting her nose to the ground.

The other three walked over to her and also put their noses to the earth.

"Bear," Owen simply said. *"Maybe an hour ago."*

"All kinds of big fuzzies up here." Pewter fluffed out her fur.

"We may be little fuzzies, but we can take care of ourselves." Mrs. Murphy puffed out her tail.

"How many times have I bailed you out?" Pewter remarked.

"You? I pry you out of jams more than you do me." Mrs. Murphy couldn't believe Pewter's ego.

"Ha!" Pewter dashed in front of the humans, energized by her own opinion of her powers.

Susan noticed. "I don't recall ever seeing Pewter this lively."

Harry watched as Pewter followed up her burst of speed with a two-foot climb up a tree trunk, then a drop down. "She has her moods." She returned to the subject at hand. "Finding a timber company that will take on a job this small won't be easy. You're talking about sixty acres, which is nothing to the big boys. And we want someone who is responsible. Right now, prices for pulp timber, which is what this pine is, are low."

"If we wait it will just fall down."

"Maybe yes and maybe no. We've got a year or two." Harry climbed in and gladly closed the door to the lime-green Wrangler. Tucker sat on her lap and Owen, Tucker's brother, sat on Susan's lap. She picked him up, placing him in the back with Mrs. Murphy and Pewter, who were already curled up in Owen's little sheepskin bed.

"I've got all G-Uncle Thomas's notes." She called him G-Uncle for great-uncle. "Those pines were planted in 1981. A long period of rain, some high winds, and they're crashing down."

"It's those bitty root systems. You wouldn't think such tall trees would have such small roots." Harry turned on the heater. "Okay?"

"Yeah, I'm chilled to the bone. Let's go into town for a big hot chocolate. I need to pick up mail anyway."

"Okay."

They bounced through the old rutted roads. Harry got out at the gate to her back pasture and opened it. Susan drove through and then Harry locked the gate, hopped back in. They cruised past the barn, down the long lane out to the paved state road.

"Any more thoughts?" Susan asked.

"Yes, actually. If we sign a contract with a good timbering company—not a management contract, mind you, just a timbering contract—for say, five years, we'll be able to attract a better grade of operator. The last thing we want is someone to go up there, take out the timber, leave slash all over the place."

"You want them to dig pits and burn it?"

"No. I want the leftovers pushed along into long piles of debris maybe five or six feet high. Let it decay. It will provide homes for lots of critters. I know why people burn the stuff, but it's wasteful. Slash provides habitat, and the cycle of renewal begins again for animals and plants."

"How much do you think we can make from the pine?"

"Well, I'd love to think we could pull out at least a thousand dollars an acre, but the market is so erratic. The black walnut's market has been really good. High prices."

"We've got two acres of black walnut up there."

"That's another thing that worries me. Let the wrong people in there and some of that enormous profit will just disappear. They'll steal the walnut."

"We'd know."

"I'd like to think we would, but it'd still be a great big mess."

"Hot chocolate first. I really need it." Susan pulled into the parking lot of what used to be the old bank building, now owned by Tracy Raz.

The bottom of the building housed a clean, simple restaurant.

As they plopped into a booth, the proprietor, Kyle Davidson, greeted them and took their order.

"Susan, one of the things I've been thinking about, especially since we did the soil tests, is why don't we, on the lower acres where the soil is more fertile, plant sugar maples, red maples, locusts, Southern hawthorne, trees that we can sell to nurseries once they are three or four years old? We can continually renew our stock from our own cuttings and we'll be efficiently using the land. Nursery stock has a much faster turnover than timber. We won't see much of a return for three years, but that's the beauty of taking out the Virginia pine and the old loblolly pine. The soil might be acidic, but most of those pine stands are a little higher up. We can use the money from the pine on the lower acres to start up the nursery stock. The sticking point is irrigation. If we suffer a drought we've got to get water to the saplings." Harry had talked out loud to her animals about this, since she often thought better out loud. However, she hadn't said anything to Susan until now.

Susan, cup in hand, drained it, brightened. "A water buffalo."

She cited a holding tank usually pulled by a pickup truck or tractor. Smaller ones could be placed on the bed of the pickup, but that was hell on the shocks.

"That's a lot of man-hours." Harry leaned back on the booth seat. "Still, it's a beginning. There's no way we can afford an irrigation system now. Leaky pipe is even more expensive, so a water buffalo makes a lot of sense."

"What about your sunflowers? Aren't you going to irrigate?"

"Actually, I'm going to irrigate everything—the alfalfa, the orchard-grass pastures, the sunflowers, and my one-quarter acre row of Petit Manseng grapes. I'll use the tractor to pull a boom sprayer. We've got that big tractor that Fair and I bought from Blair. Eighty horsepower. Perfect! I say we use the same system for the nursery stock."

"You'll rent it?"

"No. Susan, we're partners, remember?"

"Yes, but that's wear and tear on your equipment. I have to come up with something."

"You came up with 1,500 acres."

"I guess I did, didn't I?" She laughed.

Loud voices at the counter diverted their attention.

"That's a damned irresponsible statement." Toby Pittman loomed over Hy Maudant, who sat on a stool at the counter.

"No, it's not. What I'm saying is not a criticism of Professor Forland. You think the government is always the enemy. Go on, show me how morally superior you are. Then you can sit on your butt and do nothing."

"I ought to knock your fat ass right off that stool."

Kyle quickly came around from behind the counter. "Take it outside."

"Forget it. I'll go. I don't want to be in the same room with this French fascist anyhow." Toby glared at Hy, then left, thoughtfully not slamming the door.

Hy spun around on the stool, noticed Harry and Susan. "Entertainment?"

His light French accent made every sentence sound musical. This was also true of Paul de Silva, Big Mim's young equine manager, who spoke with a beautiful high-class Spanish accent.

"What's Toby bitching about?" Harry forthrightly asked as Hy picked up his cup and walked over to them.

"Sit down, Hy." Susan moved further inland, as there was quite a lot of Hy.

His light-blue eyes merrily danced from one pretty lady to the other. "Oh, you know how extremely sensitive he is. Why, when he was pruning the vines at Rockland Vineyards this March, I mentioned, I hinted, I barely breathed the suggestion that perhaps he might be a bit more aggressive to encourage growth. He threw me off the place! I swore that would be the last time I'd try to help him. No one can work with him." Hy held up his hand, the palm outward. "I remain dedicated to the revitalization of the Virginia wine industry, thanks to the brilliant effort started thirty some years ago by Felicia Rogan at Oakencroft Vinery, but I will not lift one finger, not even my pinky, to help that insufferable malcontent. If his grapes were infected with an anthracnose and I had the last ton of lime sulfur in the county, I wouldn't sell it to him."

"Runs in the family. All the Pittmans are difficult people." Harry accepted Toby but avoided him.

"What's an anthracnose?" Susan asked.

"Bird's eye," Hy replied. "It's a fungus on the leaves that looks like a bird's eye. Tricky. The grapes seem okay, but the leaves wilt. Two or three years pass, everything seems okay. Eventually, though, the infection reaches the fruit and one gets misshapen grapes."

"Sure are a lot of things that attack grapes."

"There's no foolproof crop." He shrugged.

"Weeds." Susan cupped her head in her hand.

Harry laughed. "When people talk about a natural garden, I figure they mean weeds." She turned her attention back to Hy. "By the time I apply every remedy to my little vines, I won't have a penny of profit."

He smiled. "You're too smart for that." Tapping his thick cup, he continued. "You only apply fertilizer or spray when it is needed or at the right time as a preventive. We're lucky here, so far. We've managed to keep grapes healthy."

"Persistence." She paused, then smiled slowly. "And ego."

"You need ego to do anything well." He agreed. "Gargantuan ego. Pantagruel. Yes, the Pantagruel of ego. That's Toby. I have an ego. Felicia has an ego. Patricia has an ego, but we also have sense. Toby has none." He assumed both ladies knew their Rabelais, and being well educated, they did know the work of France's greatest comic writer, who worked in the first half of the sixteenth century.

"Can anyone be a vintner without a huge ego?" Susan marveled at the complexity of the task. One had to select the correct grape for the soil, nurture it, harvest it, then sell it or actually make the wine oneself.

It remained a science and an art to create the right medley of sensation on a discriminating palate.

Harry, a foxhunter, evidenced a bit of the slyness of the fox herself. "Hy, surely Toby didn't threaten to knock you off the stool because of pruning grapes. What exposed nerve did you touch today?" She smiled flirtatiously, since Hy believed himself attractive to all females worldwide.

"Ah, yes." He leaned forward conspiratorially. "Vincent Forland. I said I thought both those men at the panel gave everyone a blueprint for bioterrorism. Irresponsible!"

"Hy, I didn't think of that at the time. It was so fascinating, but you know, you've got a point there," Harry said.

Hy shrugged a Gallic shrug, one imitated but never perfected by those not born to the greatness of France. "Mark my words, ladies. It will all come to a bad end."

"Why would that set off Toby?" Susan knew Toby had a short fuse, but he seemed extra agitated.

"Ah, Toby, the morally superior Toby. When I suggested to him that Professor Forland and Dr. Jenkins might as well work for the terrorists given that they'd told us too much, he cursed me and swore that was ridiculous. I said, no, smart. The two experts appear to be warning us, but they're scaring people. Plants as lethal agents, common enough plants, such things could be distilled by someone who knows less than Professor Forland."

"Toby seems to have a volatile relationship with Professor Forland," Susan said.

"Toby likes him, but I guess he's never really gotten over not being hired by Tech," commented Harry, who in her typical fashion didn't believe there would be emotional repercussions in her life because of Arch's return.

"He takes things so personally," Susan said compassionately.

"And now Arch is here, a partner to Rollie Barnes. That grates on Toby's high-strung nature," Harry said.

Hy nodded gravely. "This is so. You have a big heart, Susan. First, Toby lost his temper when I suggested that his esteemed Professor Forland might as well give terrorists a blueprint if he's not already in their employ. Then when I said Professor Forland could also work for Homeland Security or some other agency, he erupted. He shook his finger at me and declared Professor Forland would never stoop to cooperating with our right-wing government."

"Is that what he called our government?" Susan's cheeks reddened.

"Alas, madam, he did."

"Toby prides himself on being an anarchist." Harry felt the warmth from her cup on her hands. "But you know, irritating as he can be about stuff like that, it's good we hear it. Otherwise, we're just a bunch of sheep."

"Still, can't a man be amusing?" Hy held up his hands in bafflement.

6

Rollie Barnes touched a stock; it surged upward. His gorgeous wife, twenty-two years younger than Rollie, prudently hid her intelligence from him, for he was not a man comfortable with formidable females. For all his brains, Rollie was rather a weak fellow emotionally. This in turn made him aggressive, a quality not appreciated in its raw form in the South.

Born on the wrong side of the tracks in Stamford, Connecticut, Rollie slogged through the local community college. Yet once he found his gift, to his credit he made the most of it.

"Periosteal elevation." Rollie pronounced this with finality.

Fair, who had delivered the foal, tried not to smile. "An invasive procedure, Mr. Barnes. This little fellow doesn't need a P and E." He used the shorthand version for the procedure, one known to horsemen.

Mim would have known instantly what Fair was discussing—surgery required on the knee of the foreleg.

"I want this foal to have straight legs." Rollie folded his arms across his chest as he stood, legs apart, under a completely unnecessary chandelier in the stable.

"Honey, he likes me." Chauntal put her blonde head down to the colt, who nuzzled her as his mother turned to look.

Fair smiled. He liked Chauntal. He didn't envy her. It's easier to make money than to marry it.

"Mr. Barnes, this colt has carpal valgus: knock-knees. I think he'll straighten out in time. Right now I wouldn't do anything restrictive. I wouldn't even put a splint on him, because it's not that bad." He didn't say a P and E would be the wrong thing to do, because, being a sensitive man, Fair didn't want Rollie to take offense.

"Well, it looks bad to me." Rollie's lower lip jutted out.

"I'm sure it does, but it's a mild case. Truth is, you don't want a horse with straight, straight legs. A truly straight leg actually promotes knee problems."

"But I read that this stripping is used on knock-kneed foals."

"I guess some vets do it, but I'd really only do a P and E for an ankle problem or badly bowed legs. It really will take care of itself. This little fellow will be just fine."

Chauntal couldn't keep her hands off the lovely bay colt. "Dr. Haristeen, what is periosteal stripping?"

"It's pretty interesting, ma'am. You make a small, inverted T-shaped cut through the periosteum, right above the growth plate. You lift the edges of the periosteum, and in most young foals the leg will grow straight after four to six weeks. What the surgery really does is allow the slower-growing side of the leg to catch up. The cut releases the tension on the membrane that covers the growth plate—that's what's called the periosteum. Guess I should have said that in the first place." He smiled reassuringly.

"Well, I'm going to ask Dan Flynn." Rollie mentioned a nationally famous equine vet who lived in Albemarle County.

"Sir, you won't find anyone better. You can also call Reynolds Coles or Anne Bonda or Greg Schmidt. They're all excellent vets. Dan, as you probably know, is so famous he's in demand all over. I'm surprised one of those Saudi princes hasn't offered Dan and Ginger," he mentioned Dan's wife, a small-animal vet, "a million to practice in Dubai."

That Fair hadn't been insulted surprised Rollie, who imagined every exchange with another man as a contest of wills, wits, and, of course, money.

Chauntal, often embarrassed by Rollie, tried not to show it. Born poor in Mississippi, she was raised by people with beautiful manners, people who respected other people. Her mother, father, and sister didn't rejoice in Rollie's wealth. They thought him rude and unfeeling. They prayed their beautiful girl would have a good life. That her husband would respect her. Not that they showed anything to Rollie but pleasantness. He tried to buy them things, which they refused.

Rollie understood only money. He was a poor man for all his wealth.

"You tell me what you want to do, Mr. Barnes, and if you want to go ahead with surgery, I'll step aside for another vet or assist, if you choose. As I said, any of those folks are excellent. You can't find better."

"I'll have my secretary call you after Dr. Flynn has a look."

"Fine." Fair reached over and patted the colt.

The little fellow had a lovely eye.

"Heard BoomBoom's got a mule." Rollie smirked.

"Mules are good animals."

"Is she really going to train it? That's what Paul said." Chauntal was surprised.

"When did you see Paul?" Rollie grilled her, because Paul de Silva was handsome and sexy.

"When I went down to Tazio's to see how she was coming with the plans for your wine-press building."

This pleased him. "Ah, yes, they're an item." He turned to Fair. "She's easy to work with, and since she's at the beginning of her career, I'm getting good value for my money."

Fair thought the world of the young architect. "You made a wise choice."

This puffed up Rollie. His sandy hair, thinned a bit on top, retained its color. A bit weedy, he at least didn't sport a big potbelly like Hy Maudant. When he first made money, Rollie hired consultants to teach him how to dress, consultants to teach him what fork and knife to use. He'd mastered these intricacies.

As they walked outside the brick stable painted a soft peach with white trim, dark-green shutters on the windows of the office, the breeze ruffled Fair's thick hair.

Chauntal skipped along, slipping her arm through Rollie's. "Honey, show him your latest."

Rollie pointed down to the south side of the farm. "Merlot."

Arch could be seen walking along the straight rows of vines.

"Heard you planted them last November."

"Twenty acres of Merlot. Fifteen in Pinot Gris. And that's just the beginning."

"Arch will know just what to do," Fair noted.

"Veritas Vineyards wanted him, but I offered a partnership and that closed the deal. He's thirty-four, his best years ahead." Rollie smirked.

Fair bit his tongue, then replied, "Arch has a lot of hands-on knowledge and ambition. Those years in the Napa Valley gave him a lot of experience."

"Chauntal and I intend to make the best red wine in the state of Virginia. Great design on the label, too. 'Course, we're still in the creative stage." He pulled drawings out of his pocket. They were pretty.

Fair thought of Hy Maudant's white square label, with a gold fleur-de-lis underneath the simple logo "White Vineyards." He murmured about the colors.

"Dr. Haristeen, can we get you anything to drink, a sandwich perhaps? You've had a long morning, I'm sure."

"No, thank you, Mrs. Barnes. My next call is at St. James."

"Alicia Palmer." Rollie's eyes widened. "I've seen her, but I've never met her."

"She likes her solitude, her horses, and her Gordon setter, Max. She's a thinker." Fair wasn't one to gossip.

Before Rollie could open his mouth and put his foot in it regarding the legendary Alicia, Chauntal said, "Congratulations on your marriage." She'd heard that Harry and Arch once had an affair, but Chauntal would never mention this—not even to Rollie. Let him hear it, which he would eventually. She'd pretend surprise, which would please him. Then, too, the longer Rollie didn't know, the longer she had before he blurted out something inappropriate.

"I am a lucky devil." Fair's eyes twinkled.

As he drove down the long drive lined with blooming Bradford pears, he thought how lucky he really was, how exquisite spring could be in central Virginia, three months of color and coolness that finally surrendered to summer's warmth.

He also thought that Rollie Barnes would be eventually disappointed in Crozet. In their first year, the Barneses had succeeded in being invited to the big parties but had yet to be asked to the small, intimate gatherings, which were far more important. People liked Chauntal. They had more difficulty liking Rollie. At least his new interest in making wine aligned him with the great powers in the county.

Fair turned right on Route 810, headed down toward Crozet. St. James was a little closer to town.

7

Carter's Ridge, like a slender rib off a fish's spine, runs northeast–southwest from the Blue Ridge Mountains from which it has become detached over millennia. Eppes Creek slides into the north fork of the Hardware River near the northeast ridge of Carter's Ridge. The old bridge, washed out many times since Europeans arrived this far west in Virginia, was replaced with a trestle bridge a stone's throw east of that confluence. Route 20, a snaky, dangerous road, rolled over the bridge.

Turning left at Carter's Bridge, if one had originally been traveling south on Route 20, estates such as Red Mountain were hidden from view. One mile and a half down the road, the land opened and a beautiful valley impressed itself on the viewer. James Monroe had lived on this road at Ash Lawn, a simple, yellow, gracious Federal home at the end of a curving tree-lined drive. Morven, once home to Thoroughbreds and those who loved them, was also situated on the northern side of the road, as was Albemarle House, the center of Kluge Estate Winery and Vineyard, established in 1999.

Professor Forland luxuriated in the lavish hospitality of Patricia Kluge and her husband, Bill Moses. During the days, chauffeured in Patricia's much-used Range Rover, he inspected her Chardonnay grapes along with the rows of Cabernet Sauvignon, Merlot, and Cabernet Franc. He counseled her on using three shoots off the main stem even though two was safer.

"That third one is your insurance policy," he declared.

Given her legendary generosity, Patricia made certain that Professor Forland had an opportunity to visit other practitioners of the art. In her mind and in Bill's, it wasn't enough for her or for Felicia Rogan of Oakencroft to flourish; all should flourish. Throughout the week, she personally drove him to the vineyards of Hy Maudant, Rollie Barnes, and Arch Saunders. She also stopped at smaller places where a farmer nursed scarcely an acre under cultivation.

Patricia believed in the theory that you can give a man a fish or you can teach him to fish. She thought teaching someone to fish was by far the greater service.

The good professor made many a suggestion, and the recipients were suitably thrilled. None more than Toby Pittman.

Toby prided himself on the types of grapes he was growing. One, Barbera, a red from Italy's Piedmont region, did quite well in Virginia's Piedmont. Toby aggressively promoted the grape. Barboursville Vineyard also used Barbera. The Italians, according to Toby, pushed their grapes, and the Barbera was suffering a loss of quality. He asserted that he was doing a better job of it. When Professor Forland sampled one of Toby's casks, he agreed, with reservations.

"Be wary of too much spiciness, Toby." Professor Forland spat out the small tasting on the ground, as one was supposed to do; otherwise the small fellow would have been drunk as a skunk by the end of the day. "Now, mind you, my strongest suit is under the canopy," he alluded to his expertise being in the actual growing itself, "but I have an educated palate."

Toby waited while Patricia sampled his wine. "Medium-bodied, and I love the hint of tobacco flavor. You're an artist, Toby." Her smile dazzled him.

Patricia had that effect on men.

"As I said, mind the spiciness." Professor Forland then sampled Toby's newer type of grape, which was a Petit Verdot. "Mmm. Yes. I assume you'll be blending this with Cabernet Sauvignon when all is ready. Growing that, too, are you?"

"No. Tried. I don't like what I get. I buy from Dinny Ostermann when I can. He cultivates five acres of Cabernet Sauvignon over in Crozet. Just the right combination of sun, rain, and soil."

"For all our studies, I sometimes think Dionysus smiles on one man and not another, all things being equal." He paused, beaming at his hostess. "We know the gods smile on you, but none has smiled more than Aphrodite."

"Professor, you're very kind."

Toby, not smooth enough to have thoughts of mentioning Aphrodite, scowled. "You know how I know I'm succeeding?"

"Your wine tells you that," Professor Forland said.

"Yeah, but the way I really know is that Arch offered to buy Rockland. 'Course, it's all Rollie's money." He laughed.

"If Rollie and Arch ever got their hands on Rockland it would fry Hy Maudant's last misshapen brain cell. They can bid against each other. I'm not selling one acre. I know what I've got."

Later that evening, another extraordinary dinner was hosted where Bill had wisely sprinkled the guests with politicians from all levels of state government who could or should help the wine industry along with local growers. Since he was a worrier by nature, Professor Forland felt for the first time that the hard years for Virginia vintners were behind them at last.

In the interval between dessert and cards, he stepped outside to gaze at the gardens, answering to spring. Up the hill, he beheld a statue beckoning in the night, a focus for the eye. Everywhere he looked he was seduced by a powerful aesthetic sensibility.

Bill, cigar in hand, joined him. "Cohiba? I needed a respite." He offered him a cigar from his leather carrying case.

"Gave up smoking," Professor Forland said as Bill pocketed the extra cigar—a nice fat gauge, too, so the draw would be deliciously smooth.

"Thank you for serving on the panel, for visiting our compatriots," Bill graciously said. "Virginia has two hundred fifty vineyards. You can't visit them all, but I'm delighted you've visited the ones here."

Professor Forland inhaled the fragrant cigar odor as Bill prepared his. "Like Galileo, I recant."

"Ah." Bill smiled, pulling the extra cigar from his blazer pocket, cutting off the nub end for the professor with a sharp mother-of-pearl cigar cutter. Then he carefully held the flame a bit away from the tip so Professor Forland could light the treasure. "A little bit of heaven, isn't it?"

"Nicotine serves a purpose," Professor Forland good-naturedly remarked. "You know, when your wife and I were out today we saw Toby's operation."

"Very opinionated."

"There are worse characteristics, but, yes, he can be difficult. What surprised me is his idea for a wine he hopes to bottle this year. He buys the Cabernet Sauvignon from—let me remember—"

"Dinny Ostermann." Bill nodded with admiration. "He's one of those people who can make a purse out of a sow's ear."

"The usual mix of Petit Verdot, and Toby's got the Verdot right, too, but the usual mix is eighty percent Petit Verdot with twenty percent Cabernet Sauvignon. The Petit Verdot plays the dominating role. He wants to reverse it."

"Linden Vineyards Aeneus 2001 does that." Bill's studies showed themselves, although he wasn't a bragging sort of man.

Then again, if you catch a big fish you generally don't go home by an alley.

"Yes, yes, I know, but what really surprised me was Toby's aggressiveness. He says he can do it better."

Bill laughed. "In his own way he's as arrogant as Rollie Barnes. What'd you think of that operation, by the way?"

"Too early to tell. Spends money like water. Arch Saunders was one of my students, you know. Even taught for two years. Not as brilliant as Toby in the classroom, but a more balanced person. And sounds like Rollie is buying or renting any land with the right soils and drainage. Very competitive. Arch, too. They'll upset people, those two." Professor Forland drew deeply on the heavenly cigar. "Despite the conviviality of tonight's dinner, every now and then Toby glares at Arch and Rollie. Toby's worked so hard, alone, and here Arch comes back from California and snags a plummy partnership."

"Heard that Rollie is building his own bottling facility. And the first grape hasn't appeared on the vine." Bill exhaled a blue plume, changing the focus of the conversation.

"Optimism."

"Mmm." Bill shrugged. He endured Rollie.

Bill was a secure man with a bubbling, effervescent humor. Bill's quiet confidence and, worse, his social grace infuriated Rollie, who felt clumsy.

"Did you know that Hy Maudant bought a mobile bottling line?" Professor Forland closed his eyes as he took a deep drag, the orange glow of the cigar tip shining.

"When did he do that?"

"Today. We stopped at White Vineyards first."

"Patricia and I haven't had a minute to catch up. I'll be interested to hear what she says. Those units cost $350,000. Hy is a good businessman, the French usually are. Instead of sinking all his money into his own bottling facility, he buys the mobile unit. He already has the huge tractor to pull it. He'll use it himself and then hire it out to other vintners. Shrewd." Bill made note of the fact that Hy, a guest this evening, didn't brag about his acquisition.

"Very, as long as you have someone who can service it."

Bill turned as he heard Patricia call from inside. "Be right in." He turned to Professor Forland. "Hy will have someone who can fix it. I know Hy. By the way, I'll put together a small box of different cigars for you to take home. Unless you have a favorite."

"Ah, your sampler will tell me more about you than my poor tastes." He stopped a moment. "But I have to say the best cigar I ever smoked in my life was a Diplomaticos, Cuban."

"Yes. I like them very much, although I tend more toward Cohibas, at least after dinner. Romeo and Juliet and Dunhill make a good cigar even if the tobacco isn't Cuban. But you know, the Cubans really do have the perfect conditions for cigar tobacco. Funny, isn't it, cigars are as unique as wine and just as difficult to produce. Another fine art," he sighed. "Damned fool embargo. Hell, when the embargo was declared, President Kennedy had humidors stuffed with Cuban cigars. That's what raises my blood pressure more than anything—hypocrisy."

"The hypocrite honors morals or the law by pretending to obey."

Bill laughed, appreciating the fine point. "Another brandy?" As they walked inside, Bill draped his arm over the professor's narrow shoulders. "I married Patricia, but you know when I knew I was completely, totally, eternally in love with that woman? When she dragged me out of bed at four-thirty in the morning for weeks our first year to pick the grapes. She spared me nothing. We did much of the physical work ourselves, and I am not an early riser. But, you know, the happiness on her face, the shared goal—for the first time in my life I have a three-hundred-sixty-degree relationship with a woman, the most remarkable woman I have ever known."

"You are a fortunate man, because she's one of the most beautiful women in the world."

Bill puffed his last puff. "Beauty may bring you to a woman, but it won't keep you. She has to have beauty from within."

"Ah, like the vine. It, too, must express the beauty from within."

"Poetic." Bill smiled as they rejoined the guests in the

den, where a lively discussion was in progress about the spiritual difference between baseball, football, and basketball.

Professor Forland knew little about sports, but the sight of women as impassioned about sports as the men was not unique to him. In Blacksburg, football was a religion both genders appeared to worship equally.

However, the true achievement of Virginia Tech lay in its vibrant social life. It was once written in a national magazine when rating the best party schools in America that they couldn't include Tech. It would be unfair to pit professionals against amateurs.

As the guests left, Toby and Arch fell in step some distance behind Rollie and Chauntal.

At the bottom of the curving outdoor stairs, Toby abruptly asked, "Why'd you leave Tech for California? Being a professor is a soft job, a good one."

"Hands on. Classroom's not for me, but I didn't know that until I taught for two years."

"Didn't have anything to do with Mary Minor?" Toby used Harry's true Christian name and her maiden surname.

They reached Toby's truck, parked well below the great house. "A little, I guess."

Toby leaned against the door, crossed his arms over his chest. "What was it like working out there in Napa Valley?"

"Different world, a totally different world. But the people who have been hired by the rich people—the movie stars' people and all that, those Italians and French that actually run the vineyards—they are something. They are true blue. They had to adjust to a different climate, soils, rainfall, and a whole different way of living, but, boy, look what they are producing." He paused a moment. "Good as it is and beautiful as it is, too many people in California, even in Napa Valley. They're like locusts just eating everything up."

"Never happen here."

"Oh, yeah? Toby, Charlottesville came in as the number-one place to live in America."

"Ah, just a poll. The rest of the country, outside the South, I mean, thinks we're all a bunch of dumb rednecks."

"Hope so." Arch laughed.

Toby laughed, too, a rarity for him. "Yeah, keep 'em out. Hey, want to see what I just bought?"

"Sure."

He opened the truck and pulled down the raised center console/armrest. He popped open the lid and removed a handgun. "Isn't this something? Brand-new. A Ruger P95PR. Bought two boxes of ten-round magazines, too."

"Hey, that's nine millimeter. You going to shoot targets with that?"

"Sometimes."

"Expensive ammunition. I stick to a twenty-two for practice."

"Yeah, but feel this in your hand." Toby handed the gun to Arch.

Arch knew it was unloaded. Toby wasn't stupid. "Feels balanced." He handed it back. "I know that's expensive."

"Keep it right here in my truck. Never know when I'll need it." A puff of air escaped his lips, as the air was quite cool. "Did Forland get mad at you when you left Tech?"

"No, he understood I needed to be in the field. All he cares about is that his students make a name for themselves."

"Big ego," Toby flatly replied.

"He's entitled to it."

"Did he ever say why he didn't give me that job?"

"Thought you'd do better out of school, I suppose."

"I don't believe that."

"I don't know."

"Bet everyone knows in Blacksburg but me. University towns create more gossip than scholars."

"I don't know." Arch avoided the issue.

"You all think I'm nuts. Everyone thinks I'm like a radiator that overheats. I know that. Just because I say what I'm thinking when I'm thinking it. You all think I just boil over." He threw his hands up like water shooting up. "Whoosh."

"Toby, you'll never change." Arch kept his voice level. "Thanks for showing me the Ruger." He started toward his truck.

"I'll show you all. Just wait. I will make the best wine in this state and I'll make money, too."

Arch couldn't resist. "Not if I do it first."

"You try!" Toby's face reddened. "I'm gonna beat your ass. I'll show Professor Forland who's the best."

"Okay." Arch kept walking as Toby kept making promises of greatness to come.

Early the next morning after protracted good-byes, Professor Forland drove off in his Scion car, down the long, winding driveway, all paved, and out the main gate. He turned right, passed Keelona Farm as he headed toward Carter's Bridge. Then he simply vanished.

8

"Bullshit." Aunt Tally sharply rapped her silver-headed cane on the Aubusson rug, which slightly muffled the curse.

The light played on Ned Tucker's distinguished silver sideburns and temples as he bowed to the fabulously well-dressed nonagenarian perched on the sofa in Big Mim's living room. "I agree."

Aunt Tally used her cane topped off with the silver hound's head for punctuation as well as to help her walk. Spry enough at her age, she did find that sometimes she wasn't quite as sure-footed as she once was if the ground wasn't level.

Big Mim, equally well dressed, glided over to her aunt. "Cursing again?"

"Yes. I think bullshit ever so much more forceful than shit. And if I had time I'd be more creative than bullshit, but what Ned has just told me infuriates me, so I responded immediately. Bullshit, I say, pure, unadulterated bullshit."

The small gathering at Mim's beautiful house, redecorated last winter by Parish-Hadley, the august interior decorating firm—"freshened," as Mim liked to say—gravitated toward the ancient lady.

Big Mim was giving a small Saturday luncheon party in honor of Harry and Fair. The luncheon was on a par with a hunt breakfast, which is to say it was sumptuous. She'd been close friends with Harry's mother, as had Miranda Hogendobber, who used to work with Harry at the post office. When Harry was left without either parent while studying at Smith College, both women did their best to look after her. Big Mim's daughter, a year younger than Harry, never really forgave her mother for this diversion of attention Little Mim believed she herself deserved.

Over the years, young Marilyn managed to reach an accord with Harry. After all, it wasn't Harry's fault that her parents had died within months of each other. It was just that even now, Little Mim sometimes resented the bond between her mother and this poor—formerly poor, anyway—country mouse. Harry, a terrific athlete, shared foxhunting, tennis, shooting clays and skeet with Big Mim.

BoomBoom, six feet tall and gorgeous, was also a natural athlete. Woe to the man who invited her to play golf just to see her form at the top of her swing's finish. She'd bet on each hole and clean the fellow out. BoomBoom understood the monetary value of outstanding physical attributes.

It seemed everyone was a good athlete but Little Mim. To her credit, she could ride, thanks to thousands of dollars' worth of lessons plus her own grit. No amount of money will give one the courage to take a big fence. Little Mim took her fences without blinking an eye.

The luncheon pleased Little Mim because she was grateful her mother hadn't gone overboard. She wanted her June wedding celebrations to overshadow anything that might be done for Harry and Fair or anyone else in the county.

Miranda and Susan walked over, flanking Ned. Jim, the host, noted whose drink needed a lift.

Also gathering around Aunt Tally were Tazio Chappars, Paul de Silva, Tracy Raz, BoomBoom, Alicia, and Hy and Fiona Maudant.

"Well, Aunt Tally, once again you're the center of attention. Perhaps you'd like to recapitulate your conversation with Ned?" Big Mim goaded her.

"Ned, you start." Tally leaned forward, both hands on the head of her cane.

"As some of you know, I've been assigned to the Ag committee. I paid a courtesy call to the chair and he told me, his exact words, 'Ned, my boy, if you want to rise in government, don't drive a foreign car. Get yourself a good ole American piece of junk.' Here I thought we might discuss last year's corn surplus—the average price came to $1.95 a bushel—and he tells me to get rid of the Audi station wagon, which isn't my car, it's Susan's. I borrowed it to carry some things down to the apartment." He looked at Aunt Tally.

"Bullshit was my reply." Aunt Tally lifted an eyebrow.

"I guess so." Tracy Raz laughed.

"It is, but he has a point. Appearances count for more than reality in politics. Always have and always will," chimed in Jim, mayor of Crozet and a Democrat.

This created some friction in the family since Little Mim, a Republican, was vice-mayor. She had ambitions. Her father did not. He simply wanted to serve Crozet, for he loved the town and surrounding farms.

"I'm cooked either way, because my car is my old 1998 540i," Ned ruefully said.

"Don't buy another BMW. Not until they dispense with that ridiculous iDrive as well as the ugly bustle on the trunk." BoomBoom loved cars and read four magazines dedicated to the automobile.

"Under the circumstance, I'd say driving a BMW would be political suicide." Ned half-laughed.

"Considering that the German government has criticized our plans in the Mideast, you're right on two counts." Tracy Raz was a keen student of foreign affairs.

"Buy a truck," BoomBoom advised.

"Yes, but, Boom, if you want, you can go out and buy a damned Bentley." Ned was a little frustrated.

"I love my Bentley." Big Mim squared her shoulders.

It should be noted that Big Mim had more money than God, whereas BoomBoom only had enough for an archangel.

"Your Bentley GT is beautiful. But you know I always had trucks because of the business and now it's my only vehicle. I sold my Mercedes two months ago. I don't know why I waited this long to have one set of wheels. God knows, it's easier." BoomBoom glanced over at Alicia, whose lavender-tinted eyes glowed, a feature the camera exploited in her long-ago film days.

"The Cadillac Escalade isn't so bad." Paul de Silva, in his early thirties, liked the big SUV, popular among his generation.

"He can't drive a Cadillac. Not if he wants to go above his present station." Aunt Tally nursed plans for Ned. "It's all silly, I know, but if Ned is going to be our next governor, then he has to be clever about these things."

"I thought I was going to be governor," Little Mim blurted out.

"You are, dear, if the gods are willing, but you're younger

than Ned. Let him go first. As for all of us here, party is irrelevant. All that matters is what comes back to Crozet. Ned, I presume you want to be governor?" Big Mim asked.

"Uh—"

Susan chirped, "Have you ever known my husband to refuse a pro bono case, an honor, or more work?"

"Am I that transparent?" He was shocked.

"No." Miranda patted his arm. "But politics is the ultimate seduction, you know. One actually believes things will be accomplished. True power comes not from an electorate. 'I can do all things in Him who strengthens me.' Follow that, Ned, and you will achieve what is necessary." Miranda quoted Philippians, Chapter 3, Verse 10.

"Miranda, I thought you'd given up being a religious nut." Aunt Tally minced few words. "And while you're on your feet, Jim, another martini."

"You've had enough." Big Mim glared at the diminutive lady on the sofa.

"Oh, balls, Mimsy. I can't engage in illicit affairs anymore. All the men of my generation are dead, and a young man of seventy wouldn't give me a tumble. I can't ride astride, so I drive that damned buggy. Who can live without horses? I can barely dance. You have no mercy. Gin is comfort. And I did not insult Miranda, because I know that's why you are now hovering over me like a blowfly." She pounded the cane on the rug again.

"I'll fetch you another drink." Little Mim maliciously smiled at her mother. She couldn't help it.

"My beautiful girl here isn't a religious nut, Aunt Tally, but you know how she loves the Good Book." Tracy adored Miranda. "She has most of it memorized. How does she do it?"

"She has most of it memorized because all those years in

the post office she would have lost her mind without a mental project." Aunt Tally cast her eyes over to Harry. "And you got out while the getting was good, young lady."

Big Mim's springer spaniel walked into the room, discerned no food would fall on the floor as it had at the dinner table, and padded back out.

Little Mim returned with a fresh martini for Aunt Tally, and Blair, her fiancé, bore a small crystal glass filled with olives in case Aunt Tally wanted to pick at them. He'd speared them with tiny silver swords.

"We're off track." Alicia graciously brought them back to Ned's dilemma. "Ned, you haven't asked for my opinion, but given the company, I feel safe in expressing it. Buy a truck. Buy a three-quarter-ton Chevy, Ford, Dodge, doesn't matter, whichever one appeals to you."

"Why not a half-ton?" Harry asked. "Easier to drive and a bit cheaper to run." Harry's gaze rarely strayed from the bottom line, a good habit acquired from decades of living close to the bone.

"He's on the Ag committee. A half-ton is so glamorized these days, it's a city person's flash vehicle." Alicia displayed the sharp insights that had enabled her to survive the slings and arrows—or more often the knives in the back—prevalent in her former acting profession. "If he drives a three-quarter-ton, has a Reese hitch on the back, and is wired for a gooseneck, running lights, a running board, think about it, that's a working farm truck. When he goes down to Lee County the farmer he visits sees another farmer. And in truth, now that Susan is in the nursery business and timber business, he may not exactly be a farmer but he's married to one."

"How smart!" BoomBoom clasped her hands together.

Aunt Tally squinted at the movie star. "You're one hundred percent right, sweet pea."

"Do I have to trade in the 540i?" Ned's voice was mournful.

"No. Just don't ride it to Richmond or thereabouts." Fair, listening all this while, added his two cents. "And if you'll forgive me for changing the subject, did you see in the Richmond paper where Virginia beat out California in a number of wine-tasting events? I think I got that right. Is everyone in the state going to make wine now?"

Big Mim's eyebrows shot upward. "Jim, did you know that?"

"Darlin' girl." He added her pet name. "I did not. Ned, looks like you fell into the honeypot, or should I say the wine tub? You're on the right committee at the right time."

"Make the most of it, Ned," Aunt Tally commanded.

"It takes so much money to start a vineyard," BoomBoom noted. "Anywhere from twelve to eighteen thousand dollars per acre."

"Either you have a good harvest or you don't. Russian roulette, sort of." Little Mim finally interjected something, her mother's gaze having lost its sting as Big Mim accepted that Aunt Tally would have her martini one way or the other.

Ned remarked, "These new people can read all about grapes, they can realize they won't get good yields until the fourth or fifth year, depending on the grape variety and the weather. But they aren't country people. I don't know that they're tough enough. That's why Rollie Barnes impresses me. For all his gargantuan ego, his aggressiveness, he had the sense to know he needed someone like Arch Saunders."

A murmur of agreement filled the room.

"It's the crazy thing about being a farmer, isn't it?" Harry lamented. "You have a bumper crop and prices go down. You suffer through diminished harvests and prices shoot up. I know, I know, it's supply and demand, but when Mother Nature is your business partner, nothing is certain."

"Except uncertainty." Alicia smiled.

They heard the front door open.

"Anybody home?" A deep, resonant voice called out.

Jim hurried to the front hall and within seconds the Reverend Herbert Jones entered the room, Lucy Fur under his arm like a loaf of bread. She didn't much like it.

"Lucy Fur." Harry knew people's pets better than she knew them, really.

The extremely healthy kitty wiggled out of Herb's arms to run to Harry, who picked her up with a grunt.

"She hasn't missed too many meals when she was visiting at my sister's." Herb laughed. "Sorry I missed the lunch, but I needed to pick up the cat from Marty." He mentioned the local vet. "Shot renewal time."

"Let me fix you a plate, Herb." Big Mim kept a good table.

"I would never refuse your hospitality." He winked.

Everyone trooped back to the bright enclosed patio, which served as the luncheon site. They liked being with Herb and succumbed to the temptation of a second dessert.

Alicia, BoomBoom, and Harry summoned the strength to resist by sipping hot Constant Comment tea.

As Herb sliced his small partridge stuffed with wild rice, the fresh vegetables artfully arranged on his plate by the cook, the conversation flowed.

Lucy Fur, standing on her hind legs on the floor, raised a paw, placing it on Herb's thigh. He cut a small piece of partridge for her, put it on a bread plate, and bent over. No one said a word, since everyone there would have done the same thing. The springer spaniel rejoined them upon hearing the plate scrape the floor.

These were animal people. The differences among them were differences of income, age, gender, and the mysteries of personality. But when it came to animals, they were as one. Every single one of them, even Tazio, new to animal ownership, cherished a deep respect for all life.

"Baseball season's fresh as a newborn babe." Jim loved the Philadelphia Phillies. "Blair and I are going up to see this new Washington team."

"Yeah, I'd like to see them play, too," Fair, another baseball fan, commented.

"Orioles, now and forever." Harry placed her hand over her heart.

"Not going to be their year. In fact, it isn't going to be their year for years." Blair, no Orioles fan, enjoyed tweaking his former neighbor.

"Ha. You just wait," Harry defiantly replied.

"Well, I think the Kansas City Royals will surprise everyone," Tracy declared.

"Yeah, by being at the bottom of the barrel." Herb paused between bites.

"Those are fighting words, Rev." Tracy lifted his forefinger.

"Dodgers." Alicia had season tickets for years and used to go to the games with Cary Grant. She didn't say that, as it would have been bragging. She liked Grant enormously and one reason was he had learned baseball, no easy task for an Englishman. He also took pains to explain cricket to her, and she found she quite liked it.

"They may be a factor," Jim said judiciously.

Once Herb, himself, reached dessert, the conversation

turned to the panel discussion and terrorism in general, which they discussed at some length.

"Just think if someone contaminates the reservoirs that supply New York City. They could strike down, potentially, twenty-two million people between nine A.M. and five P.M.," BoomBoom added to the lively topic.

"Those are obvious targets," Alicia commented. "They'll strike us where we aren't looking."

"Exactly," Big Mim agreed. "Imagine if chemical-warfare specialists find a way to release a fungus that could make us sick? Not something that would kill immediately but something that would make people sick. It would incapacitate the sick, tie down the people caring for them, and damage the economy, too."

Harry added her two cents. "That's what was so fascinating about the panel: how common the types of fungus are that infect wheat, corn, grapes even. All of these could be used."

"Terrorists would use grapes?" Tazio's eyes widened.

Jim answered Tazio. "No, but let's say wheat becomes tainted. It passes on to humans. That's a one–two punch. But let's suppose our enemies are far more subtle than that. Let's say they infect hay, grass, crops. Cattle eat them. The meat becomes dangerous, and Americans consume huge quantities of beef. Meanwhile, thousands and thousands of cattle are eating poisoned grasses before the sickness can be traced to the source." Jim took a deep breath. "Now you have humans, cattle, medical people, and crops being destroyed or rendered useless for a time. You get the idea."

"I do. Become a vegetarian." Susan broke the mood of worry.

"Right. Drink wine, not water." Blair held up a glass.

9

After the luncheon, back at the farm, Harry walked through the quarter acre she'd planted with Petit Manseng, a grape used in Jurançon, perhaps the most famous of the white wines of southwestern France. She'd planted the rootstock herself in November, which would allow root growth over the winter. She planted each bare root eight feet from another. Her rows were also eight feet apart. She really wouldn't know until the growth spurt in high spring whether she had correctly spaced the vines.

She kept to the golden mean of spacing for grapes and hoped she was doing right by the Petit Manseng.

Naturally, as this was the first year, she didn't expect much. With help from Patricia and Bill and Felicia Rogan, she had settled on Petit Manseng because the small white grape stayed on the vine longer than most other types. This bumped up the sugar content even as it pushed down the acidity. Jurançon, at the foot of the Pyrenees, bears similarity to western Albemarle County. That helped Harry decide. But on one-quarter acre, once the vines were established, she should produce one ton of grapes, which translated into fifty cases or six hundred bottles. One barrel of oak is the equivalent of twenty-five cases.

Watching her pennies, Harry cultivated one-quarter acre at a cost of five thousand dollars and prayed all would be well, because, for her, that was a big outlay of cash.

She begged old oaken barrels from Patricia Kluge. One of the surest ways to produce inferior-tasting wine was too much oak. Although not a winemaker, she was a country girl and a quick study.

She loved agriculture. She liked growing grapes, but the expenses preyed on her natural financial caution. Reviving the Alverta peach orchard kept her on solid ground. And she kept her mother's pippin apple orchard flourishing. Fortunately, apples and grapes flourish with the same soil, water, sun conditions.

Tucker, Mrs. Murphy, and Pewter followed her as she bent down to check the shoots emerging from the trunks. A few warm weeks, when the air reeked with heavenly fragrances from apple trees, viburnas, different varieties of scented bushes, and these babies—she thought of them as babies—would surprise everyone with their vigorous growth.

She stood up, casting her eyes over the farm. In the paddocks the foals—true babies—dozed, and her heart melted each time she looked at the horses.

The hay peeped up, spring green, a tender color promising life, nutrition.

Her two acres of various sunflower types also glowed spring green, except for the Italian sunflowers, which she'd just planted. The sun warmed the afternoon to the mid-fifties. Her ancient three-ply cashmere crewneck sweater with darning spots served her well. Harry could never throw anything out that might be useful even one more day.

Once a year, Susan, Miranda, and BoomBoom would descend upon her to throw out tattered things. Her sock drawer alone took a half hour. She'd try to hang on to a threadbare sock by declaring it could be used to hold catnip.

The cats didn't care how they received their catnip, so long as it was forthcoming.

A car turned onto the farm road.

Tucker barked, *"Intruder!"*

A curly-haired, extroverted Bo Newell showed up. "Harry. I'll only be a minute." He checked his watch. "It's two-thirty, so I'll be out of here by two forty-five." Then he laughed.

"Do you think he has Miss Prissy in the car?" Pewter hated Bo's ancient cat, who was fond of travel and arguments.

"She tore up the leather upholstery in Nancy's Thunderbird. She's grounded." Mrs. Murphy related this story with undisguised glee, for Miss Prissy had ruined Mrs. Newell's new sports car.

"Why doesn't she just die, she's so damned old?"

"Tucker, why doesn't Aunt Tally die? They're too mean." Pewter giggled.

"What's cooking?" Harry asked the muscular Realtor.

"I've got clients from Belgium. They want me to find a farm with soil suitable for grapes. I tell you, I can't sell land that grows grapes fast enough. The word is finally out on Virginia wine. Obviously, a lot of time the best pieces are between friends. I'm trying to keep one step ahead of Rollie Barnes." He rubbed his hands together. "You haven't heard of anyone getting ready to sell, have you?"

"No, I haven't."

"What about Aunt Tally? She's sitting on nine hundred acres at Rose Hill. The windows are gone in some of those outbuildings. Course, they're stone; they'll outlast all of us, as will Aunt Tally."

"They look blind, those buildings." Harry leaned over the hood of his car. "She's not going to part with an acre. You know, Urquharts buy land, they never sell it. Now that Little Mim and Blair are going to live there after they're married, she won't surrender an inch."

"Well, I wouldn't, either." He exhaled through his nostrils. "This couple has big bucks, too."

"I'll sniff around."

"You've got a good nose." Bo's light eyes complemented his handsome features. "What do you think about Arch taking over Spring Hill Vineyards?"

"Well," she considered this question, one Fair had scrupulously not asked. "If Rollie lets him alone, he'll make it one of the best vineyards in the state, for starters. Arch is an ambitious man."

"So is Rollie."

"Yeah, but I don't know if he has the sense to leave people alone to do what they do best. Some people can't stop meddling."

"Big Mim." He half-smiled. "Although, in her defense, she improves most situations."

"And she gives out cookies." Tucker appreciated Big Mim's generosity toward dogs.

"No tuna." Pewter sniffed.

Before she could complain more, the blue jay, who had been perched on the stable cupola, opened wide his beautiful wings, lifted off his pretty perch, and dove straight for Pewter. He zoomed within an inch of Pewter's wide-domed skull.

"Fat ass!" he screamed, his squawk raucous.

"Jesus Christ." Bo jumped.

Harry jumped too. "Blue jay on steroids. He torments the cats."

"Cats? What about me?" Bo looked skyward.

Pewter ran under the shadow of the bird, who was gaining altitude. Mrs. Murphy ran, too.

"I will kill you!" Pewter raged.

The saucy fellow turned a graceful arc, then zoomed toward the two felines, who crouched. Sensibly, he did not go as low as his initial surprise attack. The cats leapt in the air, Mrs. Murphy higher than Pewter.

"Worthless. Worthless as tits on a boar." He then reclaimed his perch on the cupola, where he sang loudly to the world. *"I am the mightiest bird in the kingdom, in the universe. I fear no one."*

Harry and Bo stared up at him, his chest puffed out, his beak open. He ranted and sang. A low *"hoo, hoo, hoo, hoo"* should have alerted him, but his pride and volume blocked out Flatface's pronounced irritation.

Awakened by his song, which was harsh to her musical ears, Flatface ruffled her feathers. She slept in the cupola. Harry had fixed it so Flatface could nest up there. She could fly through the loft barn doors, which Harry usually left open at least a crack, even in winter. Also, one side of the cupola was opened enough for her to get in and out. Silence, big talons, a frightening beak, and remarkable intelligence are the weapons of all owls but are heightened in the great horned owl.

Flatface, furious, flew out from the cupola. The blue jay didn't hear her until she closed over him, grasping him in her talons.

"Drop him on me," Pewter shrieked with excitement.

"Holy shit." Bo was mesmerized.

"Flatface lives in the cupola. I think he plucked her last nerve." Harry breathlessly watched the drama.

Flatface, slowing, opened her wings wide and opened her talons, dropping the blue jay about six feet over Pewter's head. Mrs. Murphy danced on her hind legs.

The blue jay, feathers scattering, plummeted toward the two awaiting cats. He managed to open his wings and pull out of the free fall just as Pewter snatched at him.

Her reward was some exquisite tail feathers.

The blue jay hurried away as Flatface flew back into the barn. *"That will shut his trap,"* she said as she nestled in her cupola.

Simon, who watched from the hayloft doors, called up, *"You showed him."*

The blacksnake, Matilda, emerged from her nest in the back hay bales—she had laid eggs in a depression next to her nest. She cast a glittering eye at Flatface, then another at Simon before returning to her place. She was old and accordingly large, as fat around as a big man's wrist. Being a reptile, she lacked sociability. She did not, however, lack fangs, and although nonpoisonous, a deep bite from her jaws could send a human into shock. Thanks to Matilda and Flatface, not one mouse twaddled about in the hayloft. The cats might have a deal with the tack-room mice, but as far as Matilda and Flatface were concerned, one mouse equaled one hors d'oeuvre.

Matilda did say, *"Good work."*

Flatface turned her head almost upside down and winked.

Outside, the humans, cats, and dog were still talking about the blue jay's comeuppance.

"Near-death experience." Harry was on the side of her cats.

"I know some people who need a near-life experience." Bo chuckled. "Like Toby Pittman. One weird dude."

"Maybe he wears his weirdness on the outside. The rest of us wear it on the inside."

"I hope that means you're kinky."

"Bo, you think about one thing." Harry laughed at him.

"Know anything else that's as much fun?"

"Mmm. I'll give that deep thought." She waited a moment. "What do you think about Arch coming here from California?"

"Hell of a deal at his age to be responsible for a large operation. But I think he came back for you, too."

This startled Harry. "Why? Over is over."

"For some people; not for others," Bo wisely replied. "You know, he didn't know you were getting remarried. You'd think someone would have e-mailed him."

"Maybe." Harry thought a long time. "But my experience is men don't usually keep up with relationships. Arch's only friend here, if you can call him that, is Toby. All his old buddies are in Blacksburg or down in Chatham where he was raised."

Bo checked his watch. "I lied. I've been here longer than fifteen minutes. Must be the company." He climbed back into his SUV, perfect for showing clients country properties. "Keep me in mind, now, if you hear of anything."

"I will."

He closed the door, started the engine, rolled down the window. "Damnedest thing, that owl. Isn't that the way, though? I mean, something just hits you, right out of the blue?"

10

Late that afternoon, Deputy Cooper, at her desk, received a call from Cory Sullivan, an acquaintance who worked for the sheriff's department in Blacksburg. Many women in law enforcement share a special bond, as there are still men out there who belittle their involvement in the profession.

"Cooperation." Cory pronounced this as "Cooperation," accent on *Cooper.*

"Cory, what's cooking?"

"Three wrecks. No fatalities. One break-in at a convenience store, the perp on meth. One missing person, which is why I'm calling you."

"Another day in paradise." Cooper picked up her yellow pencil.

"Yep."

"Who's missing?"

"Professor Vincent Forland."

As Cooper wrote this down she clarified the information. "The viticulture expert?"

"How do you know him?"

"He was the speaker at a panel here a couple of days ago. Give me what you've got."

"His housekeeper called at two-thirty, alarmed that he hadn't returned from Charlottesville. According to her, he is extremely punctual and he told Mrs. Burrows, that's the housekeeper, that he would be home by noon."

"Two and a half hours. Kind of jumping the gun."

"Not according to her. She said she called Kluge Vineyards and they said he left at seven this morning."

"Guess he didn't give them an itinerary?"

"No. Just told Patricia Kluge that he would make a few calls along the way."

"Anything else?"

"The guy was unnatural. Never had a speeding ticket or a parking ticket."

"That's major." Coop laughed.

"Mrs. Burrows is very upset, so see what you can find out up there."

"Sure. Come up and visit sometime."

"Same here. I have tickets to Tech football next fall but, hey, don't wait that long."

After Coop hung up she checked all the accident reports in the county since seven in the morning. She checked with the state police to see if there had been any accidents on I-64 or I-81, Professor Forland's probable routes. There hadn't been any that involved him.

Then she called tow and wrecker services in case he'd had car trouble. He could be sitting at a gas station or at a car dealer's service center. Maybe he was too upset or busy to in-form Mrs. Burrows, but that wasn't her concern. Her concern was tracking him down.

On the fourth wrecker-service call she hit pay dirt. Big Jake's Towing Service had towed a Scion bearing Professor Forland's plates from the underground parking lot at Queen Charlotte Square. It had been parked in a reserved spot, and the owner of that parking space was one step ahead of a running fit on coming in to work to find her slot filled.

Big Jake, aptly named, walked Cooper to the chain-link fenced-in area where cars were impounded until their owners forked over the cash to release them.

Big Jake handed her the keys. "You sure got here fast."

"Just hit the flasher button." She smiled at him. "Where did you find the keys?"

"Behind the sun visor."

"Did you open the trunk?"

"No."

She walked to the trunk. "Big Jake, I don't know what's in here, so fair warning."

He nodded, stepped to the side as she popped the lid. A banker's box filled with notes, a flashlight, and an emergency kit seemed a pathetic amount of stuff.

Putting on thin latex gloves, she opened the car door and checked every cubbyhole and compartment. The day turned from crisp to cold, the usual April inconsistency. She flipped down the sun visors.

"You expecting trouble?"

"I don't know. I sure hope not." She hunkered down to check under the seats. From under the driver's seat she pulled out Professor Forland's thick, square, black-rimmed glasses. She then replaced them exactly where they had been. "Who comes in and out of here?"

"Me, Fatty Hazlette, Kerry, the other driver."

"Anyone touch this car?"

"No, just me. I was the one who towed it in."

"Thanks." She pulled her cell out of her jacket pocket and called Rick. "Boss, I think we've got a major problem."

11

A fence board popped off due to a combination of age and too much attention from a naughty mare. Harry, using the claw of her large hammer, pried off each end, carried the two pieces to the dump pile behind her large equipment shed. The sun was setting and she hurried to finish the job.

The pile, used for wood bits, would be picked over. Odd bits of wood can often be useful, and Harry, true to form, wasted precious little. At the end of the fall, the ground still soft, she'd scoop out what remained using the big bucket of the front-end loader. This would be burned in a pit and then covered over. For fun, she'd stick in a couple of potatoes, carrots, and onions wrapped in tinfoil. Later she'd use the rake, pull them out, and eat them for supper.

The pile today consisted of three or four wood pieces and a little wagon with the wheels off, placed to one side. Early spring meant the debris pile was sparse.

Conscious of fire, the pile was thirty feet away from the

equipment shed on lower ground. One couldn't see it unless one walked behind the shed and looked down. Harry was as tidy as Fair, a good thing because it's the little things about another person that drive you up the wall.

A flatbed load of cured fence boards rested on pallets on the far left side of the big shed. She hoisted a board on her shoulder and returned to the paddock. She nailed it in place, enjoying the helpfulness of the mares and foals. She'd paint it in the early evening when the horses were back in the barn. Otherwise she'd have zebra-striped foals.

Dozing in the hayloft, Mrs. Murphy raised her head. A car was turning off the state road, a half mile away. She heard the tires crunch on the bluestone.

Tucker, standing dutifully beside Harry, pricked up her ears.

"Cooper." She recognized the tire tread.

Pewter, asleep on the tack trunk, dreaming of today's adventure, heard nothing. Little dust motes floated upward in the air each time she exhaled. Martha sat and watched, a tiny bit of peppermint she'd found on the floor in her paws. The foals liked peppermints. Harry had dropped one, stepped on it, and figured she'd clean it up when she came back in.

By the time Harry's ears, good for a human, picked up the sound, Coop was a quarter mile from the barn, sound zinging clear on the clear day.

She tapped the last nail in place. She'd put on a little dab of wood putty later. She sunk in the tiny nail heads and didn't want the depression to show. She wouldn't use nails with large flat heads, because the playing horses might scratch their faces. Like all young mammals, foals couldn't always distinguish between playing and playing that might be dangerous.

"Hey, girl." Coop closed the door to the squad car.

"Back at you." Harry slipped the hammer into her belt. "I've got deviled eggs. I've never known you to pass up food."

Coop laughed. "Word is out."

"At least your stomach isn't. You stay in good shape." Harry complimented her as they pushed open the screen door.

"Volleyball and running."

Mrs. Murphy, on her feet now, stuck her head out the opened loft doors. Harry would close them come nightfall, leaving them open enough for air to circulate, but as the nights warmed, she'd eventually leave them wide open.

Tight barns sickened horses.

Simon, a broken Pelham chain in his paws, lay fast asleep.

Mrs. Murphy marveled at his penchant for anything shiny. He already had one broken Pelham chain, but he thought this one even better.

She shook off the last of the hay, looked straight down. Too far. She trotted back to the ladder, shimmying down, then dashed into the kitchen just as Harry put out the deviled eggs, butter, sandwich meats, cheese, lettuce, and sliced tomatoes, along with a big jar of Hellmann's mayonnaise.

A loaf of whole-grain bread rested on the thick cutting board, a bread knife alongside.

"Miranda?"

"Her latest. She says it's seven-grain. Have you ever kneaded bread?"

"No." Coop sliced two pieces for Harry, two for herself.

"Makes your hands and forearms strong. Think about laundrywomen throughout the centuries. My God, their forearms had to be bigger than bodybuilders'."

"When you think about it, we live soft lives."

"Pretty much." Harry, lean as a slab, knew that despite her farm labors she enjoyed electricity, central heating, the best dental care in the world, and all manner of vaccinations to prevent disease.

"Turkey," Tucker informed Mrs. Murphy, who smelled it the second she slipped through the cat door into the kitchen.

"If we're good, you know one of them will give us some." Mrs. Murphy sat by Harry's right side, Tucker on Harry's left.

"I'm here on business." Cooper reached for the mayonnaise jar.

"What did I do now? Or maybe it's these two beggars here." Harry glanced down at the attentive animals. "Where's Lardass?"

"Out cold in the tack room," Mrs. Murphy informed her.

"When she finds out there was turkey, she'll turn into a big grump." Tucker giggled.

Ice cubes clinked in the tall glasses. Harry put them on the table, then two Cokes. She finally sat down.

"Thanks." Coop poured her Coke, the fizz rising. "Professor Forland didn't stop by here today, did he?"

"No, why?"

"His car was towed from the underground Queen Charlotte parking today, but no sign of Professor Forland."

"Odd."

"He'd parked in a reserved space. I should say the car was parked in a reserved space. Big Jake towed it, and so far no call from the professor about his car. And his housekeeper called. He told her he'd be home, and she said he is very punctual."

"Maybe he had a heart attack or something."

"Called all the hospitals, rescue squads, state police. Nada."

She noticed how pretty the paprika looked on the deviled egg yolk. "Well, something's wrong."

"Did he ever stop by during his visit?"

"He came to look at my Petit Manseng." She pronounced the French perfectly.

A wry smile played over Cooper's lips. "God, you'll soon be as fussy as the rest of them."

"No, I won't."

"These are good."

"Hey, Miranda left a cheesecake with a chocolate bottom crust and raspberry sauce on top, French raspberries. She said the market had had a run on strawberries and raspberries shipped in from Florida and Georgia."

"Spring comes a lot earlier there."

Harry rose, returning with the cheesecake. Then she got up again.

"Now what are you doing?"

"Coke and cheesecake don't go. I'm making tea."

"Okay." Cooper happily assented. "So what happened when Professor Forland looked at your vines?"

"Nothing. He said they were healthy and he wished me luck."

"Hmm."

"Ever notice he looked like a worm?"

Cooper thought. "He did, didn't he?"

12

After a long Thursday morning, Fair stopped at the small coffee shop in Crozet. The days, incredibly busy, had flown by. It seemed like he'd checked fencing with Harry on Saturday and suddenly it was Thursday. Before he had his cup to his lips for a needed jolt of caffeine, Rollie Barnes pushed through the door. Seeing Fair at the counter, he sat next to him.

"Hello, Rollie, how are you today?"

"Cold. I thought Virginia was the South," Rollie grumbled.

"It is, but you're hard by the Blue Ridge Mountains."

"Kyle, I need a double shot," Rollie called to the owner, and then swiveled on his stool toward Fair. "Low pressure."

"Yeah, I know I shouldn't drink this much coffee. I'll get the jitters later, but I've been up since three-thirty this morning and I'm about beat." Fair wasn't complaining so much as stating fact.

"Something going on?"

"Too many people are turning horses into rich pastures. In spring if folks don't watch their horses they can founder. And I'm delivering foals that aren't Thoroughbreds. Late ones."

"Guess you heard Professor Forland is missing."

"Harry told me when I came home last night."

"Thanks." Rollie eagerly grasped the large mug when Kyle slid it to him.

"Doesn't make much sense. He doesn't seem like the kind of man to go on a bender."

"You never know about people. Everyone's got secrets." Rollie sounded learned.

Fair uttered the words that were music to Rollie's ears. "You're right."

Kyle, who'd been listening to theories about the professor's disappearance all week in the news, said, "Wouldn't believe the stuff I've heard." He paused. "He's captured by Al Qaeda. He is Al Qaeda. He's run off with Dinny Ostermann's wife. It goes on."

"People can talk." Rollie pointed his finger at the door to the coffee shop. "Who knows what goes on out there?"

Fair tapped his head. "Who knows what goes on in here?"

"Nutcase?" Kyle's brow furrowed.

"The professor?" Rollie propped his elbow on the counter.

Kyle leaned over the counter. "Or whoever snatched him."

Always one to look on the bright side, Fair added, "Oh, he might show up. Embarrassed maybe."

The door swung open at regular intervals. The lunch

crowd started at eleven and didn't taper off until two in the afternoon. Kyle appreciated a large lunch clientele.

Fair slid his money across the counter. Rollie pushed it back. "I owe you a cup of coffee. You were right about the colt."

"How's the little fella doing?" Fair smiled broadly. He loved babies.

"Pretty good. 'Course, my wife spends more time with him than with me. She's so soft-hearted."

"That's why she married you." Fair honored him by teasing him.

Rollie thought about that a minute. "Might be right. You know, I wonder sometimes what the world would be like without women. Apart from being dull."

"We'd kill each other," Fair simply stated.

"Is this a woman-as-civilizing-force discussion?" Kyle cracked as he motioned for his waitstaff to pick up the pace.

"They are." Rollie placed a crisp ten-dollar bill on the polished counter.

Kyle, having had his troubles with women, grumbled, "What the hell do they want? Maybe they do make the world kinder, I don't know, but I can't figure out what they want."

"Whatever they tell you," Fair, accustomed to Harry being forthright, advised.

"They say one thing one day and another thing the next." Kyle put his hand on his hip. "It drives me crazy."

"Everyone, man or woman, wants to feel special," Fair said. "You have to figure out what that person really needs and then figure out what they want. The two aren't always the same, you know."

Rollie stared at Fair, taking his measure as if for the first time. "Guess you do."

"My experience in keeping a woman happy—and mind you, I didn't the first time around; I learned this the hard way, by losing the best woman I could ever hope for—but give her what she wants. Simple."

"The Taj Mahal." Kyle grimaced.

"Oh, Kyle. You know what I mean." Fair leaned down, since he was now standing, and lowered his voice. "Give her what she wants in bed. Take your time. Count from one hundred backward if you have to, but take your time. Bring her flowers just because. Take out the trash. Wash and wax her car. Do stuff. Tell her she looks pretty."

"You do all that?" Rollie seemed amazed.

"Sure I do. Harry's a country girl. What makes her happy? A new pair of work boots that won't hurt her feet. And some flowers with the boots are okay, too. Maybe another woman would like the money for a new dress or something, but with Harry, practicality comes first."

"When did you know you'd won her back?" Rollie was now quite interested.

"Started two years ago when I bought the dually. Helped her buy it, really, and Art Bushey, who owned the Ford dealership then, helped me. But I knew I was across home plate when I bought her that colt by Fred Astaire. He was a yearling when I bought him, correct and good mind. She melted. After that it was a matter of time."

"Two years," Kyle matter-of-factly stated.

Rollie blurted out, "You hung on for two more years?"

"I kept asking her to marry me. I knew she'd say yes eventually. No one will ever love her like I do, and I learned my lesson. She knows that."

"I don't know if I have that stamina," Kyle declared.

"Then you don't love her enough," Fair bluntly replied, which was surprising coming from him.

"He might have a point." Rollie supported Fair. "I haven't met a man yet who doesn't have to jump through hoops of fire. Once you do it, you're okay. But I mean, they'll put you through fire."

"I just don't see the point." Kyle raised his voice and a few customers turned his way.

"Because you're a man," Fair said. "Listen to me. You don't have to see the point. You just have to do what needs to be done."

"Yeah, if you try to understand a woman you'll never get to first base. Some things you can understand, but other things, ridiculous as they are, are really important to them. So, like the man says, do what they tell you." Rollie chuckled at this.

He and Fair walked out together.

"Learned something about you today," Fair warmly said. "You pay attention."

"Sometimes."

13

"Slow down," Pewter growled, running behind Mrs. Murphy.

"No!"

Ahead, a baby bunny ran evasively to avoid the sharp claws of the tiger cat. The little fellow just made it to his warren and the comfort of his mother as the cat pounced a great final pounce.

"Brute!" the mother bunny scolded Mrs. Murphy.

"Drat!" The tiger sat down, bent her head for a better look at the large cottontail glaring back at her.

Pewter, panting, pulled up beside Mrs. Murphy. *"Nearly got 'im."*

"We'd have our own Easter Bunny." Mrs. Murphy said this loud enough to further infuriate the mother rabbit.

"Maybe the Easter Bunny will have a limp," Pewter hopefully remarked.

At this, both Mrs. Murphy and Pewter exploded in laughter.

"You cats think you're superior." The mother rabbit sniffed. *"We'll see how superior you are when the bobcat gets you."*

"Have you seen him?" Pewter feared the medium-size predator.

"He passes by. He's a killer, that one, and one day he'll have you in his jaws."

"What a pretty thought," Mrs. Murphy saucily replied as she turned and trotted back over the greening-up pastures.

"I hate that cat." Pewter fell in alongside her best friend.

"Nearly took me to heaven twice. Thank God for the red fox. He saved me first time out. And Tucker did the second time when that devil snuck up on me."

"You'd think you would have smelled him. He's strong."

"Upwind and a strong wind. I didn't know until I heard a twig crack." Mrs. Murphy ruffled her fur, then it settled. *"I burned the wind and I still couldn't put enough distance between us. He's incredibly fast. And ruthless."*

"Why'd the fox help you?"

"Because once I helped him. Also, I always tell the foxes when the hounds will be here. And now that the Bland Wade tract has been added to the holdings, or I should say the use of it all, they'll be here at least once a month, come fall."

"You never take me when you visit the foxes."

"Pewter, you're flopped in the barn or on the sofa and you don't want to move your lardass."

"That's not true. You're selfish."

"Oh la!" Mrs. Murphy tossed this off, sweeping her whiskers forward. *"Pewter. Stop."*

"Don't tell me what to do!" Pewter stepped on a snoozing rattler, a big one.

The membrane rolled back from her eyes and she coiled up, waving her tail, the deadly sound loud.

Both cats jumped sideways as she struck, white fangs

poised for action. Then they ran like blazes. The rattler, who could be fast for a short burst despite her winding motion, had no desire to kill the cats. She looked around, sniffed, for she had very good olfactory powers, then moved to a flat rock and decided to doze again in the pleasant, warming afternoon.

The cats raced and raced, finally drawing up under a small, beautiful grove of Alverta peaches on the southeast side of the old Jones home place, a half mile from the house.

Herb had made a lovely sign that read "Homecoming."

Farther west and at a higher elevation, a small mature orchard of pippin apple blossoms lent fragrance to the last days of April.

The two felines caught their breath.

"Funny. Snakes," Mrs. Murphy mused.

"There's nothing funny about snakes." Pewter loathed the reptiles.

"Cold blood. She could move fast because she'd been lying in the sun and it's maybe sixty-eight degrees or higher, you know. I can't imagine being cold-blooded."

"Is that what humans mean when they say someone is cold-blooded? They're a reptile?"

"Maybe. Maybe that's where it started." The sweet chatter of purple finches and bluebirds added punctuation to her words. *"For them, being cold-blooded is terrible. I mean, they can understand someone killing in anger or passion but not thinking it out, planning. So they call it cold-blooded."* Mrs. Murphy watched a peach-blossom petal swirl down.

The cold snap had delayed everything, but once the warmth came, the peaches bloomed at about the same time as the redbuds and early dogwoods.

It would be another week or even two, depending on temperatures, before all the apple trees blossomed, although the buds kept swelling, turning the hills lapping up to the Blue Ridge Mountains white.

"*Hey.*" Pewter noticed.

Mrs. Murphy walked to the packed-down earth for a better look. She flared her nostrils, opening her mouth, too. "*Someone dug here, then replaced it. Look how careful they were to try and make the turf look undisturbed.*"

"*Sure seems like a lot of work.*"

"*Wasn't Harry. We'd have been with her.*" Mrs. Murphy checked for footprints. "*They covered their tracks.*"

"*You can't dig and get the earth packed like that. Whoever did this dumped earth somewhere.*"

They searched but found nothing.

"*Could have carted it off in a truck.*" Mrs. Murphy found this unsettling.

Pewter, intent on searching, didn't notice a large buzzard high in an ancient poplar. The buzzard, who had a sense of humor, spread her wings for a sun bath, calling down, "*Lunch.*"

Scared twice this afternoon, Pewter had had quite enough. She ran east toward Harry's farm. The distance between the two houses, if measured in a straight line over the uneven ground, was a little more than one mile. Running, a cat could blaze home in four minutes, but the creek, if it was high like it was now, presented an obstacle.

Mrs. Murphy, following, paused for a moment at the lovely family cemetery, a huge oak within the wrought-iron fence.

"*I'm not stopping. And furthermore, why do humans put fences around cemeteries? Do they think the dead will climb out?*" Pewter huffed and puffed.

"*I think it's an aesthetic thing.*" Mrs. Murphy had never thought of why the dead were so often contained.

"I don't want to be around anything gruesome today. That rattler was enough."

"Pewter, death waits for us all."

"Yeah, well, he's going to have to wait a good, long time for me."

She was right, thankfully. But death was waiting, no doubt about that.

14

On Monday, May 1, Harry and Susan pulled out of Mostly Maples, a nursery to the trade. Harry braked hard, throwing Mrs. Murphy, Pewter, and Tucker onto the floor of the 1978 Ford truck.

"Jesus Christ!" she exclaimed.

As Harry rarely swore, the animals climbed back onto the bench seat without complaint. They, too, had seen Toby Pittman hurtle by at top speed.

"What is the matter with that man?" Susan indignantly wondered. "He's become positively unstable."

"Hell, Susan, he was never wrapped too tight to begin with. Professor Forland going missing put him right over the edge."

"Living alone."

"I beg your pardon." Harry cautiously looked both ways before pulling left onto Route 240 to head into Crozet. "I lived alone for years."

"Yes, but you're social. You have many friends and, of course, you have Mrs. Murphy, Tucker, and Pewter the rotund."

"I am not. I'm built round."

As they were in close quarters, neither Mrs. Murphy nor Tucker corrected Pewter's illusion. It's hard to fight in a truck.

"Toby has Jed, his donkey, but that's about it. His sister hasn't spoken to him in eight years. Maybe more."

Susan changed subjects. "We got our first order!" She twisted her head to look at the cars parked at Crozet Vet. "Bo Newell's there. I didn't know Bo took Miss Prissy to Marty." She named the owner and head veterinarian of the clinic.

"That cat is a holy horror. Bo might be there to see if Marty knows anything about land for sale. Grapeland." She giggled for a second. "If Elvis had only grown wine he could have lived at Grapeland."

"Harry, you're mental."

"Yeah, but I'm fun."

"I need a hot chocolate so I can better appreciate your humorous, wonderful self."

"Susan, what's this thing with you and hot chocolate?"

"I don't know, but I want a big hot chocolate with mountains of whipped cream."

"And you're the woman who obsesses about her weight?"

Susan laughed. "That's just it. I've discovered if I drink a big hot chocolate I'm not so hungry. Another thing, if I eat a couple handfuls of Virginia peanuts, I can go for hours before I want food."

"Virginia peanuts, best peanuts in the world."

Crozet, however, was too far west and north in the state to produce the famous crop.

"Did you know when the English first came in the seventeenth century they fed peanuts to their cows and horses? They didn't think it was a suitable food for humans."

"Who told you that?" Harry raised an eyebrow. She couldn't believe humans would be so stupid as to sidestep a rich source of protein.

"Barbara Dixon. I was down in Dillwyn the other day and I stopped by Barbara and Gene's. You know how she gets wrapped up in history." Susan named a foxhunting couple they both enjoyed, who were in the process of restoring an early-eighteenth-century house and stables.

"And she's from San Antonio. She just got seduced by Virginia." Harry laughed.

"Actually, I think she was seduced by Gene."

At that they both laughed, then Harry returned to peanuts. "Really, they wouldn't eat them?"

"No. Wouldn't eat tomatoes, either. Thought they were poisonous."

"Well, all someone had to do was pop one in their mouth and that would be the end of that," Harry said.

"Would you do it?"

"Uh, well, let me reconsider my statement."

They rolled along in the best mood because of their first order and because it truly was spring. Spring fever.

"Wonder when people realized they could eat peanuts and tomatoes?" Susan pondered.

"There's a project for you." Harry slowed to thirty-five miles an hour as they entered Crozet.

"I'll give it to Barbara. You know that once I ask her she won't rest until she finds the answer."

"Sue Satterfield is like that, too." Harry named a friend who had been a teacher and was a good friend of the Dixons.

"Maybe I should give one the tomato question and the other the peanut question." Susan touched Harry's shoulder. "Hey, don't forget about my chocolate."

"Damn." Harry had turned into the post-office parking lot. She swung around to wait for traffic to pass.

"Miss it?"

"Sometimes. I miss the people. But I don't miss the hours, I don't miss the Federal regulations. You know, Susan, this is crude, but I can't help it: we are reaching a point where you won't be able to wipe your ass without the government telling you when to do it, how to do it, and what times to do it."

Susan roared. "I'll tell that to Ned."

"Tell him, while I'm on the subject of wiping, to just wipe ninety percent of the laws off the books. They're useless, obstructionist, and furthermore costing us all far too much money. Just tend to the roads, encourage business and agriculture, keep the state police strong, and stay out of everyone's life."

"I'll be sure to tell him. That can be his maiden speech. Ought to be a big hit among a group of people whose job security depends on making more laws."

"Then what in the hell is he doing there?" She continued to look both ways. "Where are these people coming from?"

"North of the Mason–Dixon line," Susan mused.

"Can't we send them back?" Harry smiled, then glanced at the clock in the dashboard, still ticking away after decades. "Lunch. Forgot about the time."

"Then you'd better get me to the café before everyone sits down. I'll never get my hot chocolate."

"We can sit at the counter. While I'm waiting for these Yankees to pass you have time to write, 'will die without hot chocolate' and pin it to your blouse. The notebook is in the door pocket."

"And leave us in the car? No fair!" came the chorus.

"Pipe down. Finally." Harry pulled out, turned left, then turned immediately right into the old bank parking lot. "We could have gone into menopause waiting."

"Don't even breathe that word." Susan grimaced, notebook in hand, although she hadn't written anything.

"We're a long way away."

"Maybe so but, boy, my mother suffered, and they say it's hereditary."

"I'll buy you a hat with a little fan in it. I, personally, am not going to go through anything."

"O la!" Susan cracked the window enough for plenty of air.

Harry did the same on her side. "We won't be long."

"You always say that." Mrs. Murphy dropped her ears slightly.

"Yeah, and someone comes in and the next thing you know it's who-shot-John." Tucker used the old Southern expression for catching up with the news—news to men, gossip to women, although of course the information was exactly the same.

"Yeah. Not fair. We could die of heat prostration in here." Pewter tried the medical route, which wasn't convincing since the temperature outside was fifty-two degrees. It might get to sixty at the most inside the truck with the windows cracked.

"They're going to abandon us! Just like children in Rio de Janeiro's slums." Mrs. Murphy sounded plaintive.

"They shoot them." Pewter licked her lips with not glee so much as pride of imparting shocking information.

"They do not." Tucker was aghast.

"Yeah, they do. I heard Fair talking about it to Harry after the news. You were asleep. They shoot them because the children are criminals. I can't imagine why they steal or maim, can you?" Pewter sarcastically replied.

The animals erupted into a heated discussion about why humans kill their young as opposed to why and when animals kill their young.

As Harry and Susan walked away, Harry turned, "What's gotten into them?"

"They'll settle."

"Either that or I'll need to reupholster the seat."

"Your truck will be fine."

Small stones breaking through the crumbling old macadam crunched underfoot. "Hey, did I tell you that Fair brought me a new pair of Wolverines and two dozen pink tulips? He is so sweet."

"Yes, he is. When did you switch to Wolverine?"

"When Timberlands slid downhill. They're so cheaply made now. I have that pair I bought in 1982—"

"The one your old German shepherd chewed the back off?"

"Yes, but I had Frank Kimball put on a new piece of leather with a roll for my Achilles tendon. It worked."

"For over twenty years. I'd say Timberland ought to get your business."

"That's just it. I went to A&N, tried on a few pair of work boots, and Susan, they just aren't the same. I was so disappointed. So then I tried on Montrails at the Rockfish Gap Outfitters in Waynesboro, and they are really good but really expensive. Had to pass. Then I went to Augusta Coop and tried a pair of Wolverines. Pretty darned good and affordable, but I was so worn out by trying on all these work boots, I gave up. But I did tell Fair."

"Harry, only you can agonize over work boots. It's not the expense, you're obsessing."

"You say." Harry became enlivened. The topic of money usually had that effect on her. "The Montrails were $130! The Wolverines weren't so much less, maybe thirty dollars, but I thought they were a lot of boot for the money. 'Course, I won't know until I work in them. I'm on my feet all day. I can't do with bad work boots or ones that are going to fall apart from horse pee and poop and tractor oil. I have good reason to agonize."

"You're right." It was easier to agree.

They pushed open the door to find the usuals perched on their stools at the counter, where Hy entertained Karen Osborne. Her marriage to Pete deterred Hy not a whit.

Harry sat next to Karen, and Susan sat on the other side of Hy, since those were the only vacant stools.

Susan begged Kyle for hot chocolate, pronto.

"Karen, how are the horses?"

"Good. All the spring visitors want trail rides. I cherish my lunch hour." She smiled.

"I'll bet. I don't see how you can run a hack barn. Takes a special person. I couldn't do it, deal with people who know nothing about horses but who want to ride."

"It helps that I have good horses."

Susan called down to Karen, "In any endeavor. My mother used to say, 'A second-rate horse makes a second-rate rider,' and you sure see that in the hunt field."

Hy, in his element—surrounded by women—flattered them. "I don't see how you girls can jump those big fences."

"We don't, Hy, the horse does," Harry answered as she held up her forefinger, which meant one cup of orange pekoe tea.

Kyle nodded as he foamed the whipped cream on Susan's

hot chocolate, since she was perishing before his very eyes for want of it.

The door swung open and Toby stomped in. "Hy, what were you doing in my vineyard today?"

Hy, surprised, swiveled around on his stool. "I wasn't there."

"The hell you weren't. I saw your white truck. No one else has a gold fleur-de-lis on his truck."

"Toby, if I were going to see your vineyards, I'd call on you first. I wasn't there."

"That was your truck." Toby's face reddened.

"The fleur-de-lis is small. Did you drive up to this alleged truck of mine?"

"No. I saw it from a distance, but I know your truck."

"And from that distance you determined it was my truck?"

"Liar! It was your truck. You were on my property and I damned well want to know why!"

Hy, out of deference to the ladies, stood up, stepping away from the counter as everyone held their breath. "I told you, I was not at your farm. I don't think anyone who works for me was at your farm, but I will check as soon as I return home. If they were, I will tell you immediately as well as why. Give me your cell number."

"What I'm giving you is fair warning. If you so much as put a foot on my land I will shoot you. I know why you're there. You want to ruin my grapes. You can't stand that I'm growing better grapes than you are. Stay off my land or I'll put you under it!"

"You're utterly deluded." A look of apprehension crossed Hy's face.

Toby yanked back his right fist, slamming it hard into

Hy's jaw. Hy had a glass jaw. He sank like a stone, cold-cocked.

Kyle flew around the corner, but that fast Toby ran out the door.

"Goddammit!" Kyle cursed.

"I'll take care of him." Karen called for one of the waiters to throw her a clean towel. She poured her water on it and knelt down, placing the wet towel on Hy's forehead.

Both Harry and Susan knelt down with her.

Kyle called the sheriff. Deputy Cooper just happened to be near the new post office. She pulled a three-sixty, hit the siren and lights to cross the road without waiting for the endless traffic.

When she opened the door, Hy was coming to, blood seeping from his mouth for he'd bitten his tongue when he was hit.

"Hy. Hy. Can you hear me?" Cynthia bent over in front of him.

"Uh-huh," he weakly replied.

She passed her hand in front of her eyes. "Follow my hand."

His eyes followed the motion of her hand as everyone in the coffee shop talked at once.

"Come on, Hy, let's put you in a booth." Kyle searched for an empty booth.

As there wasn't one, he was about to ask people to move, when Hy stood up unsteadily.

"I'm okay. Hurts, but I'm okay."

"Let me look at your tongue." Karen reached to hold open his jaw as if he were a horse.

Hy saved her the trouble by sticking out his tongue.

"Not too bad," Susan remarked, and Karen concurred.

"Are you dizzy?" Coop inquired. She wanted to make sure he hadn't suffered a concussion.

"No."

"Headache?" she asked.

"No. What I am," he dabbed his bleeding tongue, "is mad."

"Would you like to press charges?" Coop never assumed anything.

"Yes. Throw the book at the bastard." Hy's face flamed crimson.

"Why don't we go outside in the fresh air and you can sit in the car with me, windows down. We'll go over everything." Coop then told Harry, Susan, Karen, and Kyle she'd take statements from them in time. But they didn't have to stick around. She'd find them.

As she put her hand under Hy's elbow, he said, louder than he realized, "He's been furious at me ever since I won the best new entry at the wine-tasting last year. He can't stand it."

Coop walked to the door with Hy. "Sure you don't want some ice in a towel?"

"No," Hy growled. "Toby is dangerous. I want him locked up."

"Hy, that's easier said than done, but come out in the fresh air. I'll do what I can."

"Why is it difficult? Assault and battery. Straightforward."

"Toby is clever." Coop left it at that as she opened the door.

Harry hoped to hear more of the conversation, but the door closed.

Karen Osborne shrugged. "Certifiable." She didn't say whether she thought Toby was nuts or Hy or both.

15

"Warm winters." BoomBoom leaned over the paddock where Keepsake nursed Burly.

"1990 to 1995 were especially warm. Had the drought years in there, too." Fair, having come from Big Mim's to BoomBoom's farm, rubbed his stubble.

His thick beard irritated him because it grew so quickly. He kept an electric razor in his truck to try and keep up with it. If he had time, he shaved in the morning with a safety razor and then again when he came home from work. He felt his wife was entitled to a smooth face at night.

"It really hasn't been that cold since 2000 either. We've had a lot of snow and ice but not long periods of cold. Strange."

"Guess there really is global warming. I don't know if I read it in *The Wall Street Journal* or *The London Financial Times*, but there was an article about hybrid vehicles. Said those emissions would be just as hot as gasoline."

"Since you get more miles to the gallon, maybe it would slow global warming," BoomBoom, a true gearhead, replied.

Fair smiled as Burly left Keepsake to run a few circles, buck, then stop to stare at the two humans, only to repeat the process. "Personality."

"To burn." She laughed. "I've fallen in love with the little guy and I don't care if he does have big ears."

"So did Clark Gable." Fair laughed, then said, "Driving so much gives me time to think. I think we don't have any choice but to be done with the internal combustion engine."

"God, all those beautiful engines." BoomBoom's hand involuntarily flew to her breast. It didn't have to fly far. "I do love engines." She sighed. "But we can't very well destroy the planet because of it."

"It's kind of like if President Rutherford B. Hayes had declared the future of America was the whale industry because of whale-oil lamps. I expect some technology will replace the internal combustion engine, but I can't imagine what or if it will happen in my time. You know, Boom, I think the proliferation of some of the equine disease we see is the result of the warming."

"You mean West Nile?" She named a disease, often fatal, that infected horses and humans.

"That. What gives us some wiggle room there is that the virus has to go from the crow to the possum—usually a possum—and then the horse. People can get it directly from crows but not from horses. Fortunately, the fragility in the transfer of the virus means if we break the cycle in just one jump between species, we ought to knock it. But there's something coming down the pike every day, it seems." He shook his head.

"It's odd, too, that so many of these new diseases—or what seem to be new to our hemisphere, anyway—evolve so quickly." BoomBoom, a highly intelligent woman, read widely and often.

He nodded in agreement. "AIDS wins the prize there. But the old standbys are making a comeback: tuberculosis, syphilis, even measles. They return more resistant to treatment."

"No one can blame those diseases on animals. Human-to-human transmission."

"Actually, there's not much that can be pinned to animals, because so few humans in the developed nations live close to them. 'Course it's different in Asia, Africa, and parts of South America. Every time a new disease appears on the horizon, I have to laugh, because the medical profession is in such a hurry to trace it to a monkey or a snail or a lemur. It's as though humans still can't face the fact that we are perfectly capable of being agents of disease." He checked his watch. "Didn't mean to take up so much of your time."

"I've never spent a minute with you that I didn't enjoy."

He smiled. "I don't know about that, but you're kind to say it."

"How's Mim's crop this year?"

"Beauties. She bred to Polish Navy, Mineshaft, Yankee Victor, and Buddha."

"Mim has a head for breeding. Alicia says that because Mim and Mary Pat were so competitive with each other, each pushed the other higher." BoomBoom mentioned Mary Pat Reines, now deceased, an excellent horsewoman.

"She had a good year last year. She came within a hair of taking the Colonial Cup." Fair cited a famous steeplechase race. "The Polish Navy colt is a beauty, great shoulder on that guy. She says he's going to be her old-age hunter."

"Did she happen to say when old age would begin?"

"Next Thursday." He burst out laughing.

Once BoomBoom stopped laughing, she said, "This global-warming thing—I was wondering if it will speed up all kinds of infections, in animals and plants. I was reading a book on the Black Death, and the ideal temperature for the bacillus to thrive in is between fifty and seventy degrees Fahrenheit."

"Pretty much the same as the ideal temperature for humans."

"Now there's thought that not only can the rat flea carry the plague, but the human flea can, too. Something like thirty-two different flea varieties can carry the plague. Hope I got that right."

"Warming might hasten disease spread, but I think more than anything you need the right kind of host and the speed of air travel."

"What do you mean, 'the right kind of host'?"

"A large population, living in filth, bad water supply, in-adequate nutrition—they become the perfect host. All it takes is one visitor from a developed nation who is physi-cally compromised to pick up the pest, be it virus or bacil-lus, get on a plane, and disembark in Berlin, Paris, London, New York, take your pick."

"It's a terrifying prospect." She paused. "The panel with Professor Jenkins and Professor Forland got me to thinking—could an enemy reintroduce the plague?"

"They don't have to reintroduce it, Boom, it's here. For-tunately our hygiene is good, but given some disaster like the great San Francisco earthquake, the rats will come out of their holes. Some of those rats will carry the plague. At least, that's what I believe."

"Any word about Professor Forland?" BoomBoom asked since she'd just spoken of him.

"No. No one knows what to think."

"He's dead. That's obvious to me, anyway."

"God, I hope not." He inhaled, then exhaled. "Why? Sure, it crossed my mind, but I can't think why someone would kill him."

A light breeze ruffled BoomBoom's long blonde hair. "There are always reasons to kill someone, Fair. Greed. Jealousy. Revenge. Profit. Religion. Politics. Sex. Even sheer carelessness. You kill someone by accident, don't want to pay the consequences, so you remove the body."

"I guess. Pretty dismal."

"The history of humankind is dismal, with a few bright exceptions."

"I see it just the opposite. We've progressed in every field. There are periods of backsliding and regression, but no one can suppress progress for long."

"A long discussion." She paused. "Back to Professor Forland. The news reported his car was found in Queen Charlotte Square parking lot. There are businesses there. McGuire Woods law firm has their offices there. There are apartments. He could have had good reason to be there."

"If Rick and Coop can find it."

"Or Harry." She smiled.

"Don't even say it!" He shook his forefinger. "Don't give her any ideas."

"Me? She's as curious as a cat. She won't be able to resist trying to find out what's happened to Professor Forland."

Sighing, he leaned on the fence with both elbows. "You're right. I guess the leopard can't change her spots."

Strangely enough, Arch Saunders was using that same phrase in talking to Harry, whom he ran into picking up mail.

They hadn't seen each other alone since Arch's return. Given that he hadn't been in Crozet a full month, that didn't seem odd, as he had a great deal to do in a short time. Harry, too, was extremely busy.

At first their conversation was polite, not too personal, then Arch asked her why she remarried Fair.

She replied that she loved him and he'd grown up a lot.

"The leopard doesn't change his spots," Arch said, a trace of bitterness creeping into his voice.

She compressed her lips, then changed the subject. "How do you like it at Spring Hill?"

"I'm going to make it one of the best vineyards in the state." He added, "Lot to do, though. Like this morning I found downy mildew on some vines Rollie bought last fall. I didn't like the way the rootstock looked. Rollie didn't know enough to screen for it."

"Can you fix it?"

"I can control it. I can spray with Ridomil. I have to spray every vine every twenty-one days, and it's expensive. But it's the only way."

"Good luck." She opened the door to the old F-150, the cats and dog on the bench seat.

"Hi there, Mrs. Murphy, Tucker, and Pewter."

"Hello," they replied.

After good-byes, Arch watched Harry drive off. He thought she looked even better than she did when they dated.

That same afternoon, Hy Maudant called Toby Pittman.

"Toby, one of my men, a new man, Concho, did drive on your premises. He didn't see anyone so he left."

"Why'd you send him?" Toby angrily replied.

"I didn't. He's new, like I said. He's Mexican; his English is a little rocky. Anyway, he'd been visiting vineyards to schedule the use of my mobile bottling unit."

"That's half a year away," Toby said.

"Which is why I'm scheduling now. By the fall it will be too late."

"Thought you said his English was bad. Why would you send him out to make arrangements?"

Beginning to fume, Hy snapped, "Because I had a form drawn up. All Concho has to do is hand it to a prospective client. And furthermore, I said his English was rocky, not so bad he can't understand. He improves every day."

"Why would you send him here?"

"He's new! He doesn't know we don't get along. He was just going from vineyard to vineyard like he was told to do."

"You sent him to spy on me."

"You're crazy." Hy was losing patience rapidly.

"And you're a murderer," Toby accused loudly.

"What?"

"I bet you killed Professor Forland."

"You really are insane. Furthermore, he's missing. That doesn't mean he's dead."

"He's dead, all right. I know him. He would never disappear for a few days. You killed him because you're a jealous, scheming son of a bitch and you knew he was working with me. You can't stand that I'm better than you. That—"

"He visited everyone. There's no point in continuing this conversation." Hy slammed down the phone.

Fiona walked into the library from the next room. "Whatever is it?"

"He's mad. Totally insane." Hy's arms flailed in the air. "Toby Pittman accused me of murdering Professor Forland. They need to put him away."

The phone rang. Fiona picked it up.

Before she could say "Hello," Toby shouted, "If you or any of your men come on my farm I'll kill you."

"This is Fiona."

He paused. "I won't kill you, Fiona, but you must be dumber than snot to stay married to that low-rent bastard."

Now she slammed down the phone. "He called me 'dumber than snot.'"

Red flushed Hy's cheeks. He started for the door. "No one is going to insult you. I'll kill him before he kills me."

She grabbed him. "Hy, calm down. I believe he really will try to kill you."

"I'll kill him first."

"He's not worth the fuss."

Hy hit his palm with his fist. "Well, I am not putting up with him insulting my wife."

"He's off his rocker. Crazy people are more dangerous than sane ones."

And the sane ones are bad enough.

16

"Goddamned snotty Virginians. They want to see me fail. Well, I won't give the sons of bitches the satisfaction!" Rollie kicked his expensive wire-mesh designer wastebasket, sending white, pink, blue, and green pieces of paper all over the navy-blue old Chinese rug.

Arch breathed deep relief because Rollie wasn't mad at him. "Spring Hill won't fail. First, I caught it in time. Second, as we buy up land or rent it, we'll grow different varieties of grapes. That will be an insurance policy. If one type has a bad year, the others should make up for it. Kind of like the balance between stocks and bonds." He tried to use terms Rollie would understand.

He was surprised at how sensible the prickly fellow was, considering the news. Rollie wasn't assigning blame. He appeared to grasp, tenuously, that nature had her own agenda.

"Order the stuff?"

"Should be here tomorrow morning."

"Anyone else know?" Rollie raised one eyebrow.

"I called Hy Maudant."

"Why him?"

"He's very knowledgeable. He grew up in the vineyards in France and attended their agriculture school. Also, he's established and he can tell me how best to contact other vineyards: should I make personal calls, use the phone, use e-mail. He's very helpful." His inflection rose slightly at the end of the sentence, the traditional method in English for asking a question or appearing less than certain.

"And?"

"He doesn't have any downy mildew, but he said he's found the beginnings of black rot in one lower-lying section of his vineyards. Not much, he said, but he's already up-rooted those vines and begun the spraying. 'Course, he'd spray anyway."

"Why is he tearing them out?"

"Hy isn't going to take any chances, and once the plant is infected, it's always infected."

"But if you control it, can't the vines bear decent fruit?"

"They can. Depending on when you catch the fungus, but, boss, why take the chance? Those vines aren't going to produce over the years like the clean ones. Kill them."

"Hell of a lot of money."

"Growing the perfect grape is not for the fainthearted." Arch laid it on the line.

Rollie leaned over his desk, his weight on his knuckles. "For your information, I've got a set of balls. Do you think I'm going to fold my hands because of some stupid spores?"

"No." Arch measured his words. "Nature is a brutal business partner sometimes. That's why I think spreading the risk is the way to go. The more land you have under the umbrella, the better off you are."

"Mmm, I'll buy land if it's necessary, but I'd rather buy up someone else's yield. Let them do the work."

"Kind of like a portfolio, gotta balance it out." Arch nodded. "The Ridomil should do it, but I've got to apply it about every twenty-one days depending on rainfall."

Rollie dropped back into his seat, the leather squeaking. He was about to dismiss Arch and get back to his work when a nasty idea popped into his overheated brain. "Could someone do this to us?"

"Infect our vines?"

"Yes."

"Why would someone want to do that?"

"Competition. Drive me down or out."

"I don't think anyone would do that, because of the danger of the spores spreading to their own vineyards. They can be carried on the wind during their release times."

"Could be someone who isn't making wine but who hates my guts."

"That would be one dead person. He'd have to be pretty stupid once the rest of the growers found out."

"But is it possible to infect other people's vines or crops?"

Arch rubbed his chin. "Yes. Don't think downy mildew would be the way to go, but if someone was really determined, yes, I expect they could damage grapes or any other crop, really.

"If an employee were disgruntled, he could spray water without mixing in Ridomil. That would be one way to do it. You'd think your vines were protected but they'd be vulnerable."

"A crooked person could sell infected stock," Rollie said.

Arch shifted his weight from one foot to another. "There's all kinds of ways to screw somebody."

Rollie twirled his thumbs around each other. "Professor Forland didn't say he saw anything."

"There wasn't enough leaf when he was here. There's always something ready to get your grapes. Birds, deer, foxes, too. At least the foxes just eat the lower ones. The birds and deer can clean you out."

"Can't we cover the clusters when they develop?"

"No." Arch shook his head. "You have to go to the canopy and you have to keep spraying. Shoot the deer or put up deer fences. There's no other way."

"All right." Rollie waved his hand, dismissing Arch abruptly as his phone rang.

Arch stepped outside into the high golden sunlight of early afternoon. It could have been worse. Maybe Rollie was learning to trust him a little. It made up in small measure for the sadness, anger, envy he felt when Harry drove away. She made him angry because she didn't want to talk about anything to do with their affair. Typical Harry, just stuff the emotions. And she made him sad because he knew he'd never find another woman like Harry.

17

Low blue-steel clouds roiled over the top of the Blue Ridge Mountains. The dampness slithered into the bones as the temperature began to slide.

Mrs. Murphy, Pewter, and Tucker started their jaunt innocently enough. Harry was inspecting her new grapevines, since the word about downy mildew had passed quickly from grower to grower. Everything looked fine, the buds getting fuzzy and bright green. She then walked among the different types of sunflowers beginning their first great growth spurt. From there she checked her hay, then a back pasture with rich, rich alfalfa. Harry knew she could make good money on the alfalfa. She hopped the creek to walk the fields at the old Jones home place. Those pastures were enriched by the cattle Blair had kept. She put in orchard grass, alfalfa mix. She whistled while she worked. Young, healthy life was everywhere. She was on her way to the peach orchard, hoping all was well there.

Much as the animals loved Harry, they did not share her passion for grass crops. Orchards proved more interesting. They looked forward to the sunflowers maturing because of the bees and the birds. Pewter had staked her corner of the Italian sunflower patch. She felt certain she could lure her nemesis, the blue jay, there. That was a long way off, but Pewter planned ahead. Meanwhile, the bird dive-bombed her with impunity.

Bored with Harry's bucolic rapture, they returned to the creek, walking upstream toward the edge of the Bland Wade tract. Potlicker Creek coursed through the tract, its clear sweet waters deep in parts.

A doe leapt out. They chased it, their egos in excess of their abilities. Tired, the three sat down for a breather under a towering sycamore, little May apples covering the ground.

"Think a cat has ever killed a deer?" Pewter asked.

"I guess it's possible," Mrs. Murphy said.

"Never." Tucker panted still.

"And why not, dwarf dog?" Pewter sassed.

"Deer are too big and too fast."

"I can run as fast as a deer." Mrs. Murphy lifted the fur on her spine.

"For a short time, but the deer can go for miles and miles. You're built to run really fast, then cut at a one-hundred-eighty-degree angle. You can do backflips over your pursuer, if you want. Deer can't do that." Tucker thought it best to flatter.

"Ever notice how we hunt the same as foxes? Crouch, stay still, then pounce," Pewter mused.

"It's because we hunt the same game." Mrs. Murphy respected foxes even though she was known to quarrel loudly with a few.

Tucker lifted her talented nose. *"Storm coming."*

Pewter inhaled deeply. *"Fast."*

"Let's go home." Mrs. Murphy started trotting south, down the foothills.

The others fell in with her. As they broke cover, they beheld the ominous clouds cresting the mountains.

"Damn!" Pewter hated thunderstorms, and the not-so-distant rumble gave her the shivers.

They flew over the wildflower meadow, dipped into the woods on the other side. They were perhaps two miles from home, but the storm was closing fast. The wind hit twenty knots out of the blue. Bam, trees began to sway.

No one spoke as they ran hard. They sped past the old black-birch stand—white birches couldn't grow this far south—then darted through a pocket meadow.

Mrs. Murphy skidded to a halt. *"Hold up!"*

"Like hell." Pewter kept running, turned her head, saw that Tucker had stopped, her nose down in the high weeds and grass.

"Pewter, look for a den or something. We won't make it home in time," Tucker instructed the cat, whose pupils enlarged.

Pewter didn't protest. She wanted shelter. She dashed to the edge of the pocket meadow, circumventing it in hopes of finding any old den. *"Nothing,"* she shouted.

"We'd better run, Tucker. There's a den in the big rock outcropping a quarter mile further on. It's our only chance," Mrs. Murphy called over the wind.

"Come on!" Pewter was really scared.

The three ran just as huge raindrops smashed into freshly opened buds. Higher up, spring came later. There was no shelter from emerging leaves. Raindrops hit the ground like wet minié balls.

They reached the boulders, now black and slick, jutting outward. They dashed inside the small cave.

"No!" Pewter puffed up like a blowfish.

Mrs. Murphy and Tucker stopped in their tracks, the rain firing like a fusillade outside. Too amazed to speak, they bumped into each other as they put on the brakes.

Sitting on her haunches was a four-hundred-pound brown bear nursing two cubs, much as a human would nurse a baby. Her poor eyesight could make out the three small intruders. Her nose told her it was two cats and a dog.

Pewter trembled. What was worse, the storm or the bear?

The cubs, born in January, had been the size of rats. Their amazing growth filled them out to the point where they looked like teddy bears. They blinked, trying to make out the little visitors.

Mrs. Murphy bravely stood her ground. She realized the nursing mother couldn't spring to reach her, and bears shambled anyway. Only at a trot or a run could they move along. The cat determined she had time to talk, and if conversation proved discomfiting, she'd brave the lightning.

"Excuse us. We got caught in the storm." A searing flash of lightning underscored her words.

"I can see that." The gravelly voice betrayed no anger.

"Bears eat little mammals," Pewter unhelpfully blurted out as she backed away.

"I'd much rather eat berries and honey. Say, you don't know where there are bees' nests, do you? Close by. Can't range too far with the children, although they're growing like weeds."

"If you go down to where Potlicker Creek feeds into Harry's Creek—that's what I call it—right on that corner is a dead oak, really big, and the woodpeckers have been at it. Huge nest of bees."

"Goody." She smiled, revealing fearsome teeth.

"Wild bees are so aggressive. Don't they hurt you?" Mrs.

Murphy thought it best to keep her engaged in subjects interesting to her.

"*They can't sting me. And I know how to protect my nose and eyes. Did you know that wild-bee honey is much stronger than that of domesticated bees? Now, I like both, I can tell you, but the wild-bee honey packs a powerful sweet punch.*"

"*How's fishing been?*" The intrepid tiger cat remembered how much black bears like to fish.

"*Good. Crawfish haven't been bad, either. Sometimes they taste like nuts. I just love them. I love to eat.*"

"*Me, too.*" Pewter relaxed a little, but she kept one ear cocked, hoping the storm was diminishing.

"*I can see that.*" The bear laughed.

"*See or smell anything unusual lately?*" Tucker asked, to keep the ball rolling.

"*Smelled a human at the peach orchard couple of nights ago. They have such a rancid odor, poor things. So easy to track and bring down. Not that I want to kill and eat humans, mind you; even if I did, think of the chemicals. They eat all that processed food. They're a real health hazard.*" She wrapped her arm around one of the twins, who'd stopped suckling, falling asleep on her breast. "*I don't mind humans. If they leave me alone, I leave them alone. The world is big enough for all.*"

The rain kept coming down, but the lightning and thunder moved down the ridge.

"*Do you have twins every year?*" Tucker inquired.

She laughed. "*No, I only have a litter every other year. I couldn't bear it,*" she giggled at her own pun, "*more often. Being a mother is an awful lot of work.*"

The rain softened.

"*Did you see what the human was doing the other night at the peach orchard?*" Tucker asked.

"Burying another human," the bear simply said. It was no concern of hers. The three domestic animals looked at one another but said nothing.

"Well, we'll be on our way. Thank you for giving us shelter," Mrs. Murphy politely said.

"Yes, thank you." Pewter and Tucker both remembered their manners.

"My pleasure. I love my babies, but they prattle on. I enjoyed our conversation."

The three scampered out, running the whole way to the stable. Although soaked, once they scurried into the center aisle they were exhilarated.

"We've got to go to the peach orchard," Mrs. Murphy said.

"Not in this rain," Pewter replied.

"She's right, Murphy," Tucker agreed.

Harry tromped in from the opposite side, water coursing off her trusty old Barbour coat. "Where have you been? I looked all over for you all. I was scared to death."

Tucker ran up, sat down, and looked adoringly at Harry. *"Mom, we need to go to the peach orchard, if it ever stops raining."*

"You all look like drowned rats." Harry took off her coat, hanging it on a tack hook to drip. She picked up a thick barn towel and wiped down Tucker. She tossed it in the plastic wash bin, fetched another, and cleaned both cats with it.

As she was rubbing down Mrs. Murphy, Simon leaned over the hayloft. *"What a mess."*

"Thanks," Pewter grumbled as she sat on her rear end, stretched out a hind leg straight, flaring her claws. *"I'll never get the mud out."*

18

The next day sparkled as though the thunderstorm's dark gray clouds, like giant S.O.S pads, had scrubbed everything clean. Fields glistened, the late dogwoods bloomed even as the regular dogwoods lost their blossoms. Lilacs opened. Fresh air filled lungs, invigorating everyone.

Up at 4:30 A.M., Harry knocked out her chores by noon, hopped in her 1978 Ford pickup, and cruised over to Alicia's to see how her foal crop was doing.

When she drove along the long, winding driveway where the massive trees lent their authority to the place, she noticed the yearlings racing about in the front pasture. Last year's group of Thoroughbreds showed such promise. Harry was eager to see how the foals of two and three months were doing. She'd been so busy she hadn't much time to visit around, although she did manage to see Burly. How funny to see the long-eared little mule nursing on Keepsake, an elegant Thoroughbred. If Keepsake was embarrassed by her offspring she chose not to show it.

Alicia's colors, green and gold, were painted in a band around the middle of the white gateposts to the stable. Once at the graceful white clapboard stable, the colors, in a small band, encircled the posts, which supported the eight-foot overhang. The stable, built at the turn of the twentieth century, evidenced all the charm of pre-World War I America.

"There's Max." Tucker, on her hind legs, joyfully noted the appearance of Alicia's beloved and impressive Gordon setter.

Max, unlike Irish setters or English setters, actively guarded his human. He happily hunted, too, but at a more conservative pace than his ribald Irish cousin or his stately English cousin.

Mrs. Murphy and Pewter liked Max well enough, but they were more interested in bolting out of the truck to chase the barn swallows swooping in and out of the stable.

Harry noticed both Toby Pittman's and Arch Saunders's trucks parked in the lovely large square at the front of the stable.

"Wonder what's up," she said out loud.

"Yeah, none of those guys want Thoroughbreds. Arch can't ride." Mrs. Murphy eagerly waited for Harry to turn off her motor.

The moment the motor was cut, Harry opened her door. Before she swung her leg out, the cats bounced on her lap then to the cobblestones. They flashed into the stable before even Max knew they were there.

"Ignore them." Tucker waited to be lifted out.

"I do," Max replied as he walked forward to greet Tucker.

Harry, who had called Alicia beforehand, checked

around outside, then entered the barn. She walked to the office, where paneled walls were covered with gold-framed photos of Mary Pat Reines: in the hunt field; over fences at Keswick's Horse Show, Deep Run's Show, Devon; photos of her horses winning conformation shows, her steeplechasers in the winner's circle. There was one photo of a twenty-two-year-old Alicia in informal attire at a foxhunt.

Arch Saunders and Toby Pittman sat on the newly covered sofa while Alicia sat opposite them in a club chair, a scarred coffee table between them.

"Alicia, I can come back." Harry realized this was an impromptu gathering, because Alicia said she'd be alone. When Harry had called, Alicia raved about a colt she had by Distinctive Pro, a New York sire, and a filly by More Than Ready, standing at Vinery Stud in Kentucky.

"Come on in."

The men stood as Harry entered, then sat when she sat in the other club chair.

Toby returned to his subject. "He means to destroy me. All of us."

Arch grimaced but kept his mouth shut.

"Have you spoken to Sheriff Shaw?" Alicia calmly inquired.

"He won't listen to me. That's why I came to you. Everybody listens to you and to Big Mim. But Mim's mad at me. You talk to the sheriff. Get him to investigate."

"Why is Mim mad at you?" Alicia asked.

Toby distractedly tapped his knee with his forefinger. "I told her she was making a big mistake in not turning some of her land into vineyards. And I said with her wealth she could be a big player early."

"And?" Alicia knew there had to be more to the story.

"I told her that Patricia and Bill were so powerful they'll

be like Nelson Bunker when he tried to corner the silver market. She said Patricia and Bill weren't like that. If they were they wouldn't have driven Professor Forland to visit other vintners."

"That's true, Toby." Alicia wondered why Toby couldn't exercise the minimum of diplomacy.

"Things were going along okay until then. I gave her my theory about Professor Forland's disappearance. She said I should be careful about making false accusations and I called her a rich bitch."

"Harry, Toby thinks that Hy plans to ruin his vines. He said Hy sent Concho to spy on his place."

"Hy knows a lot. He's smart enough to cover his tracks. He'll have the best vineyard in Virginia by ruining the rest of us!"

"Arch, you haven't said anything." Alicia smiled at him.

"Hy is very knowledgeable." Arch remained noncommittal.

Harry wondered what Arch was doing here with Toby.

"Guys, forgive me, I don't know so much about growing grapes. If Hy wanted to harm your vines, how would he do it?"

"Simple!" Toby's eyes blazed. "He'd sneak into the rows, dig up a vine, and plant an infected one. Could be infected with anything. God knows, there're enough diseases to go around. But all he has to do is introduce diseased stock. You know, Arch has some downy mildew."

"Hy dug up vines with black rot." Arch tried to introduce this as a counterweight to Toby.

It was, but Toby, too upset to appreciate it, launched off the sofa and stood up. "Ha! He put that there himself to throw us off!"

"I see." Alicia maintained a calm tone.

Arch spoke again as Toby dropped back so hard into the sofa that Arch bounced up slightly. "There's bad blood between Hy and Toby. Hy could introduce infected stock or insects, but I don't think he would, because it could backfire."

"What do you mean backfire? He would bring me down." Toby gripped the edge of the sofa cushion.

"He might bring himself down, too." Arch kept his eyes level with Alicia's. "Hy knows that one mistake, one spore on his pants leg, and he risks his own vines. That's why I think his revenge—if he really is planning to do something—will be in a different form."

"Like what, for goddamned example!" Toby raised his voice, then lowered it. "Sorry, ladies."

"That's all right, Toby. This is unsettling. After all, your livelihood could be in jeopardy."

"Like what?" Toby tried to sound reasonable.

"Well," Arch measured his words, "Toby, you can't do anything but worry about Hy, at least that's how it looks to me. So as I see it, he's winning. Your mind is not where it belongs—on your vines, on your business."

"Hard not to worry when he killed Professor Forland."

"Toby, you don't mean that," Alicia blurted out.

"Yes, I do. Professor Forland was on to Hy. He knew he was intent on ruining me." Toby offered no explanation as to how Professor Forland could know this, but then Toby, seemingly irrational, was not asked for one.

The humans were quiet for a moment, since no one knew what to say to this ludicrous accusation.

As the humans talked, Mrs. Murphy and Pewter ran the length of the stable, leaping up at the barn swallows, who swooped down to bedevil them. Great fun that it was, it became tiring.

The two cats repaired outside to take a sunbath, the mercury hovering at sixty-five degrees with not a hint of breeze. The skies, robin's egg blue, arched over a perfect spring day.

"Look at those stupid dogs," Pewter sniffed.

"Better hope it's a cast-off shoe, or someone will pay." Mrs. Murphy wondered how any self-respecting creature could sink his jaws into one end of a shoe and tug while the other dog did the same at the opposite end.

The growling sounded ferocious.

"Ha!" Pewter laughed, because Max had dragged Tucker, who refused to release her grip, across the cobblestone walk.

Never one to lay about, Mrs. Murphy roused herself, stretched, then shook. She sauntered to Arch's truck; the window was open, but that was a higher leap than she cared to make. She knew she could do it if pressed, but no one was chasing her, nor was there anyone for whom she could show off. Instead she leapt onto the hood to peer into the interior. Then she jumped up on the cab top, leaned over to slide into the open window. Tricky, but easy for her.

His captain's chair was empty. A nice pair of sunglasses rested on the dash. The passenger seat overflowed with notebooks, soil maps, a tin containing small vials for soil samples, a laminated page with pictures of insects. A worn leather vest lined with fleece had slid onto the floor.

Nothing interested Mrs. Murphy there, so she hopped back to the hood, then to the ground, and jumped up on Toby's new green Dodge to look through the windshield. His interior, pin-tidy except for mud bits on the driver's floor, offered no tidbits. She had hoped for some Fritos or even a sandwich. The center armrest was pulled down. She repeated her feat of going from the cab top into the wide-open window.

Pewter lifted her head to watch. Curious, she sat up.

"Hey," Mrs. Murphy called. *"Come here."* She had popped up the lid of the armrest.

Pewter walked over. *"What?"*

"You gotta see this."

Pewter measured the distance to the truck's hood. Her rotundness crossed her mind. She might be able to jump on the back bumper, haul herself into the truck bed, then jump onto the cab hood. This lacked appeal.

"Open the door."

Truck doors were easy pickings for a smart cat. Mrs. Murphy pushed forward the latch, then pushed open the door. The bell announcing the door was open while the keys were in the ignition started ringing.

"I'd cut the wires to that darned thing. How can someone be so dumb they don't know their truck door is open?" Mrs. Murphy hated the sound. *"Pewter, look here."*

Pewter peeked into the middle armrest storage bin. A brand-new Ruger P95PR 9mm handgun nestled inside, the blued steel accentuating the efficient design of the powerful weapon. Some ten-round magazines were also there.

"Golly," she exclaimed.

"That could put a serious hole in someone." Mrs. Murphy felt uneasy, not because of the $445 gun but because of Toby's mental state. The animals could smell fear and agitation when they were around him.

"Run!" Pewter heard and saw Harry come out of the main entrance, followed by the other humans.

The two cats shot out of the seat, ducked under the truck, and scooted out the back. They reached the dogs before the humans noticed them.

"I know I closed this door." Toby started to slam the

door shut, then noticed the center console open. "Hey, hey, there's my new gun. I thought I'd lost it. How can it be here?"

"Ghost trick," Arch said. He knew better than to make a joke about Toby's state of mind.

Alicia and Harry walked over while Toby lifted out the good-looking gun. "In my truck."

Fearing his moods, Alicia smiled. "I find things all the time. Little leprechauns live in Virginia, I swear it."

His eyes bulged a moment. He started to say something, when Arch stepped in. "You're lucky to find it. That's a nice piece."

Toby studied the blued steel, the textured nonslip hold. "You know, the Army Tank-automotive and Armaments Command picked five thousand of these for a field assignment.

"There's even a Picatinny rail under the barrel so I can mount a weapon light."

"That's something." Harry admired good equipment.

"Well, ladies, back to it." Arch smiled and got into his truck.

Toby, still puzzled about his P95PR, climbed into his truck, placed it in the center console, and closed the lid.

After the men drove off, Alicia showed her babies to Harry, who thought they were everything that Alicia said they were.

"Who's the elegant fellow?"

"Ah, that's by Lycius. He's by Mr. Prospector out of Lypatia, who, as you know from your study, was by Lyphard. You know how much I prize that Lyphard blood. He lived a long and useful life, that stallion."

"Who is the mare?"

"Party Girl. Remember when you were a kid, Mary Pat

imported that gorgeous Irish mare, Peat's Girl? She wanted to hunt her, but the mare met with an accident in the pasture, fractured her cannon bone. Not the whole way, more of a splint. Anyway, Mary Pat didn't want to pound on her even after she healed, so she turned her into a broodmare. This is the fourth generation."

Harry was impressed. "Why don't you hunt her?"

"Well, she was never made." Alicia used the term "made," which meant she was never trained. "And I haven't been back long enough to sort all this out. So I thought I'd breed her and hunt this fall something already made. Of course, when I go looking, the price will triple."

"Let me handle that," Harry offered.

"I will. You're charged with finding me a bold field hunter who is also stunning. I hate pedaling to the jumps. Give me a forward horse. And if you want to work with any three- or four-year-olds, let me know."

"I'll do it." Harry smiled, for she loved these kinds of challenges. As they walked back toward the stables and a hot cup of tea, Harry remarked, "Toby's one brick shy of a load."

"Certainly seems to be the case."

"Alicia, Toby must have indigestion from all the shoe leather he's eaten."

Alicia laughed her silvery laugh. "From putting his foot in his mouth."

Harry opened the stable door; the sunlight glinted off her wedding band. She smiled. "Will you speak to Rick?"

"I will, but I expect our sheriff knows Toby is suffering from some kind of mental distress." Alicia headed back to the large office to make a hot pot of tea.

"Why was Arch here?" Harry sat at the coffee table.

Alicia answered, "Toby wanted a witness who isn't a

friend but not an enemy. That's how he phrased it. Very odd."

"It was good of Arch to come."

"I expect Arch knows Toby is falling apart. His presence did somewhat calm Toby." She paused, her beautiful face delightful to behold. "How is it having Arch in Crozet?"

Harry, relaxed with Alicia, told her, "It was funny. He showed up two weeks before my wedding. No one knew he'd made a deal with Rollie. Why would we? He was on the other side of the country and wasn't in touch with anyone in Crozet—the old gang, I mean.

"Mim knew first, of course. She called me. Then I called Susan." Harry shrugged. "It didn't seem like a big deal to me."

Alicia smiled. "Good, but I bet Susan wanted amplification."

Harry waved her hand. "Girl talk. Susan loves it. I can't stand it. Funny, she's my best friend. We're so different."

"Maybe that's why you're best friends."

"Could be. Fair asked me last night if Arch's return changed anything. Why?" Now Harry threw up both her hands.

"Harry, for a smart woman you can be dumb." This was said with good humor.

"I know." She did, too. "I told him I had fun while it lasted but that was then and this is now. I didn't bring up BoomBoom. We'd been all through that." Harry stopped, gulped. "Did I put my foot in it?"

"Of course not. No one comes into your life without a history."

"Whew."

"And Fair is divinely attractive." Alicia's eyes danced.

"BoomBoom, too. She's so . . . uh, womanly. I never felt I measured up. I used to wonder if I was really a woman."

"Harry." Alicia was surprised.

"Well, I'm not very feminine."

"Of course you are. You're outdoorsy. Natural." Alicia sipped more tea, then thoughtfully added, "Feminine and masculine are social constructs. Male and female are physical reality. As long as a person frets over whether or not they are feminine enough or masculine enough, they'll always be someone's victim."

"What do you mean?"

"An insecure person looks for another person or an organization to affirm them. My business," Alicia referred to her acting career, "is full of gorgeous people who really don't believe in themselves deep down."

"You did."

"Yes."

"How did you do it?"

"I had the great advantage of country life as a young person. I was grounded, literally. And I had Mary Pat to guide me at a critical time in my life." She leaned forward. "Harry, I don't think of myself as especially feminine, despite my public persona. And I don't care. I'm happy within. If the world sees me as a middle-aged sex bomb," she laughed uproariously, "that's their problem."

"Alicia, I wish I were more like you."

"Harry, be more like *you*." Alicia reached over and touched her hand. "There's only one Harry Haristeen. Be that wonderful person."

When Harry finally drove back through St. James, she thought of something her mother used to say to her when she didn't immediately accomplish what she wanted. "God's delay isn't God's denial."

"Hmm." She grunted to herself. She'd lived long enough to know that friends and even strangers give one marvelous gifts and insights quite unexpectedly.

"Is she going to hum? I hope not." Pewter shifted in her seat.

"You know, kids, I miss my mother," Harry said with deep feeling.

19

"Tick." Pewter maliciously stuck one claw into Tucker's fur.

"Ouch." The dog felt the point dig under her skin.

"See." Pewter flicked the offending insect onto the kitchen floor, where she gleefully speared it as the blackish red goo oozed out.

"Thought Fair put that stuff on your neck." Mrs. Murphy, like all cats, could rid herself of ticks more easily than a dog.

Fleas were another story.

"Washed off when we were caught in the thunderstorm." Tucker hated ticks. *"He put it on the first of the month, which was only the day before."*

"But it's still coolish and damp. They love that. You'll be infested if you go into the wrong places." Mrs. Murphy worried about her buddy.

"Yeah, like the world." Pewter stabbed the tick a second time.

"That's a happy thought," Tucker grumbled.

"*What about that gun in Toby's truck? No happy thought there?*" Mrs. Murphy asked the corgi, whom she and Pewter had informed of the P95PR.

"*I'm surprised Harry didn't jump the gun, forgive the pun, and assume he was going to shoot Hy—or himself maybe. She's still reading about things that can attack her grapes. She's occupied and no danger to herself,*" Tucker replied.

Harry, in the kitchen, stepped on the bleeding tick and slid. "What the—" She looked down. "The scourge of the earth."

"*Tucker had the tick. Probably carrying Lyme disease.*" Pewter was a font of optimism.

"*Shut up.*" The corgi flattened her ears.

"*I'm terrified. I'm so scared I might widdle,*" Pewter said.

"*You only do that on the way to the vet's office,*" Tucker fired back.

"*I do not,*" Pewter huffed.

"*I'm amazed none of us did when we ran into the bear's cave.*" Mrs. Murphy thanked her stars the mother had a full belly and was nursing contentedly.

"*We were lucky. But like she said, she'd rather eat berries, honey, and sweets. Likes grubs, too. How can any animal eat a fat white grub?*" Pewter grimaced.

"*Chickens love them.*" Tucker liked chickens, although their clucking could get on her nerves.

"*Wonder if Harry will get more chickens? That last hen was Methuselah's chicken. I bet she was the oldest Rhode Island Red in the world.*" Pewter fondly recalled the ancient bird who cackled with delight to the last day of her uneventful life.

"*When Harry puts straw in the chicken coop we can bet on more chickens.*" Tucker watched Harry wipe up the tick goo.

"All right, you all, I'm going to warm up Miranda's corn bread. Wish we hadn't missed her."

Miranda Hogendobber had driven by when Harry was at St. James. Finding no one home, she placed a large tin of corn bread on the screened-in porch with a note.

"Susan!" Tucker barked as she heard Susan's Audi station wagon turn off the state road onto the farm road.

Harry checked the old railroad clock on the wall, knew it was too early for Fair, but put up coffee since someone was coming. She trusted Tucker.

Within minutes Susan burst through the door, tulips in a pot. "Can you believe the color?"

Harry inspected the yellow tulips with deep red throats, red lines fanning out to the end of the petals. "They're incredible."

"My garden," Susan boasted. "For you."

"Thanks." Harry kissed her on the cheek. "Coffee, tea, Co-Cola, what?"

"Fresh coffee."

"Still percolating."

"I could use it. If it's not coffee, then it's my hot chocolate."

"You'll like this coffee. It's Javatra from Shenandoah Joe's."

"What are you having?"

"Co-Cola. Want some corn bread?"

"Well..." Susan wavered.

"Miranda's corn bread."

"Yes," came the decisive reply.

As the two stayed there happily slapping on butter and jam, drinking their beverages, the cats leapt up to sit in the window by the sink. Tucker repaired to her bed.

"I've been riding All's Fair." Harry mentioned the four-year-old gelding by Fred Astaire that Fair had given her as a yearling. "He did very well last year just walking along. I like to bring them along slowly, but he's got such a good mind."

"That was a wonderful present from your husband. I forget how old Tomahawk and Gin Fizz are getting."

"I forget how old I'm getting."

"Don't push it. We aren't forty yet."

"We aren't far, honeypie."

"Say, I came by to tell you that wine people are lunatics. Are you sure you want to grow those Peti-whatever out there?"

"What happened now?"

"Tanking up at the Amoco—"

Harry interrupted, something she rarely did. "Did you refinance your house?"

"Ha." Susan laughed drily. "Prices are so high that Ned and I talked the other night to see if we could get by with one vehicle and we just can't. Those trips to Richmond he takes devour the budget. He sold the BMW by the way, in Richmond, of course." She paused. "Filling the wagon. I hear these voices. Hy and Arch. Not angry but increasing in volume. Hy was worked up because Toby, I don't know when, sounded very recent, had been ugly to Fiona on the phone."

"Toby's really losing it," Harry interjected.

"Arch was telling Hy that Toby's gone to pieces over this Forland thing and to let him be. Hy said that Toby's rude and irresponsible, and everybody lets him get away with it. He's not going to put up with him. When Hy called to explain why Concho was on Toby's property, Toby blew up. Then he called back and blew up at Fiona. Hy's version, anyway, and Hy said we all needed to slap Toby down hard."

"What did Arch say?"

"He kept trying to soften Hy. I mean, it wasn't an argument. More that they didn't see eye to eye. Arch said he didn't much cotton to Toby, either, but there was no point in making a bad situation worse."

The phone rang. "Drat." Harry rose to pick up the old wall phone. "Hello. Hi, honey, where are you?"

"I'm on my way to Toby Pittman's," Fair replied. "I hope it won't be too long and then I'll be right home."

"What's going on over there?"

"His donkey, Jed, cut his hind leg. Toby sounds hysterical. Probably stitch him right up and be on my way."

"Susan says hello. Hurry home."

"I will."

She hung up the phone and relayed the information to Susan.

"Sure hope Fair isn't treated to one of Toby's lectures."

"I heard the one about Andrew Estave the other day."

"Andrew who?"

"Andrew Estave was hired by the Virginia Assembly in 1769 as winemaker and viticulturist for the colony. Virginians grew our first grapes in 1609, but we had a mess of problems. Anyway, over comes the Frenchman and he couldn't get the European grapes to do diddly, but he came to an important conclusion, which was that Virginians needed to use native grapes."

"Then what?"

"With Toby or with grapes?"

"Grapes," Susan laughed.

"Jefferson, the man of a million interests, brought over Philip Mazzei, an Italian wine merchant, and he was doing okay but the Revolution wrecked everything. Tell you what, when Toby gets wound up on this stuff, you can't tone him down. You should have heard him today at Alicia's. He accused Hy of trying to destroy everyone's crop. He accused him of killing Professor Forland!"

"What is he doing making these accusations to Alicia?"

"He wanted her to speak to Rick. He said the sheriff wouldn't listen to him. Arch was there, too. Alicia was cool as a cuke, as you'd expect."

"She probably witnessed major tanties in Hollywood." Susan used tanty for tantrum.

"She rarely talks about her film career. I'd like to know what Ava Gardner was like and Glenn Ford and . . ."

"Wrong generation. She was huge in the seventies and eighties."

"But those actors were still around. They interest me a lot more."

"Why?"

Harry shrugged. "I don't rightly know."

"I do. Better material. The studio system was still strong; they developed the actors, and the stars had better material. Also, stars didn't have their own production companies like they do today. I mean, I realize why they do it, but usually the stuff they select is just a star turn. Boring. I don't care how handsome or beautiful or even talented those people are; if they're in every frame of the picture, if the supporting roles aren't strong, I'm bored out of my head."

"Guess that's why we don't go to the movies." Harry failed to mention she had no time. "You were interested in film when we were kids. I sometimes wonder why you didn't go into it."

"Movie-star looks, that's me," Susan joked.

"You're pretty. But I wonder why you didn't go into some facet of the business?"

"Pregnant with Danny."

Harry crossed one leg over the other. "Hey, we are the generation that was told we could have it all: motherhood, career, deep personal satisfaction."

"They lied."

The phone rang.

Harry rose. "Bet it's more of a problem than he thought. Either that or it's Mim or Miranda." She looked at the clock, which read five after five. "Hello." A long silence followed this as her shoulders stiffened and her eyes widened.

Tucker, smelling the change, the worry, crawled out of her bed to sit next to Harry.

The cats turned from the window.

Susan put down her coffee cup.

Harry then replied, "Is there anything I can do?" Another silence followed. "Honey, I can't believe this." More silence as she listened intently. "I promise. You come home the minute you can. I love you. Bye." Ashen-faced, she hung up the phone.

"What?"

"Fair couldn't find Toby at the barn. He walked out into the vineyard. He heard a truck engine start up and caught sight of Hy driving away—fast."

Susan's eyebrows shot upward. "And?"

"Toby's dead. Shot a couple of times."

20

A soft wind swept over Rockland Vineyards; the new leaves swayed slightly, as did the hair on Toby's head. With his eyes wide open and his mouth slightly ajar, he appeared alive until one noticed the ever-widening circle of blood soaking his chest, another one at his stomach. He had slumped against the base of one of his vines in the row.

Fair studied the situation. Toby appeared to have taken a few steps backward after he was shot, because a few drops of blood speckled the grass. He was as freshly dead as he could be, unless Fair had shot him—then Toby would be dead for seconds instead of minutes.

Rick and Coop showed up within ten minutes, which gave Fair ten minutes to further observe Toby and to wonder at the abruptness of death.

When he called the sheriff with his cell phone, Fair mentioned that Hy had flown out of there, but he didn't know whether he'd turned left or right once out on the state road at the Rockland entrance.

In the far distance he could hear sirens; he expected officers were running down Hy.

Both Rick and Coop checked the ground as they approached the body.

"Did you hear shots?" Rick asked Fair.

"No. I was walking up from the barn. Maybe I was two hundred yards away, if that. It's a rise, but I did see Hy drive out once I reached about one hundred fifty yards."

"Did you hear Hy drive in?"

"No," Fair replied. "But I was in the barn looking for Jed." They stared at this name; he added, "Toby's donkey. I could have missed sounds, truck engines, even shouting. Once out of the barn I could hear well enough."

Coop squatted down near the new Ruger pistol in Toby's hand. She didn't touch it but sniffed the barrel. "Fired."

"What brought you here?" Rick asked Fair.

"Toby called. He said Jed cut his hind leg and I needed to come immediately. He was bleeding profusely."

"No donkey?" Rick rubbed his chin.

"No."

"What time did you reach the barn?"

"Four-thirty, give or take a minute," Fair told Rick.

"What time do you think you reached here?"

"Four forty-two. I checked my watch the second I saw him collapsed like that."

"Did you touch him?"

"Yes. If he showed any signs of life I would have done my best. An animal is an animal, and even though I'm a vet, I can fix up a human if it's a crisis."

"Mmm," Rick nodded as Coop moved behind Toby's body.

"One bullet still in him and one came through," she said.

"See if you can find it. Just put down a marker if you do."

As Coop was looking, the rescue-squad sirens wailed.

"This is a hell of a thing," Fair said.

He wasn't shaken by the corpse. He was a medical man, after all, but the fact that he had literally walked up on a man killed only moments before was unsettling. Erratic as Toby had been, Fair certainly didn't wish him dead.

Rick's phone rang. "Yeah." He listened intently. "Okay. Take him in." He clicked off just as Coop yelled, "Got it."

"Good. Got Hy. He tried to get away but finally gave up when he realized he had one squad car behind him and another blocking the road ahead."

"Did he have a gun?"

"No." Rick knew the chances of this being an open-and-shut case were rapidly dimming.

Coop studied Toby, sighed, and walked up to Fair. "You okay?"

"Yeah. Feel sorry for him."

"It was quick." Coop believed that was worth some solace.

Rick jotted down a few details.

"Do you two need me?"

"I know where to find you if I do. Why?" Rick replied.

"I'd like to find Jed and stitch him up. I'd hate for the poor little fellow to bleed to death."

"Go ahead," Rick said.

As Fair retreated back to the barn, Coop flipped open her notebook. "What do you think?"

Rick shrugged as he heard the rescue-squad vehicle turn

onto the farm. "Hy Maudant will hire the best lawyer in the country."

"Yep."

"Anything else?"

He glanced at her. "I'd hate to die unmourned."

21

Crozet shook as though one of the small earthquakes from the Blue Ridge Mountains had rumbled. The news of Toby's demise was on everyone's lips. Humans, being what they are, appear to enjoy horror on some level. The details of his corpse's disposition added additional allure to the sorry story.

The following morning Fair was in the operating room. He called Sheriff Shaw to ask if Harry could search for Jed. He wanted BoomBoom to accompany her. He emphatically did not want his wife out there alone.

The mercury stuck at fifty-four degrees at eight in the morning; the light breezes gave the temperature a cool tang. Since Boom was six feet tall and strong, Harry was glad she agreed to come along. For good measure both women packed a .38 to humanely end Jed's suffering if he were found in bad shape. Fair told Harry that Toby was very upset and kept repeating that Jed had deeply cut his hind leg.

The two women walked through Toby's small barn.

"These little blue pellets do kill the flies, but they crunch." Harry noted the blue dots on the center aisle.

"I don't like them underfoot," Mrs. Murphy declared.

"Ever try those hanging lanterns filled with kill juice?" BoomBoom asked.

"The smell will kill you, too." Harry looked around again. "No flies here and no Jed."

"Silent as a tomb," BoomBoom said.

Tucker, at their heels, shuddered. *"Wish you hadn't said that."*

"I had hoped that Jed would come back to his stall. Well, let's work in circles around the barn. When we can't see each other, let's come back here and go to plan B."

"Sounds good to me," BoomBoom agreed as she stepped into the feed-and-supply room. "Toby certainly was prepared for summer. I've never seen so many rolls of flypaper or blue-crystal bait."

Harry stuck her head in the open doorway. "One donkey, and Toby was prepared for a zillion flies."

After an hour of checking through the vineyards and around the house, they reconvened back at the barn.

"Harry, we'd better work in quadrants. There's a lot left to cover, and we won't be able to see each other," BoomBoom, logical as always, suggested.

"Different quadrants or together?"

"Together. Let's stick together."

"You've got a point there," Harry agreed.

"I'm going back to the truck." Pewter had already had enough of the search and was desirous of her mid-morning nap.

When neither Mrs. Murphy nor Tucker mocked her, she

changed her mind. After all, she might miss something, and then she'd have to hear about it ad infinitum.

BoomBoom zipped her Barbour jacket up to her neck as the wind picked up. "Kind of raw. You expect May to be warmer than this."

"Yeah. The closest farm with horses is the old Berryhill farm. Let's walk that way first. If there's a mare in season—and this is the time they go in naturally—the little fellow will have picked up the scent long before we will."

"That kind of scent can travel a mile on a perfect day," Tucker, the scent expert, agreed.

"What worries me, Harry, is we haven't seen so much as one hoofprint."

"Yeah." Harry walked alongside the tall woman. "But there's been so much traffic on the farm roads that would wipe them out—most of them, anyway. And he's not shod, so he won't leave a deep print. But if there had been hoofprints, Fair would have seen them."

"He could have stayed on grass."

"He'd have to jump fences," Harry remarked.

"He can jump." Boom smiled.

They carefully examined the ground to the northwest of the barn, moving consistently in that direction.

"Remember when we were kids, how Grandpa Berryhill collected old farm tools? Everyone thought he was crackers. Be worth a fortune now." Harry liked things that were practical and enjoyed Mr. Berryhill's demonstrations of wooden cider presses, carding utensils, and butter churns.

"Line all died out. Not a Berryhill left."

"Kind of cruel, really. They were so prosperous, and then a dark cloud settled over them and just rained misery."

"You never know."

"No, you don't." Harry tramped down a soft, rolling

meadow leading to low woodlands, a serviceable three-board fence dividing the open land from the woodland.

Harry grabbed the fence, because the grass, still slick, made the footing dicey. "I can't help wondering if Hy had something to do with Professor Forland's disappearance, only because Toby studied with Forland and still seemed enthralled with him in some way."

"Nah. Doesn't make any sense." BoomBoom put her left hand on the top rail and gracefully soared over the fence with a push off.

Harry, not to be outdone, did the same. "Well, nothing makes sense until you find the links."

Pewter scooted under the bottom plank, as did Mrs. Murphy and Tucker.

The woodlands, cool and damp, reverberated with the sound of birds calling out their territory boundaries. Most daytime species already had eggs in the nests. Some birds sang for the pure pleasure of living.

"*Bigmouths,*" Pewter grumbled.

A piercing cry overhead alerted Mrs. Murphy to the red-tailed hawk. "*She may be a bigmouth, but don't insult her. She's fearless.*"

Pewter did respect big birds. "*Nasty beak.*"

"*Ever notice how each bird has the right kind of beak for the food it eats?*" Tucker found birds fascinating.

"*Must be tough being a human with that flat mouth,*" Pewter said. "*They can't eat off the ground. They can't eat without their hands; well, I guess they can, but what a mess. Their jaws go up and down and that's about it.*"

"*True, but they're omnivorous, which gives them a big advantage. They can eat grains and vegetables, fruits and meats. Cats are obligate carnivores. We must eat fresh meat or cooked meat. I really do envy them their range of choices, because it al-lows them to survive about anywhere,"* Mrs. Murphy said.

"Doesn't matter where they live, they can't live without us. We kill the pests," Pewter bragged, then yowled, *"It's wet here. My paws are soaking wet."*

"Poor darling," Mrs. Murphy sarcastically remarked.

"Pewter, you ran through a thunderstorm," Tucker reminded the fat gray cat.

"That was different. I had no choice." Pewter climbed on a fallen log. *"Pick me up! Harry, you come back here and pick me up!"*

"What's she screaming about?" Harry turned to see Pewter marooned on her log.

For spite, Mrs. Murphy splashed past Pewter, puddle water now on her immaculate gray coat.

"I hate you, Murphy."

"Who cares?" The tiger ran ahead of BoomBoom.

Harry, worried that they'd come back by another route, returned to Pewter and picked her up. "Jesus, Pewts, go on a diet."

Tucker mumbled. *"What a phony."*

"I heard that." Pewter wrapped her paws around Harry's neck as the human pushed through the mucky area.

After ten minutes of slogging through the lowlands, passing jack-in-the-pulpits on the edge of the swampy parts, hearing ground nesters in the swamp grass, they emerged at the edge of the old Berryhill place.

"I don't remember the place ever looking this good," BoomBoom commented on the restored Virginia farmhouse, the freshly painted white clapboard gleaming along with the new additions.

"The Hahns sure have done a lot in a year." Harry bent over, glad to put Pewter on the ground.

Pewter stood on her hind paws, reaching up to Harry's knee. *"I'm traumatized. Carry me some more."*

"I'm going to throw up the biggest hairball." Mrs. Murphy pretended to gag.

"Ha! You'll throw up worms," Pewter sassed back, now following Harry, who hadn't fallen for her ploy.

"We get wormed once a month, remember?"

"Doesn't work for you. Only works for Tucker and me," Pewter saucily declared as they walked through the newly fertilized pastures to the stable, a tidy four–four stall structure that matched the house, Federal-period style.

"Let's check here before we knock on the door." Harry walked into the stable, which was clean. Three horses, contented, lounged in their stalls. Each door sported a brass nameplate.

Munching away in a stall, the door still open, stood Jed.

"Bingo!" BoomBoom called out as she found him first.

Harry trotted over to her, and they closed the stall door. "He's perfectly sound."

"So he is."

"Not a scratch." Harry felt her stomach tighten.

Mrs. Murphy, with presence of mind, asked the happy little fellow, *"Did you cut your leg yesterday?"*

"No," came the one-syllable reply.

No one ever accused Jed of high intelligence.

"Who let you out?" Tucker picked up the line of questioning.

"No one."

"How'd you get here?" Pewter joined in the questioning.

"Jumped the fence."

"Jed, did you see anyone on your farm besides Toby?" Mrs. Murphy asked.

Jed laughed. *"No, didn't see anybody. Heard two trucks. I knew Toby'd be occupied, so I boogied on."*

"Why'd you jump out?" Tucker sat down.

"Dunno. Felt good."

Harry and BoomBoom ran their hands over his legs. Jed didn't bat one loopy ear.

Mrs. Murphy looked at Tucker, then Pewter. Finally, she said, *"Jed, Toby is dead."*

Jed's lower lip dropped down. *"Huh?"*

"He was murdered yesterday."

Two big tears welled up in Jed's large, pretty eyes. He let out a bray that startled Harry and BoomBoom.

"I loved Toby."

"I'm sorry, Jed. I'm sorry to tell you this." Mrs. Murphy was sympathetic.

"Harry will take you home until everything gets settled, Jed. Don't worry about anything like... you know." Pewter certainly didn't want to say what might happen to an animal no one wanted or, worse, pretended to want.

Many a knacker pretended to give a good home to a retiree or a homeless quadruped, only to cart the creature off to the slaughterhouse and pick up about eighty cents to a dollar a pound. Bad enough to cart an animal to a slaughterhouse. It's another sin to deliberately lie to people who trusted you.

Harry patted him on the neck. "Poor Jed. It's like he knows."

"Let's see if Christy's home." BoomBoom wiped Jed's eye with a handkerchief from her coat pocket.

They walked out and knocked on the back door of the farmhouse.

"Just a minute."

They heard footsteps, then the door opened and pretty

Christy Hahn opened it. Thirty-four and trim, she possessed a bubbling personality. "Come on in, Harry and BoomBoom. What a nice surprise."

"Actually, Christy, we've got to walk back to Pittman's farm. Jed's been missing, and we thought he might have come here and he did. When did he show up?"

"What?"

"He's in your barn; the stall door is open. We closed it."

"I bet he's in Hokie's stall. I turned him out early." Christy thought for a second. "Is he all right?"

"Fit as a fiddle." Harry smiled.

"Come on, girls, step inside. It's raw out today." Christy tugged them inside.

The three animals, muddy paws and all, walked inside, too. They had to stay in the mudroom.

The kitchen, completely remodeled by a New York interior-design firm, dazzled Harry and Fair.

"This is beautiful. The cabinetwork looks original." BoomBoom noted the white-oak cabinetry.

"It is. Came from England." Christy was pleased by the compliments.

Harry had other things on her mind. "Excuse me while I call the sheriff, then Fair, will you?"

As Harry gave Rick the particulars, then called Fair, Christy showed BoomBoom the downstairs of the house. The whole interior was English country. The floors had been sanded, stained again. The walls glowed with subtle colors. The patina on the furniture whispered "money."

BoomBoom couldn't wait to tell Alicia.

The two women reentered the kitchen.

"Perfect timing." Harry smiled. "The sheriff told me to take Jed. I'll go back home and bring the rig over."

"Harry, why don't you let me take Jed? Your horses aren't

accustomed to looking at or smelling a donkey. Mine have at least gotten used to Burly."

"What's going to happen to Jed?" Christy folded her hands together.

"I don't know. Toby has a sister in Charlottesville, but they didn't get on. I doubt she'll want Jed. We'll work something out. He'll be safe and sound."

"It's upsetting." Christy shivered involuntarily. "This dreadful murder next door."

"They hated each other. It's a sad end."

"Scares all of us," BoomBoom replied.

"It will take me about an hour and a half. Will you still be here?" Harry inquired.

"I'll be here."

Harry and BoomBoom opened the back door to the mudroom.

Christy offered, "Let me drive you back to Pittman's."

"We'd better walk, because we have the cats and the dog. Muddy paws," Harry said.

"That's what station wagons are for." She smiled, grabbed a Buffalo plaid jacket off the hook by the back door, and walked out to lift the hatch on her red Volvo XC70.

Within minutes they were back at Pittman's farm.

"Thanks, Christy," Harry said.

"I'll look for you all later."

As she drove off, BoomBoom turned to Harry. "Why would Toby lie about Jed?"

Why, indeed?

22

Fair had left the house at four in the morning without a cup of coffee. He delivered a healthy filly out on Route 810 and was now glad to be pulling into the coffee-shop parking lot.

The three men emerged from their vehicles simultaneously. Bo took one look at Arch, then at Fair.

"You sorry son of a bitch!" Bo growled.

"What the hell did I do?" Fair kept levelheaded.

"Not you. Arch." Bo stepped in front of Fair toward Arch, who wisely came up next to Fair.

"Bo, it wasn't my idea."

"Bullshit!"

"It wasn't my idea."

"Arch, you are the most competitive piece of shit I know. You cover it up. You're worse than your goddamned arrogant, idiot boss!"

"Bo, tell us how you really feel." Fair tried to lighten the moment.

Bo's sense of humor rarely failed him, even when angry. He stopped. "You're right. You're right." He took a deep breath. "Why'd you do it?"

"I told you, Bo, Rollie sent me downtown to Toby's sister yesterday. And she's a damned mess."

"Over Toby?" Fair's curiosity grew with each exchange.

"Hell, no. She hated his guts. He was the one who told her she was manic-depressive and needed heavy-duty tranqs."

"She is. All the Pittmans are crazy," Fair agreed.

"True, the whole goddamned family is nuts. They've been nuts since before the Revolutionary War. If any family ever made a case for free abortion on demand, it's the Pittmans." Bo added his two cents.

"I don't suppose either of you would like to tell me why you're cussing?"

"He's cussing. I'm not," Arch answered Fair.

Of course, he'd used the word "damned," but that must have slipped his mind.

"Arch went down to Tabitha—what's her married name now? She's married to some crackhead."

"Martin. Don't know that he's a crackhead, but he's as cracked as she is."

"Maybe they're in treatment together," Fair said, again joking.

"Guess what? It's not working." Arch showed a flash of humor. "All right. Here's what went down. Rollie waited about ten minutes. He said under the circumstances that was all that was necessary. I then offered to buy Toby's farm from Tabitha once the estate was settled."

"And?" Fair raised an eyebrow.

"She said it would take a year to settle it all."

"By which time the grapes will be ruined. Someone has to tend to them and harvest them. All that work." Bo's cheeks flushed.

"That's what I told her. So anyway, after a long, drawn-out process during which I heard everything she loathed about her brother, I offered to rent the farm. When the estate is settled Spring Hill will buy it."

"Did she sign a contract?" Bo, keen to the letter of the law, leaned forward.

"She did. Look, Bo, I know you've got this Belgian couple looking for suitable land for a vineyard, and Toby's place is perfect. The vines are established; the land drains quickly. He's got equipment. It's perfect. Rollie might have been insensitive in timing, but you know if we hadn't grabbed it, you or someone else would have." He stopped a minute. "Truth is, Bo, we beat you to it."

Bo grimaced slightly but didn't reply.

"Competition is the lifeblood of trade." Arch smiled slowly.

Fair agreed, then remarked, "Arch, what do you think about Toby's murder?"

"I'm not surprised." Arch folded his arms across his chest. "Toby pushed Hy and I guess Hy snapped."

"Do you look heavenward and say, 'Toby's at peace now'?"

"Not me," Arch said.

"Guess you're right," Bo said.

The three went inside and slipped into a booth. Bo had a double order of waffles with local honey poured over them; Arch ate eggs and bacon, as did Fair. A moment of contented silence followed, as it so often does. The world becomes charming on a full stomach.

Finally Bo asked Fair, "Anyone hear anything about Hy?"

"No, and Fiona isn't talking to anyone but her lawyer. She engaged McGuire Woods."

"That was smart." Arch put down his heavy white coffee cup.

McGuire Woods, a large, prestigious firm, had depth in every manner of law in which one could become entangled.

"Smart. See, that's where I keep running into a wall." Bo leaned back. "Hy is damned smart. Why would he be so incredibly stupid?"

"Maybe there was more to it than we know. I mean to Hy and Toby's bad blood," Fair offered.

Bo shook his head. "Still, Hy acted like an idiot. It just doesn't compute."

"Guess we didn't know Hy." Fair lifted his cup for more coffee, which the waitress supplied.

"Does anybody know anybody? Really?" Bo enjoyed philosophical discussions.

"Do you know yourself?" Fair smiled. "My way of looking at the world is: deeds, not words. I watch what people do and I don't listen so much to what they say."

"Good program," Arch agreed.

Bo turned to Fair, and directly asked, "What the hell *were* you doing at Toby's?"

"He called all upset and told me I had to rush right over because Jed cut his hind leg. When I got there I couldn't find Jed. What I found was Toby."

"Where's Jed? Did they find him?" Arch asked.

"Don't you watch the morning news?" Bo inquired.

"I'm out in the fields by six," Arch replied.

"Seven o'clock news reported Jed was found yesterday at

the old Berryhill farm. All's well with Jed, I guess." Bo shrugged.

"What about his leg?" Arch asked Fair.

"Not a scratch."

"Huh?" Bo dropped his arms.

Arch stared down at the table for a second. "Poor guy. Toby was really losing it."

"What? Toby was hallucinating?" Bo sharply asked.

"Who knows? But strange as he could be, Toby in his right mind wouldn't see a wound that wasn't there." Arch's voice rose. "It is weird. It's like Forland's disappearance pulled a loose thread and the whole cloth unraveled."

"The Pittmans are peculiar, as we've noted," Fair added.

"For Christ's sake, every family in Virginia is peculiar. You all have been nursing your peculiarities since 1607." Bo poked a finger at both Virginia men but in good humor.

"Hey, you weren't born a Virginian, but you got here as soon as you could," Fair poked back.

"I deserve that." Bo smiled. "Well, I don't know about you two, but I have to earn a living."

As Arch paid the bill to mollify Bo—he paid Fair's, too, which was gracious—Bo begged Fair to call him if anything suitable became available for the Belgian couple.

As the three men drove their separate ways, Rick, Coop, and an entire team combed Toby's house. The department computer whiz hunched over the new computer Toby bought in the winter. Toby had bragged about its ASUS motherboard.

So far, every single thing that turned up in the computer, on his desk, and on his bookshelves related to grapes, agriculture. He had everything Professor Forland had published plus unpublished materials, works in progress. One had to be proficient in organic chemistry to read the late professor's work. Toby was. The computer whiz was not.

Toby Pittman's entire narrow existence—like that of his mentor, who had a somewhat wider sweep—was dedicated to the grape, to making wine.

In vino veritas.

23

Hy Maudant was back at White Vineyards by Wednesday. Bail had been set at one million dollars. When Hy's attorney paid it without comment, all of Crozet—indeed, all of Albemarle County—gasped at how rich he must be.

Hy strolled out of jail an almost free man. Paying the bail was his way of giving everyone the finger. Since he did not discuss his net worth, this cool forking over of the money made him appear *really* rich, powerful, and confident.

That's what he wanted people to think.

He no sooner arrived home than within twenty-four hours another crisis struck: a very late springtime frost.

Usually frost disappears by mid-April, not to return until mid-October. In recent memory, a frost blanketed central Virginia once as late as May 22. But on the other side of the dreaded—courtesy of the IRS—April 15, farmers and vintners usually breathed a sigh of relief.

This May 11, man and beast awoke to silvery meadows.

Hy immediately called in ten huge helicopters to hover over the vineyards at 120 feet. The ground temperature was twenty-eight degrees Fahrenheit. He ordered the machines an hour before daybreak. Had the frost been predicted, he would have called them the night before.

Jack Frost snuck up on everyone, especially the weatherman.

The helicopters, each at the cost of five hundred dollars per hour, pushed warmer air down to the ground. Four hours later, with the help of the choppers and the sunshine that bathed the hills and valleys, the mercury rose to forty degrees.

Hy saved his grapes. Whether or not he could save himself remained to be seen.

Arch Saunders, not three miles away, had a devil of a time renting helicopters, because Kluge Estate Vineyard, White Vineyards, Oakencroft, and King Vineyards had rented everything within a three-hour flight radius of Albemarle County.

He finally managed to procure four, at six hundred fifty dollars an hour each. By the time the noisy machines flew off like giant dragonflies, Arch figured they'd lost ten to thirty percent of the crop. Rollie was furious.

The following day, May 12, the countryside glowed in sixty-seven-degree warmth.

Harry had no recourse to helicopters, but her Petit Manseng proved a tough variety. The grape survived through the centuries not only because of careful cultivation but also because of hardiness. Indeed, Petit Manseng was so old it had been used to baptize Henry IV of France in 1553.

Early on the evening of May 12, thanks to Daylight

Savings Time, Harry had enough light to keep working. The varieties of sunflowers, redbud clover, and alfalfa that she selected were either native to the area or especially rugged.

Central Virginia weather could provide cold winters as well as sizzling summers. It was a crapshoot.

As Harry finished up, returning to the barn to check on the horses, she wondered at the shock those early English settlers must have felt in the first quarter of the seventeenth century. The American climate was harsher, the indigenous peoples were so different from Europeans. The wildlife and plant life, much of it, was new to them.

"Fair." Tucker heard his truck.

"He's been working so hard. The pace should be easing off by now," Mrs. Murphy remarked.

Pewter sauntered into the barn. *"I'm here."*

"So?" The tiger half-closed her eyes.

"Don't you want to know where I've been?"

"Sleeping in the house." Tucker trotted to the open barn doors to await Fair's arrival.

"If that's my reception, I'll keep my news to myself." Pewter walked out, pausing a moment for effect, then headed toward the back porch door, the flab of her belly swaying to and fro.

"If she thinks I'm going to beg, she's wrong." Mrs. Murphy watched the gray cat.

"Yeah, but what if she really knows something?" Tucker often fell for Pewter's machinations.

Mrs. Murphy considered this but forgot about it when Fair pulled up in his truck.

The two animals ran to greet him. He knelt down to make a fuss over them as Harry emerged into the fading sunlight.

"I'd like a kiss, too."

"With pleasure." He scratched Tucker's ears, then ran his forefinger along Mrs. Murphy's cheek before standing to embrace his wife. "Long day?"

"Yes, but the frost didn't hurt us, thank God."

"Got some other folks." He opened the driver's door again, running his hand where the seat back joined the seat bottom.

"What'd you lose?"

"Quarters. Fell out of my pocket."

"Don't you hate that?" she commiserated. "Always happens at one of the toll booths on Route 64 in West Virginia."

As they entered the kitchen, the phone rang.

Fair picked it up; his shoulders stiffened as he listened, then he said, "Good-bye."

"What was that all about?"

"Hy Maudant." Fair grabbed string cheese from the fridge.

"What does he want?"

"He said he saw me walking up the hill when he drove out. He's sorry he didn't stop, but he was, in his words, 'not in full possession of himself.' He said he was so rattled by the sight of Toby that he ran."

"How very convenient that Toby had his own gun in his hand."

Fair ate a long piece of string cheese, handing some to his wife. "Sure was. Saw Bo Newell the other day, and Arch, too, at the coffee shop. Wound up having breakfast with them once they got over themselves, and Arch actually paid. I figured he'd pay for Bo but not me. He'll never forgive me for winning you back."

"Honey, that was years ago, Arch and my time together. Tell me what happened."

"Oh, well, Bo said Hy wouldn't be that stupid."

"It's hard to believe he wasn't. He killed Toby and put Toby's own gun in his hand. What's so difficult to believe about that?" She played devil's advocate, because she'd begun to wonder herself.

"There's something to that, but it's not so far-fetched to think someone would lose their composure walking up to a freshly killed man. And there's something else that bothers me. I would have heard the shots. I didn't hear a thing."

"The other thing is, Toby called about Jed, and Jed's fine. How quickly did you get there after Toby called?"

"Couldn't have been ten minutes. I wasn't that far and I put the pedal to the metal."

"How long do you think Toby had been dead?"

"Minutes. Literally minutes. He had to have been shot just before I reached the barn." He took a long breath. "I pick on you when your curiosity spikes. Now it's me."

"I'm so glad you recognize that." She gloated ever so slightly.

"Something is missing."

"Professor Forland."

"The two aren't connected."

"We don't know that." Harry reached for more cheese.

"True, but say that Toby's murder is exactly what it seems to be: the end result of an ongoing feud, of bad feelings. There's still something we don't know."

"That's not consoling."

"No, it isn't."

Pewter, who had soaked up every word, turned to Mrs. Murphy and Tucker again. *"Don't you want to know where I've been?"*

"Oh, Pewter." Mrs. Murphy dismissed her.

"All right, then." Miffed though she was, Pewter looked like the cat who swallowed the canary.

24

"I don't know." Big Mim stood in the middle of the quad in front of her old stable, originally built in 1802.

The new stable under construction, its back facing north, was sited at a right angle to the old stable.

Tazio Chappars had designed the new stable so it harmonized with the old, using the same graceful proportions and the same roof pitch.

The 1802 structure, which was brick and painted white, bore testimony to the enduring quality of the materials and the design. Both stables had excellent drainage.

The new one had pipes running underneath to two huge buried holding tanks, four thousand gallons each. Each drain in the new stable was covered with a perforated lid. This kept out much of the debris while allowing a stable hand to lift it and clean it out with a plumber's snake.

The new stable, instead of being infested with wires, had

a small dish facing due south so Paul de Silva could use his computer without electricity.

A backup generator was housed in an insulated room that also contained a large hot water heater. A small heat pump for the office would be hidden outside behind the office once construction was finished and bushes could be planted.

The work stall had recessed lights, some of which were heat lamps controlled by a separate switch.

The brilliant design never shouted. The tranquillity of the stable would be further enhanced by the landscaping once the last truck rolled away.

Harry, next to Mim, admired Violet Hill, the stunning four-year-old blood bay that Mim loved.

"You know what you really want to do." Harry thought the filly one of the best movers she had ever seen.

"Mom will tell Big Mim to do what she wants to do," Mrs. Murphy, resting under the eaves of the old stable, commented to Press Man, the springer spaniel puppy Mim had purchased to enliven her old, much loved springer spaniel, currently asleep at the house.

The little guy, all of five months, thought Mrs. Murphy hung the moon because she talked to him.

Mim's barn cats hissed and swatted at Press.

Tucker observed Paul now running alongside Violet Hill, encouraging the beautiful horse to extend her trot, which she did.

Pewter, also under the eaves, kept her eye on purple finches eating fennel seed from a feeder hung not far from the barn.

"Paul, thank you. Any more and you'll have completed the marathon." The elegant older woman laughed.

"Anyone else you'd like to see, Señora?"

"No, thank you."

Handsome, tightly built, and light on his feet, the young trainer walked Violet Hill back to the old stable. She would be wiped down, then turned out.

Mim, like Harry, believed horses needed to be out.

"I can't decide." Big Mim crossed her arms over her crisp white cotton shirt.

"If you send her out," Harry meant on the steeplechase circuit, "she may do very well. She has a large heart girth, large nostrils, and a big throat latch. I like that. Makes it easy to get air into those big lungs. But it's a risk to the mind."

"Yes."

"She may like 'chasing, you never know."

"Yes."

"But, as you know more than I, it can change a horse's personality forever. Some can retire to hunt. Others can't do it."

"She could always be a broodmare. There's not that much wolf blood out there." Big Mim named her sire, an Argentine import.

"You'd look fabulous in the hunt field on a blood bay."

A light flickered in Big Mim's eyes. "I've never had one, you know. Not in all these years."

"Blood bays are unusual. A true blood bay."

A long, happy sigh escaped Mim's lips. "I'll hunt her. She's been bold over the small fences here. She loves being outside; plus, we get along. Wonderful smooth gaits. That's good on these old bones."

"You've ridden her, then?" Harry thought to herself how deep the bond ran between a true horseman and the horse.

"With Paul on Toodles. Dear old Mr. Toodles is so calm. I think he talks to her."

"Lucky?"

"Not much. She certainly notices everything, but then, Thoroughbreds do. Saddlebreds, too. They're so intelligent. I can't believe people think otherwise." Mim stopped a moment. "She didn't even shy when a big, red-shouldered hawk flew low over here. Scared me. She stopped, then walked in. I am just besotted with this horse."

"I would be, too," Harry honestly replied.

"I'm so glad you dropped by. I've been wanting you to see her again. Fair's quite taken with her."

"I know. That's one of the reasons I came by. He's talked about Violet Hill so much that I had to see her. I haven't really seen her much since she was a yearling. As you know, Fair is one of her—and your—biggest fans." Harry followed Big Mim as she walked to the old stable. This pleased Mim, because she knew Harry was being genuine.

Wrought-iron benches bearing Mim's colors, red and gold, in a center medallion beckoned.

Mim sat on the long cushion, with Harry next to her.

"Well?"

Harry laughed. After all, Big Mim knew her when she was in her mother's womb. She launched right in. "Toby Pittman was killed with his own gun."

"Yes." Mim knew from Rick as well as her husband about the disposition of the body.

"Fair never heard the shots. He should have heard them."

"True, but he could have arrived just after Hy killed Toby." Mim's logic was strong. "And when the coroner examined the body he found signs of struggle. Marks on Toby's wrist. A smashed finger, as though he'd been held on the ground and his hand pummeled against the earth. He had a broken cheekbone, as well."

"How come Fair missed that? He's observant."

"Toby had on a long-sleeved shirt. And according to Rick his face wasn't caved in. It might have looked like a red mark where he was hit. One other thing: three shots were fired."

"Ah." Harry crossed her feet at the ankles. "Maybe he did get a shot off at Hy."

"They haven't found the bullet. Not on the farm or in Hy's truck. It would help if that third bullet were found."

"Do you think Hy killed Toby?"

"Yes."

The third bullet preyed on Harry's mind. She wanted to find it.

When she did, finally, it nearly killed her.

As the humans talked, Mrs. Murphy, enticed by the chirping, also came out on the lawn.

"I was here first." Pewter had a territorial moment.

"I can watch the birds as well as you can."

Up on the bird feeder, the purple finches, who had been joined by goldfinches, eyed the cats inching forward.

"Want to fly away?" the brightest purple finch asked the others.

"They can't get us," answered a goldfinch.

"I know. But we could poop on them." The bright purple finch cracked a fennel seed.

"Yay!" the others answered, lifting off the perches as if in fear of the felines, only to circle, then fly over, releasing their contents.

"No fair." Pewter skedaddled back under the eaves.

The two dogs laughed, which did not improve Mrs. Murphy's humor as she took a direct hit.

Driving home, the three animals listened to the radio. Mrs. Murphy, grumbling, cleaned furiously.

"Square in the center of the back. That's hard to reach," Tucker commiserated.

"Finches are supposed to be mean." Pewter got off lightly with a sprinkle on her paw. She'd already cleaned it.

"Birds are birds," a disgusted Mrs. Murphy said, then further complained, *"I wish she'd turn off that country music. I hate that stuff."*

"She's singing along, and even she doesn't much like it. Must be in a mood. Fat chance." Pewter so rarely heard popular music that she wasn't yet irritated by it. *"Guess you two still don't want to know where I went."*

Exasperated, Mrs. Murphy narrowed her pupils. *"We're dying to hear."*

"You're sarcastic. I'm not talking to you when you're like that."

"I really want to know." Tucker had no stomach for a cat fight.

With great satisfaction, Pewter said, *"Stealth bombers."*

25

"That wasn't here before." Pewter indicated some sticky strips, old-time fly catchers, twirling from a few lower branches.

"Maybe you didn't notice." Tucker knew she shouldn't have said that the minute it popped out of her mouth.

"I saw everything!" Pewter's pupils became slits for a second. *"I'm not human. They can't see the nose on their faces."*

Mrs. Murphy inhaled the odor of the abandoned Alverta peach grove that Harry was reviving. The tang of the tree bark, the lingering scent of tiny dots where blossoms had been, where the delicious fruit could ripen, all informed her. This small orchard, bursting with life, was inviting. Few folks remained who grew Alverta peaches. Harry understood the need for crop diversity. Agribusiness, however, was becoming monocrop farming, a dangerous development genetically.

"You're silent as the tomb," Pewter sassed.

"I see the stealth bombers." Mrs. Murphy noted the glassy-winged insects that looked like the famed combat jet.

"Some died on the sticky strips." Tucker marveled at how many little corpses there were.

"Along with every kind of fly in the county." Pewter loathed flies. They tried to deposit tiny white eggs in her tuna.

Mrs. Murphy asked the gray cat, *"Footprints yesterday?"*

"I don't think so." In truth, Pewter hadn't noticed.

"There are today." Tucker put her gifted nose down on the large treads left by work boots.

"Tire tracks?" Mrs. Murphy asked Pewter.

"No."

"Anyone could park behind the equipment sheds and walk up here. We wouldn't know. It's too far away." Mrs. Murphy sat staring up at the insects on the sticky strips, listening to the variety of insects flying. *"What a strange bug."*

A scarlet tanager chirped as he sat on a branch farther down the orchard row.

"Anything with six legs is strange." Pewter wasn't making the connection.

Tucker walked into the orchard, followed by Mrs. Murphy.

The orchard faced south, to soak up the warmth and light. A northern exposure would be too fierce at this latitude. A rise behind the small orchard protected the peaches from the north winds.

Peaches could grow in central Virginia, but the farmer had to protect the tree much more than apple trees.

Tucker reached the disturbed earth. Mrs. Murphy sat on the edge of the packed dirt.

Pewter, on her haunches, fretted, then joined Mrs. Murphy, asking, *"What? What's noticeable?"*

"This grave-size slight depression." The tiger paced the long side, seven feet, of the depression.

"*That's what the bear said.*" Pewter recalled the unintended visit.

"*I half-believed her and half didn't.*" Tucker kept sniffing the earth. "*Bears can be such fibbers.*"

"*I believed her. I didn't know how we could get Harry here, and then all that other stuff happened.*" Mrs. Murphy put her nose down, then asked Tucker, "*Can you smell a body?*"

"*If it's above six feet, I can. Below I can't. So if there's a body in here, whoever buried it dug deep.*"

"*We have to get Harry here.*" Mrs. Murphy started for home.

The animals trotted down the sloping pasture, crossed the rutted-dirt farm road, slipped under the old fencing, the locust posts holding firm.

Tucker started running. The cats followed her lead, over another pasture, then under more old fencing. They saw the Jones graveyard below to their right. Usually they'd linger there a moment, for it was so peaceful and often wild animals were there, as well, so they could chat. Not today.

Upon reaching Harry's Creek, Tucker plunged in. She enjoyed a good swim. Mrs. Murphy followed, although she hated getting wet.

Pewter halted a moment, opened her mouth to complain, her deep pink tongue bright against her gray color. Her two friends reached the creek bank.

"*Bother,*" she mumbled to herself, jumping in, dog-paddling for all she was worth, her ears flat against her head held high.

Mrs. Murphy turned once on top of the creek bank. Satisfying herself that Pewter wouldn't drown, she kicked into high gear to catch up with Tucker, hustling toward home.

Corgis, fast, can turn on a dime, too. Mrs. Murphy flew alongside the determined canine.

A wet Pewter, sputtering with fury, lagged fifty yards behind. Beads of water sprayed off her fur, turning into tiny rainbows.

The two front-runners skidded into the barn not two minutes after crossing the creek a half mile away.

Harry had to be in the barn or house, because they didn't see or smell her outside.

Sure enough, Harry, on her hands and knees, was in the wash stall. The drain cover was removed, the trap sat on the floor, and she scrubbed down into the eight-inch-wide pipe with a long, thin stiff brush. The drain rarely clogged, because she repeated this procedure once a week, and because years ago when she rehabbed the barn she put in large pipes.

"Come with me!" Tucker barked.

Pewter brought up the rear.

"Pewter, you look like something the cat dragged in," Harry laughed.

"This isn't funny. Stop what you're doing and come with us." Pewter ignored Harry's jest.

"She's right, Mom. Just leave everything. You can put it back later." Mrs. Murphy leapt onto Harry's shoulders.

"Murphy." Harry felt creek droplets soak through her white T-shirt. Pawprints festooned the shoulders. "Oh, well." Harry reached back to pat her friend.

Mrs. Murphy licked her hand while Pewter continued to urge Harry to get up and go.

"Come on. Follow me," Tucker pleaded.

Harry replaced the drain trap as Mrs. Murphy dug into the human's shoulders to hang on.

"Those claws hurt."

"You're lucky I don't really use them."

Pewter encouraged Tucker. *"Try the running-away-and-coming-back routine. She usually pays attention to that."*

Tucker barked loudly, dashed down the center aisle, returned, barked more. She repeated this until Harry gently placed Mrs. Murphy on the floor.

"All right."

"Let's go!" As Tucker hustled out the opened doors, light streamed in.

Harry grew up on this farm. Animals surrounded her. Given the limitations of her species, she knew as best she could that all three were worked up and needed her attention. It wasn't until she was halfway to the creek that she realized this was going to be a hike. But her friends, insistent, prodded her on. When she hesitated at the creek swollen with spring rains, Tucker boldly nipped at her heels.

"Tucker, I get the picture. And don't you dare tear up my new work boots, you hear me?"

"Come on. Come on. It's not that bad. We'll show you the best place," the mighty dog cajoled.

Although the ford was the best place, the banks were steep. Tucker, without glancing back, catapulted off the bank.

Harry watched Tucker's tail-less rump disappear under the water. When Mrs. Murphy followed suit, Harry ran back about twenty yards, picked up speed, and pushed off the bank. She made it to the other side, hearing a crescent of the bank's lip tumble into the water.

"I'm not going in here again!" Pewter wailed.

Neither Mrs. Murphy nor Tucker paid any mind to the gray cat.

Harry looked across the creek. "Pewts, go on back to the barn."

"Carry me!" Pewter wailed piteously.

"Dear God, give me patience," Harry muttered, then gauged the distance, walked back thirty yards this time, ran hard, and sailed over. She picked up Pewter, now purring, put her on her shoulders. "Hang on."

Crouching low on Harry's broad shoulders, claws sunk in, Pewter gushed, *"I love you."*

Taking into account her feline burden, Harry hit the turbocharger and made it, although her right foot just found purchase on the bank. Part of the softened earth gave way and she lurched forward as Pewter leapt off. When she righted herself, she had to laugh, for the gray cat had the good manners to wait for her when she could have run ahead.

Mrs. Murphy and Tucker, frustrated, sat down until Harry and Pewter drew closer. Then they again took the lead.

Sweat rolled over Harry's forehead by the time she reached the peach orchard. The sun, high, drenched with golden light the tiny first nubs, the dark bark incised with thin horizontal lines raised at the edges.

The two cats and dog darted into the peach rows. Harry shrugged but dutifully followed.

Tucker stopped, as did Mrs. Murphy, nearly dry from running. Pewter was perfectly dry.

Harry blinked at the sight of the sticky strips. She examined one. She walked to the next one, peering intently.

Noticing the stealth-bomber bugs, different from the others, she almost got her nose stuck on the yellow strip.

"What in the hell is going on?" she exclaimed.

Tucker barked, *"Come here."*

Harry did. She beheld the earth and her heart dipped deeper than the sunken dirt.

26

Because of the peach rows, the sheriff did not bring in a backhoe. Two men rhythmically dug into the reasonably workable dirt. If it had rained within the last week the task would have been easier, but at least the earth wasn't hard.

Coop and Rick reached Harry within a half hour of her call. So did Fair. He canceled his last appointment—hoof X-rays for a purchase exam.

Mrs. Murphy, Pewter, and Tucker sat by Harry and Fair, although as the men dug deeper the pleasing aroma of decay enticed Tucker. The humans couldn't smell it until one man's spade hit a rib cage.

He stepped back, eyes watering.

Rick and Cooper moved to the grave's edge. The other digger stopped, too.

It was time to call in the forensics team. By early evening they knew they had Professor Forland.

Harry and Fair were aghast at the news but not entirely surprised once it was apparent the remains were human.

Coop had dropped by to tell them.

"Do you know how he was killed?" Harry asked.

"He had been shot, but that doesn't mean that's what killed him. The coroner will know soon enough." She then spoke to Fair. "You found Toby, and we found Professor Forland on your property."

"So I'm under suspicion?"

"You are." She adored Fair, but she was also a very good law-enforcement officer.

"Are you going to arrest him?" Harry's hands shook slightly.

"No. I'm just letting you know where things stand, and," she paused, "I'm sorry."

As soon as Cooper drove off, Fair called Ned. "Ned, I need you."

After Ned agreed to represent Fair, Harry called Patricia Kluge and Bill Moses, since they were the last people to see Professor Forland alive, apart from the killer. Harry then asked Bill if she could bring over a strip of the flypaper with the strange insect.

If Bill didn't know what it was, he'd find out fast enough, since he had every conceivable program for his computer relative to wine-growing.

Then Harry, Fair, Mrs. Murphy, Pewter, and Tucker glumly sat in the living room.

Finally Harry said, "We'll get to the bottom of this."

"I hope so, honey. Innuendo can ruin one's reputation. Sometimes I think the facts are irrelevant once the media gets hold of you."

"We'll come through." She put her hand on his. "In the meantime, we carry on. Business as usual."

He was glad she was by his side. "Right."

Pewter, on the back of the couch behind Fair, faced Mrs. Murphy, who was behind Harry. Tucker curled up at the end of the sofa.

"Thought of something," Pewter piped up.

"What?" Mrs. Murphy's tail swayed slightly.

"Jed heard two trucks."

Tucker lifted her head. *"Hy's and Fair's."*

"He couldn't have heard Fair's truck. Jed had jumped out and was on his way by then. That's why Fair couldn't find him." Pewter sat up.

Mrs. Murphy looked at Pewter, then at Tucker. *"She's right."*

27

"It cuts the water supply, cuts off the nutrients going through the xylem, like our veins." Bill Moses studied the sharpshooter on his computer screen.

Harry had taken the strips to Bill and Patricia. Hy Maudant might know of the glassy-winged sharpshooter, but Harry had considered his position and hers. Also, Patricia and Bill could quickly command help if needed. Right now, Hy could not.

Patricia leaned over her husband's shoulder as he brought up a picture of the odd-looking insect. "How long does it take to get established?"

"That's just it." Bill hunched forward as he scrolled up more information. "The sharpshooter shouldn't be here at all. We're too far north."

"But it is here." Harry absorbed their rising concern.

"It just doesn't make sense." Bill then answered his wife's question. "If this insect introduces the bacteria into the vine, it can kill all of them in one to two years. According to this, some vines may survive five years, but the glassy-winged sharpshooter shouldn't be able to survive frosts."

"What were the sharpshooters doing in my peach orchard?" Harry asked.

"Because the bacteria can infect peaches, plums, almonds, as well as grapes. It may not take hold in your orchard, but you don't want to wait to find out."

"No." Angry, Harry's heart beat faster. "No. And why does someone want to harm my peaches? There are hardly any Alverta peaches left. Bad enough Professor Forland's body was there. I just can't believe it."

"Right now your Alverta peaches seem to be a magnet for evil." Patricia put her arm around Harry's shoulders, then asked her husband, "Bill, how does the disease spread? I know the insect carries it, but how quickly can it spread?"

Bill scrolled up more information. "Mmm, a sharpshooter can fly a quarter of a mile. Once established, the insect population explodes. And the bacteria can be transmitted to the host within an hour's worth of feeding."

"That's a long time to eat," Harry ruefully joked.

"What else?" Patricia moved from Harry to lean over Bill again.

"One good thing: not all sharpshooters are infected."

"So maybe these bugs are clean?" Harry said hopefully.

"We should call the USDA."

"Yes. We need to send some of these strips to Virginia Tech, too. They'll work fast." Bill looked back at the screen. "Today. We have to do this today. In the 1880s, the sharpshooter destroyed thirty-five thousand acres of vineyards in southern California. When the sharpshooter migrated to the Hill Country of Texas after five unusually warm winters, it killed every vine in every vineyard, and that was after 1995."

"My grapes are more than a mile from the peach orchard." Harry felt a ripple of despair. "Isn't there anything I can do to protect my peaches or my grapes?"

"Put up sticky strips to keep an eye on your insect population. There isn't a tried-and-true remedy." He stood up. "I'll run these strips down to Blacksburg."

Blacksburg, home of Virginia Tech, was in the Shenandoah Valley, a good two-and-a-half hours away.

"I'll take some to the USDA office, then," Patricia said. The agency kept a small office off Berkmar Drive in Albemarle County.

"I'm going back to my peach orchard. Maybe I can trap whoever is doing this. Put up a sticky strip for a human."

"Harry, don't do that," Bill commanded. "I mean it. You don't know who did this. Considering everything that's been happening, it could be dangerous."

"Killed for a peach." Harry rolled her eyes.

Bill's brows furrowed. "People have been killed for less. Until we really know who killed Professor Forland, we'd better be as vigilant around people as around these sharpshooters."

Patricia punched a button on her cell phone for a prerecorded number. As she waited she asked Harry, "Are you going right home?"

"Yes."

"Sixty-four?" Patricia named the interstate.

"Yes."

Patricia diverted her attention from Harry. "Hello, this is Patricia Kluge. Is Deputy Cooper there?"

Within seconds, Cooper picked up. "Deputy Cooper here."

"Coop, will you meet Harry at her farm in a half hour? Apart from last night's grisly discovery, someone has been tampering with her peach orchard, and it could have disastrous consequences for many of us. She'll explain when you get there."

"I'll be there."

"Harry, get moving." Bill kissed her on the cheek.

As she drove out, Harry noted that Kluge Estate sat at the same elevation her farm did, from eight hundred to one thousand feet. That elevation was perfect for apples and certain grape varieties.

Virginia ranked sixth in the nation for growing apples, and the state was moving up in the grape-growing numbers, too.

When Harry arrived home, two disgruntled cats and one joyful dog greeted her.

"You left without me." Pewter coolly received Harry's hug.

Mrs. Murphy wasn't much better. *"We should be with you at all times!"*

"Hi, Mom. Hi, Mom." Tucker ran in circles.

"She is so obsequious," Pewter remarked.

"Dogs—" Mrs. Murphy didn't finish her sentence, as she heard the squad car coming down the drive.

As soon as Coop pulled in, Harry hopped into the squad car along with her three animals. She told the deputy about the sharpshooter as they drove.

They had to drive back out, turn right on the state road, and go a mile to the old Jones driveway.

"You going to rent this place?" Coop asked as the gray number-five stones rattled off the skid plate.

"Up to Herb. He owns ten acres and the house."

"When's he moving out?"

"Well, that's the thing. He swears he will retire next year, but we all know that's not going to happen."

"Think he'd rent it to me?"

"What a good idea!" Harry's countenance brightened, as she was happy to have her mind off events if even for a moment. "Ask him."

"I will."

As they passed the house, turning left by the cattle barns, the dust from the road kicked up behind like a rooster's plume.

"After all the rain we've had this spring, I can't believe how dry this road is."

"That's central Virginia, isn't it? Walk ten paces and you're standing on a different kind of soil. One type drains well and another doesn't."

"I didn't think you were interested in such things," Harry replied.

"I'm not a farmer, but I am observant. Part of my job." She smiled as she pulled over. "Wish these squad cars had four-wheel drive. Wouldn't be as good in a car chase, I guess."

They got out then walked the rest of the way to the orchard. Yellow tape cordoned off the grave site. It would be removed and the dirt filled back in once Rick felt certain they hadn't overlooked anything.

"How many strips did you say there were originally?"

"Twenty." Harry touched Cooper's arm. "Coop, you know I'm not a scaredy cat."

"I resent that," Pewter complained.

"You're tough as nails."

"I'm afraid."

Cooper carefully held the bottom of a strip, examining the sharpshooter. "Someone has snuck onto your land.

Maybe two someones: one to bury the body, the other to bring in insects."

"I feel like they know my schedule. Fair's, too."

Cooper considered this. "It's possible, but your house and barn are two miles away as the crow flies. And you can't see the peach orchard. You can't even see it from the old Jones house."

"I know." She interlocked her fingers. "I feel like I'm being set up."

"Fair," Cooper replied. "It's more like Fair is being set up."

28

Twilight lingered in the spring. An hour of fading light enlivened by brilliant sunsets brought many Virginia residents outside to watch. Cloud wisps looked as though painted with a flat brush swirling upward, turned white then gold. After ten minutes the horizon line over the farther mountains deepened, but over the Blue Ridge themselves a brilliant turquoise line appeared as outlining on what were once the highest mountains in the world.

Fair noticed the sky, streaks of pulsating scarlet mingled with gold and copper, as he walked back from the barn with Harry. "My God, that's beautiful."

Harry looked up. "Sure is."

"When that sun goes down the chill comes on fast, doesn't it? Always amazes me."

"Yeah, but then we get into summer and the nights are languid. I love that feeling of warm nights with a light breeze to keep the bugs off."

"Girl, you've got bugs on the brain." He wrapped his arms around her waist as they watched the sky.

"I do, Fair. I'm baffled. And I can't help but think, two men are dead, both of whom had a great deal of knowledge about pests, about black rot, about grapes."

"I still don't see those deaths being connected."

"If Professor Forland were studying insect-borne diseases, he could have told Toby."

"He probably did. But all the vintners or their managers are scientists of a sort. Hy, Arch, Bill, and Patricia know how to look through a microscope to identify diseased tissue or what chemicals to use to kill their fungus on that."

"Yeah, you're right."

"Isn't that something about Toby's sister refusing to claim his body? What's wrong with people?" Fair shifted the subject. "Doesn't matter if they weren't on good terms. He's still her brother."

"Maybe she killed him," Harry flippantly replied.

"At this point, honey, I'm ready to believe anything."

"Inheriting a large farm under intense cultivation isn't a slim motive." Harry watched a great blue heron fly overhead, croaking as she headed for her nest.

"What an awful voice. You think she'd shut her bill," Pewter remarked.

"Ever notice how ugly people are often more vain than good-looking ones? Maybe it's the same with birds. She thinks she has a lovely voice," Tucker observed.

"I'd feel better if I didn't think the two murders were related." Harry wasn't giving up on this idea.

"Suppose this was about bioterrorism: wouldn't it be easier to send out anthrax?" She flipped up her coat collar. "You've been to seminars about this. Professor Forland certainly scared people at the panel. Maybe he was working for our government."

Fair thought awhile, then took her hand as the twilight faded, heading back to the warmth of the house. "Anthrax can be contracted through a cut. The bacterium enters the skin. If I handle a contaminated hide—not even the animal itself—I could contract anthrax if I have a break in my skin. You can breathe it in and you can get it from contaminated meat."

"What are the signs?"

Do I have to listen to this? Pewter wrinkled her nose.

"If a human ingests the bacterium, the intestinal tract becomes acutely inflamed. Vomiting and fever, followed by vomiting blood and severe diarrhea, occur. And this kind of infection usually results in death in a very high number of cases, from twenty-five to sixty percent."

"That's a big spread."

"Yeah, it is." He opened the porch door just as Flatface flew out of the barn for a night of hunting, "But you have to consider the health of the individual who contracts it and the level of health service available. Someone who ingests anthrax in the Sudan will have a much worse time of it than someone who becomes infected in Canada. Obviously, chances of infection in Canada are next to nothing."

"What about a cut?"

"Raised itchy bump like an insect bite. One or two days later a painless ulcer occurs on the site, a bit of necrotic skin in the center. The lymph glands swell. About twenty percent of infected people die. However, the last case of cutaneous anthrax occurred in our country in 1992. You see it in the developing countries. The real problem is airborne anthrax." He turned on the flame under the teapot. "Breathe that stuff in and the bacterium races through your lungs and then is passed into your circulatory system. Fatal septicemia comes on very fast. The incubation time is anywhere from one to six days."

"Wouldn't that make more sense as a bioterrorism weapon than stuff distilled from fungii?" She put a pot of water on the stove. Tonight was a good night for spaghetti.

"Seems so to me, especially since the anthrax spores resist environmental degradation. But the trick to creating anthrax that can kill huge sections of the population is the size of the spores. A chemist has to transform the wet bacteria culture into dry clumps of spores. But when the spores are dried they glop together into larger lumps, and then they have a static electric charge, so they cling to surfaces just like laundry with static cling. If the spores do that, they won't float through the air."

"Could a smart loner figure it out?"

"The method of reducing the spores to the optimum size for penetrating the human lung once free of static electricity has been closely guarded by what used to be the Soviet Union and by our government."

"But the secret really is out, isn't it?"

"Yes." He handed her a packet of spaghetti. "One way to find out who knows the secret is to capture anthrax that has been used in an attack. Then you'd be able to tell how closely the stuff genetically resembles the weapons strain our government made before 1969."

"Why 1969?"

"We agreed to destroy our stored biological weapons then. At one time, honey, our country had nine hundred kilos of dry anthrax made per year at a plant in Arkansas. I have not one shred of doubt that some was saved after we supposedly destroyed it all."

"And it's possible some was stolen, isn't it?"

"Yes, and over time those spores divided. Remember, they are living things, so they divide. And think about all the anthrax the Soviet Union made. That's not all gone, either."

"Gives me the creeps."

"Ought to give every single American the creeps." He paused. "How about I make clam sauce after I make you a cup of tea?"

"Okay. Want a vegetable?"

"You're heading somewhere with this. Fess up." He poured water in the teacups. "Uh, I don't want a vegetable, but I'll take a salad."

"I don't think the murders have one thing to do with bioterrorism, and one of the reasons is that anthrax is easier, is available. I just wanted to hear the particulars. So I'd feel more convinced of my direction."

"Gut instinct?" he questioned her simply.

"It may be that Professor Forland's specialized knowledge plays into his murder—Toby's, too, perhaps—but that's not what's underneath all this. I just wish I could find the reason."

"Not knowing is always worse than knowing. To change the subject, what's the dress code for Mim's party tomorrow?"

"She doesn't want us to call it a party. She says it's a gathering of friends to relax and celebrate the redbuds."

He smiled. "Right. We both know Mim."

"Coat and tie."

"You, too?"

"Probably be better than the ancient tea dress I trot out."

"You wear the coat and tie and I'll wear the dress."

"Fair, they don't make women's clothes large enough for

you." She imagined him in a dress, and it was a funny picture.

"What about all those drag queens?"

"You are twisted." She tapped the back of his hand with her spoon.

"That's why you married me." He leaned over and kissed her.

"I have a surprise for you. I bought you a new tie."

He laughed. "Then it's not a surprise, is it? You just told me."

They laughed together.

29

"And that's the difference between red and white wine," Arch explained to Miranda at Mim's redbud party. She always threw an "impromptu," or as impromptu as Mim could be, celebration of the redbuds when in full bloom. Given the wild bounce in temperatures, it was only now that the gorgeous trees opened their cerise buds.

"I never knew that. Is the pigment of the skin extracted when you make the wine?" Miranda, not a drinker at all, was nonetheless interested. She had just returned from a visit to Greenville, South Carolina.

Arch puffed on his Dunhill pipe, the burly bulldog bowl emitting a beguiling odor, a hint of spice among the rich dark tobacco. He found smoking just one pipe in the evening very relaxing. "You need the right kind of grape for your region, but the aging is every bit as important. The fruity reds, the ones so much in vogue," he shrugged, "I don't like them. Depth and complexity are the mark of a master and *terroir*—place. The grape, the wine, expresses the place. Americans don't understand that. We're so busy talking about the variety, the shape, the topography, the climate. People confuse soil with *terroir*. *Terroir* is soul. The wine—red, white, rosé—expresses the soul of the place. The Italians and French I worked with in California taught me that."

Lingering by the bar, Harry and Susan drank Jim's special lemonade. "Are things settling down?" Susan asked, although she'd spoken to Harry that morning.

"Yeah, but the whole thing creeps me out." A piece of lemon pulp caught in her teeth.

"It would upset anyone." Susan pointed with her forefinger to her own tooth so Harry would remove the lemon pulp, which she did. "Look how upset Christy was when Toby was killed, and that wasn't even her property. Everyone's on pins and needles."

"When that happens other stuff surfaces, ever notice?"

"Yes." Susan smiled as Reverend Jones approached. "Soon time to go fishing, Herbie."

"It is." He smiled broadly. "You know, I believe Jesus favors fishing. After all, He went out as the men cast their nets."

"And as I recall, a great storm came up," Harry said.

"And He calmed the waters." Herb glanced outside as a stiff breeze zipped through the rooms at that moment. "And I think He might consider calming this one. Look."

The two women saw inky clouds swiftly moving from the west.

"You know, I think I was wrong. Jesus wasn't fishing when the storm arose. He went out after preaching. Miranda will know."

"She can quote the Good Book better than I can." Herb

smiled, although he did know this story by heart. "Miranda, we need you."

Miranda left Arch and joined them. "I'm so glad to be back from South Carolina, even if we are about to be blown off the map."

"Not the same without you." Susan genuinely complimented her.

"Okay, what's the story about Jesus calming the seas in a storm?" Harry, as usual, stuck to whatever was on her mind.

"Ah, yes, Matthew, Chapter eight, Verses twenty-three through twenty-seven, and the same story is also recounted in Mark and in Luke. John doesn't mention it, but he doesn't mention a lot of things." She jumped as a mighty clap of thunder rattled the china. "Must be right over the post office and soon to be here."

"But not a drop of rain—yet." Herb noticed Blair shutting up the doors and, out of the corner of his eye, Arch and Fair talking by the coffee table. "Excuse me, ladies, I'll help shut up the house before we get blown to kingdom come."

"Clouds black as the devil's eyebrows." Miranda gave a shiver.

" 'Why are ye fearful, O ye of little faith?' " Harry quoted the most famous line from the story.

"Why, Harry Haristeen, I'm impressed." Miranda smiled.

"I can also quote the Pledge of Allegiance, but that's about it." Harry heard the first great splat as raindrops big as plums hit the windows. "Glad Paul put up the horses."

"Yours in?"

"Put everyone in for a little rest from one another."

A blinding bolt of lightning struck perhaps a half mile away. The lights flickered, then died. Within seconds another bolt struck a lone shed out in one of the large pastures.

The color was pale pink, and Harry saw spots when the powerful lightning touched the lightning rod.

"Jesus Christ," Susan blurted out, for it was pitch black except for lightning flashes.

"Candles," Mim called, as Little Mim and Gretchen, her majordomo, followed, the matches and lighters flicked to help them.

Within five minutes, beeswax candles glowed in hurricane lamps in the various downstairs rooms.

"She is always prepared." Miranda admired her childhood friend.

However, even Big Mim wasn't prepared for the crash when Fair flew backward into the coffee table. People's drinks splattered all over the floor, along with a candle, which Jim quickly picked up before it could burn anything.

Arch, without a word, turned on his heel, walked down the front hall, opened the door, and went outside into the storm.

Fair followed, also without a word.

Harry put down her lemonade, then sprinted after them.

"There goes my hair," Harry grumbled to herself, as she was soaked in seconds.

Susan stood at the door, rain lashing in, and shouted, "Harry, come back in here. Let them settle it." She then hurried to the closet to rummage for a raincoat or umbrella.

Harry didn't waste energy yelling at the men to stop. Her shoes sunk into the earth; the rain was coming at her sideways. She could barely see the hand in front of her face.

"You son of a bitch!" Fair slugged Arch.

Both men, in the prime of life, hurt each other when they landed a blow, which wasn't as often as they would have liked, since footing was slick. They fell down, scrambled up, traded blows, only to slide into the grass again.

Fair, more powerful, taller, in a little bit better shape, and with a longer reach, connected with Arch more than Arch could hit him.

Men, donning raincoats, hurried out of the house behind Susan, the borrowed umbrella now blown inside out.

Ned opened his car door and turned on the headlights, for it was pitch black.

The headlights created a ghostly tableaux in the unrelenting rain. Blair, also tall and strong, grabbed Fair, as Jim and Ned pulled Arch away, blood pouring over his left eye, only to be washed clean by the rain.

Harry walked on Fair's other side, Susan with her, as Blair opened Harry's truck door, passenger side, and Fair climbed in.

"Thank you, Blair," Harry simply said as she scrambled into the driver's seat.

"You okay?" Harry, now cold, shivered as she turned on the engine. She waved to Susan, who followed the others back into Mim's house. Ned and Jim, however, walked Arch toward the stables, no doubt to clean him up. Also, the enforced march was calming Arch down.

"Broke the heel of my shoe." Harry grinned, water still running down her face from her wet head. "A genuine tragedy." She took Fair's swollen hand. "Hurt?" She noticed his left cheek was bright red also.

"I'll put it in ice when we get home." He looked down the front of his suit. "Ruined my new tie."

"I can fix that, too, once it dries out." She prudently did not ask him what the fight was about, because it would anger him all over. In time, he'd calm down and she'd find out.

The cab of the truck was warm now that the motor was

running. Harry, driving slowly in the undiminishing rain, made it home in a half hour. It usually took ten minutes.

They stripped off their clothes on the screened-in porch, the slate floor cold underneath their feet.

Harry, shivering, hung his bedraggled tie over a peg. They then both burst into the kitchen.

"*Two drowned rats.*" Pewter opened one eye from her bed.

Fair dashed into the bathroom, returning with two large bath towels. He wrapped one around Harry and the other around himself.

As he did so, Harry devilishly said, "Honey, looks like your part got shrink-wrapped."

Teeth chattering, he managed to say, "Things do contract in the cold."

"I can fix that." She laughed as she opened the refrigerator, took out ice, putting it in a bowl. "First, let's work on your hand."

30

The storm purified the air. At sunrise the mountains turned red, then pink, and finally gold. The trees at the very top were beginning to bud. Spring marched onward.

Mrs. Murphy marched onward, too. She liked hunting alone. Pewter complained the farther from the house they traveled, so the tiger pounced on field mice without the whining of the fat gray cat to warn them of a feline presence.

She reached the confluence of the two creeks, Potlicker with Harry's Creek. The oak torn open by the bear served as a shattered sentinel.

The hard rains had knocked blossoms off trees and bushes but also brought down the pine pollen, a relief to anyone suffering from spring allergies. Mrs. Murphy saw globs of yellow pollen swirling in the creek. She peered down at a deep spot where the water, swollen from the hard rains, came perilously close to the bank. She liked watching fish, turtles, and crawfish, but the current and silt nixed that.

She walked along the eastern bank. Even with the beaver dams and lodges, some damaged by the debris moving in the water, she couldn't cross the creek. Not that it mattered. There was plenty of game on this side of the creek.

Two mourning doves flew overhead as the sun rose higher. Flatface, the great horned owl, silently winged toward the barn. The mighty bird dipped her wings as Mrs. Murphy looked up at her, then continued on her way. Mrs. Murphy respected Flatface for her hunting prowess and for her good sense. Good hunters usually respected one another, including humans. The bad ones pulled everyone down with them, unfortunately.

A surge of water sent a small wave crashing against the bank. The cat jumped high, then turned and trotted away from the creek. Getting her paws wet in the pastures and soggy ground was one thing, being sprayed by the creek was another.

As she headed down toward the back pastures of the farm, she thought she heard a motor on the other side of the creek. The water muffled the sound. She stopped, listened intently, then burst into a run, heading straight for the old hickory in the center of the back pasture. She leapt onto the textured bark, dug in her claws, and rapidly climbed up.

She strained to hear. The rise of the land on the western bank blocked sight of the farm road. She definitely heard a truck. Frustrated, she listened as the motor cut off. Ten minutes passed, the motor cut on again, and the truck, in low gear, drove away.

Whoever had been on the Jones land didn't stay long.

Mrs. Murphy backed down the hickory. Back at the barn, she climbed into the hayloft, where Simon slept, tiny snoring noises coming from his long nose. She noted the Pelham chain prominently displayed. Simon loved his stolen treasures.

She padded across the expanse, half open and swept clean; the other half was filled with high-grade alfalfa-orchard grass mix. Harry always kept a hayloft's supply of good forage in case someone needed to be kept in a stall. Luckily all the horses were easy keepers and didn't need fancy grain mixes. One or two scoops of crimped oats mixed with sweet feed kept everyone happy.

Simon liked the oats, too, eagerly dining on what the horses dropped along with the bits of dry molasses. Harry, after wetting her hand, tossed in a small handful of molasses if someone was picky. Never failed.

Mrs. Murphy inhaled the tang of a working barn, the best perfume in the world. She passed Matilda, the enormous blacksnake, curled up in her hole in a hay bale. Mrs. Murphy gave Matilda and her hay bale a wide berth. This year her eggs, next to her own snake apartment, seemed fatter than last year's. Like most farmers, Harry knew that her best friends apart from the domesticated animals were owls, blacksnakes, bats, honeybees, praying mantises, most spiders, swallowtails, and purple martins. Each of these creatures rid the premises of pests, whether small rodents or insects. The bees kept things pollinated. Abundance rests on the wings of bees.

Mrs. Murphy got along with most of these creatures, but Matilda gave her the willies. She hopped from hay bale to hay bale until she sat on top of the carefully stacked, sweet-smelling mass.

"You asleep yet?"

"Fat chance with your big mouth." Flatface glared down at her.

"Any eggs up there?" Mrs. Murphy liked owlets.

"No. I can have babies more than once a year, you know. I'll raise a ferocious brood when I'm good and ready."

"Better to plan these things," Mrs. Murphy agreed. She harbored a great secret, which was that a few years ago, when Harry took her in to be spayed, the vet—not Marty, of course—spayed the wrong cat. But they had shaved her belly before mixing up patients, both tiger cats.

"All the crops that Harry has planted will bring flying and crawling pests from everywhere. The grapes alone will keep the day birds chubby. And wait until the sunflowers lift their heavy heads; won't be for a while, but those seeds bring bugs and bad birds. We both know who the bad birds are. There will be so much to do." Flatface forgot about having owlets.

"Thought you hunted at night."

"If someone tasty shows up during the day, I can be roused." She laughed her deep *"Hoo hoo, hoo hoo hoo."*

"The crows will be a problem."

"You and Pewter will be on duty for them. They are very intelligent. You have to give them that."

Mrs. Murphy sniffed, *"Pewter has the attention span of a gnat. Worse, she's obsessed with the blue jay."*

"A most arrogant bird, besotted with his plumage and his topknot." Flatface sighed, then changed the subject. *"Thought I might pick up something juicy this morning once the storms passed, but my protein sources are still holed up,"* she said.

Mrs. Murphy moved to the subject she truly wanted to discuss. *"You didn't happen to fly over the peach orchard?"*

"Yes."

"I heard a truck maybe five minutes before I saw you. Did you see it or who was in it?"

"White truck with a gold lily painted on it."

"Hy Maudant," Mrs. Murphy exclaimed.

Later that day, the contents of Toby's computer, finally transcribed, reached Rick Shaw's desk with a thud.

Cooper looked up. "Can you imagine how many trees died for that?"

"Very funny." Rick sighed, fished out a Camel, and lit up despite the "No Smoking" signs that the county government felt compelled to post in every county government building.

"Let me help." She rolled her chair next to his. They started reading.

"Sure a lot of chemical equations," Rick mumbled.

"Soil stuff. Sugars in the grapes. That kind of thing."

"How do you know that?" Rick asked, surprised.

"Took organic chem in college."

"Why?" He was incredulous.

"I liked it."

"I thought people only took that under pain of death or to get into med school."

"Always knew I wanted to go into this field. Thought it would help me read toxicology reports, stuff like that. It does, too."

"Anything unusual?"

"Pretty much what you'd expect from Toby." The distinctive, inviting odor of tobacco enticed her to bum one of Rick's Camels.

Rick's phone rang, he picked it up, listened, then hung up. "Ballistics. The bullet in Professor Forland was from—Toby's gun."

Startled for a moment, Cooper said, "Well, that's not what you'd expect from Toby."

31

The next day winds swept down from the northwest, and the temperature cooled dramatically. At ten-thirty in the morning, the mercury hung at forty-eight degrees.

Harry and BoomBoom walked through the little sunflower shoots, the grapevines—tiny little dots showing—and the hay fields. Both women wore canvas Carhartt jackets.

BoomBoom turned her back to the wind. "May."

"At least we aren't in Utah. It's snowing there." Harry was glad she wore gloves.

Tucker tagged along, but the cats thought the toasty kitchen was the only place to be.

Gorgeous, immense cumulus clouds majestically rolled overhead. From white to cream to dove gray with slashes of slate, the cloud billowed.

"Feels like rain later." BoomBoom flipped up the collar on her jacket. "Well, you can't be bored living in central

Virginia if you like observing the weather." She continued walking along the row of Italian sunflowers. "These little shoots can bear the chill. Sunflowers are tough."

"So are we." Harry smiled. "Sorry you missed Mim's party."

"Me, too. Alicia and I were in Richmond at a fund-raiser for the Virginia Horse Council." She pulled out her gloves now that the wind stiffened. "Fund-raising is the second-oldest profession."

"With none of the pleasure of the first." Harry gleefully kicked a little clod of earth.

"Do you think they like it, really?"

Harry shrugged. "It's a job. I suppose there are some pleasurable moments. I mean, people usually don't keep on doing something they hate."

"I don't know. I'm not sitting in judgment, mind you, but I don't know. There's probably a sense of power over men but disgust, too. Their need is so overwhelming; men are such fools about it."

"Yeah. But I think we need sex just as much, only we're taught to suppress it."

"Some women suppress it so much it vanishes." BoomBoom swished the air with her hand. "The older I get, Harry, the more I know about some things and the less I know about others. At least, I've learned not to make grand statements except when it comes to things like horses."

"I'm waiting."

"Whenever I doubt there's a God, I look at horses." BoomBoom gazed at the foals with their mothers.

Harry smiled broadly. "Don't forget corgis."

Both women laughed as they headed toward the barn, the limbs on the trees swaying, the birds sticking close to home.

"So you didn't hear what happened at the redbud party?" Harry enjoyed testing this out.

"No." BoomBoom stopped and looked right at Harry. "What did I miss?"

"Here's a blow-by-blow description." Harry laughed at her turn of phrase, then launched in.

When Harry finished, BoomBoom, voice slightly raised, said, "You are so evil. You could have told me the minute I got out of the truck."

"More fun to wait. I knew no one had gotten to you or you would have said something."

"Do I have to beg to find out what the fight was about?"

"No. I had to wait until this morning. Fair doesn't get angry often, but when he does he takes a while to cool down. How they reached this point I don't know. All I know is Fair says that Arch told him he didn't deserve me. Fair agreed. Then Arch told him he'd cheat again, used the phrase we've all heard: 'the leopard doesn't change his spots.' Fair told him that would never happen. Arch said something worse. Don't know what, but Fair said, 'Go screw yourself, because you're not going to screw my wife.'"

BoomBoom, astonished, gasped, "Fair said that? That is so unlike him."

"Shocked me, too."

"I guess." BoomBoom drew out "guess."

"It's all pretty embarrassing. Fair left early yesterday morning to call on Big Mim. He also sent a large bouquet. He called me after he left. Mim was lovely about it, of course. Aunt Tally was still there. She didn't go home in that awful rainstorm. Well, she kissed Fair and told him she hadn't had that much fun in years and he was perfectly right to defend his wife's honor."

"What did Arch say?"

"Fair wouldn't tell me, but I called Aunt Tally on her cell this morning. She'd heard from Bo, who was standing by the coffee table when all this started, that Arch said," Harry paused, color rising to her cheeks, "I was the best in bed that he ever had. Fair didn't deserve me."

"He said that?" BoomBoom's eyebrows leapt upward.

Harry shrugged. "Guess so."

A long moment passed as they neared the barn. "Well, are you? The best in bed?"

"Boom, I don't know."

"The things I find out about you."

"And, of course, you're a saint."

"I didn't say that," the tall blonde responded.

Harry burst out laughing.

BoomBoom laughed, too. "You know, it's not sex with men that bores me. It's their anxiety about it. I find that exhausting and tedious."

"Yeah, but they can't always control the lever, you know. Stands up at the wrong time, sits down at the wrong time. Even if a man finally gets the girl of his dreams, his member isn't a hundred percent reliable."

"Big damned deal." BoomBoom evidenced no sympathy.

"Hey, imagine if your breasts stood up and flopped down sometimes at will, sometimes against your will."

BoomBoom stared down at her magnificent appendages. "Dear God, what an awful thought."

"Anxiety. I rest my case." Harry grinned triumphantly.

BoomBoom laughed. "Given all that's going on, I'm glad we can laugh." She breathed deeply. "Talk to Bill Moses any more about your sharpshooters?"

"I did. He said it's bizarre. They can't survive a Virginia winter. And, I quote, 'Should they infect your vines, the damage will be minimal because they'll be dead first frost.' I asked about the vascular damage—I hope I'm using the right word, but you know, the little plant veins that carry the nutrients around. Bill declared they can't do enough damage in the short summer they might live. I sure hope he's right. And he reminded me that not all sharpshooters are infected."

"We didn't see any today in your grapes."

"Wind blows everything away. I'm worried a little. And I'm worried about my Alverta peaches, too."

"Everyone else is focused on grapes," BoomBoom replied. "Hey, if I make the mistake of using the word oenology when I should say viticulture, the old hands lift an eyebrow."

Harry smiled weakly.

"Tell me. I should know, but I don't," BoomBoom asked.

"Viticulture is growing grapes. Oenology is making wine. Such a big damned deal." Harry threw up her hands.

"Intruder!" Tucker alerted.

The women reached the barn at the same time as Arch. He turned off the big Dodge diesel engine and climbed out.

"Harry, BoomBoom, hi." He stood with his feet apart, his old cowboy boots creased across the top. "Harry, I apologize. I apologized to Fair at work. I was completely out of line. I'm not making any excuses, but," he shook his head, bewilderment on his face, "I thought I was over you, I guess. But when I saw you after four years, well, I guess I still have some big feelings, and I took them out on Fair. I'm really sorry."

"It can be difficult." Harry tacitly accepted his apology.

He breathed out of his nostrils. "I've got to get back. Rollie keeps me on a short chain." He smiled ruefully. "He's heard about the sharpshooter, so now we've inspected every leaf...which we should."

BoomBoom asked, "Do you think it can do a lot of damage here?"

"I don't know. I hope not. The last thing we want is trouble in the industry just when we're getting somewhere. What worries me is if it's mutated or is moving up because of warming trends." He stepped up into the high cab, shut the door, leaned out the window. "I'll make this up to you, Harry. Oh, you found the sharpshooters in your peaches, right?" She nodded "yes" and he asked, "They doing all right?"

"I think so."

"Good." He waved and drove off.

As he drove back down the drive, Harry watched the exhaust curl out of the tailpipe. "That took a bit of courage coming here."

BoomBoom sat down when they walked inside the tack room. "I thought Toby was cracking up. Now I wonder about Arch. Not that he shouldn't apologize."

"Shaky. Edgy. Everyone's off balance."

Tucker dropped like a stone on the old horse blanket on the floor for her use. *"He's afraid. I smell it on him."*

Harry interpreted the dog's talk as a request for a treat, so she gave Tucker a twisted rawhide chew, then sank into the director's chair opposite BoomBoom. "Another reason I know things aren't good is Coop's not around. She's working overtime and she's not saying much. I check in every day."

"Did she talk to Herb?"

Harry brightened. "She did. Forgot to tell you. He said fine. She'll move in as soon as she can get a day off. There's so much busy work to do—switch over the power, the phones, all that diddlyshit."

"One of these days we won't need wires. We'll own one

phone number and everything will be keyed to that," BoomBoom predicted.

"Think so?"

"I do." She suddenly broke into song. "I've got your number."

"You're as nuts as the rest of them." Harry laughed a true deep, dump-the-stress laugh.

"I'm not insane, honey, just unsane. I greatly recommend it during trying times."

32

"Right temple, neatly done. No note." Rick filled in Cooper when she reached Tinsley Crossroads three miles from White Vineyards.

She approached the truck. Hy sat upright behind the wheel, his head tilted all the way back, his Adam's apple prominent, the .22 pistol still in his right hand. The powder burns on his right temple left a smell of singed flesh and hair, but the entrance was relatively clean. The exit proved messier, with tiny bits of brain and pulverized bone on the seat. A few specks stuck to the passenger window, but the sight wasn't gross. Coop had seen some really grotesque corpses.

She walked around the truck. The bed contained a small box of twine and a small box of flypaper. A paperback book about insects had a page turned down. She flicked to the page using the blade of her penknife. It was a photograph of the sharpshooter. Then she knelt down, flipped over on her back, and crawled under the truck. When she slid out, the crushed stone from the road dotted her damp back. The roadbed remained moist from Sunday's hard storm.

"How long before the print boys get here?" She returned to Rick.

"Fifteen minutes. I called them a half hour ago. Traffic's bad right now." He brushed off her back.

"He hadn't driven in deep mud, but there's mud on the skid plate." She then asked, "Was the motor turned off?"

"Yes. Everything seems quite deliberate." Rick lit up, handing the fag to Coop so she could enjoy the first drag.

"Thanks." She inhaled, then handed the cigarette back to her boss. "Who found him?"

"Bo Newell. He was driving those Belgian people around. Guess they won't be buying here. I sent them on. I'll get back with Bo later."

"Body temperature?"

"He's around ninety-five degrees right now, give or take." Rick had put on latex gloves, checking for a pulse, the instant he arrived on the scene.

"Most folks will take this as proof he was guilty." Rick watched a blue plume of smoke rise slightly then flatten out, which meant pressure moving down, probably rain later.

"I try not to laugh when I hear the gossip. Ever notice how desperately people want to believe, want to have an answer, but don't want to work for it?"

"That's why we're on the county payroll. We have to work for it. In the meantime they can make up whatever they want to make up. They aren't held accountable."

"Think he was accountable?" Coop inclined her head toward Hy for a second.

"Suicide? He took care of it that way?" Rick crossed his arms over his chest. "It's logical."

"Are you going to treat this as a suicide?" Coop asked, her inflection rising.

He replied, eyebrows raised, "What do you think?"

She waited, looked at Hy, then back at Rick. "Nope."

"Damned straight. I'm treating this as a suspicious death."

"Too many, too close."

"I hear the wheels turning." Rick pointed his forefinger at her.

"They are, boss, but I need traction."

"What we know is, everyone who could have killed Professor Forland or Toby doesn't have an airtight alibi." He tapped his toe on the crushed-stone road surface. "Fair has an alibi for Forland. He was asleep in bed. Harry can testify to that. Toby and Arch have or had no one who could clear them about their whereabouts in the middle of the night. Rollie has Chauntal. Then, of course, wives can and do lie to protect husbands. For Toby's murder, while signs point to Hy, we can't completely rule out Fair."

"I think Fair was set up, because of Toby calling about Jed. We're missing a big chunk here."

"Yeah, I know. And now the bugs." He nodded in the direction of the truck.

"Flypaper?"

"Coop, we're close to this guy. Really close, if we can just find the right piece to the puzzle."

"In time," she grimly replied.

"Thought of that, too."

"Traction."

33

Fiona had borne up through her husband being accused of murder. Now she bent under the crushing weight of his death.

Rick carefully described the scene and the fact that the gunshot may have been self-inflicted.

Cooper, as was her habit, stood quietly beside Rick but made mental notes. Once back in the squad car she would write everything down. Usually she carried her pad with her, but under the circumstances that seemed cold.

"Hy would never kill himself. He's Catholic." Fiona sobbed, her embroidered handkerchief at her gushing eyes.

Plenty of Catholics had killed themselves over two millennia, but neither Rick nor Cooper thought it wise to mention this. The fact that Fiona hadn't collapsed was impressive to the two enforcement officials. Events had leached pounds from her, but her haggard face retained vestiges of mature beauty.

"Did you notice anything out of line the last few days?" Rick sighed. "You and Hy have been under a punishing strain."

Her bloodshot eyes searched his. "Do you still think Hy killed Toby?"

"I have to stick to facts. Hy was our main suspect in the death of Toby Pittman."

Coop stepped in. "Something horrible is happening, and for whatever reason it's happening among those who possess highly specialized knowledge concerning disease in grapes and other crops."

Fiona wiped her eyes, took a deep breath. "Hy was passionate about making wine. He got into a big argument with Rollie Barnes yesterday at the co-op store about using machines to destem grapes. He ran into him at the café. People have been shunning us, Rollie included, so Hy's been extra sensitive. I don't even know how they started talking, but Hy lost his temper and declared the only way to make wine was to destem the grapes by hand. No bad grape should ever fall into the basket. With a machine they do. Hy came home livid, as it apparently turned into a real shouting match. He thinks everyone is against him." A long pause followed. "And they were."

Coop's voice soothed. "I'm terribly sorry, Fiona."

"Sheriff, Deputy, I know my husband did not kill Toby Pittman. Yes, a wife isn't considered a good judge in these circumstances, but the least I can do for Hy," she choked up, then gained control, "is to clear his name, and by God, I will."

"Why don't we wait with you until Alicia arrives?" Rick suggested, as he didn't want to leave her alone.

Knowing that the Maudants had no children and were fairly new to Crozet, Coop had taken the precaution of calling Alicia Palmer on the way to White Vineyards. Alicia and Fiona were pals. Alicia dropped everything, so Rick and Coop expected her at any moment.

The sound of the Land Cruiser on the drive sent a ripple of relief through Coop. Alicia would know what to do.

Before the beautiful woman came through the door, Fiona asked, "When can I have his body?"

"I'll get the autopsy performed today. I'll call you as soon as it's over. You understand this is necessary?" Rick spoke in a low tone.

"Yes, I understand." She sat upright, speaking deliberately. "I want you both to know that my husband did not commit suicide."

Alicia entered without knocking, greeted the sheriff and deputy as she walked over to Fiona. She leaned down to embrace her friend, and that's when Fiona gave way.

As Fiona's sobs shortened, Rick briefed Alicia on the disposition of the body.

"I'll take care of the details." Alicia held Fiona's hand.

"Fiona, please forgive me for pressing you at this time, but it's crucial. We must go through Hy's papers and computer."

"Must it be now?" Alicia spoke for her friend.

"Yes. Alicia, if this isn't suicide, others may be in danger," Rick stated.

Fiona nodded that it was all right.

Alicia asked, "Is she in danger?"

"I don't care if I am," Fiona flared. "Let them come and get me. I don't want to live without Hy. I don't care!"

Coop calmly reminded her, "You have to live long enough to clear his name."

Fiona blinked, nodded, and said, "You're right."

34

Hy Maudant's funeral, a desultory affair, was attended by twenty-five people that Friday. St. Luke's seemed cavernous with so few mourners in the pews, but the Reverend Jones rose to the occasion. He didn't want to praise a murderer, but he didn't wish to condemn him, either. While Herb didn't know conclusively if Hy had killed Toby, he felt the evidence against him to be overwhelming. However, the Christian God is a merciful God, and Herb wanted to console Fiona and leave some shred of dignity with the departed.

Whenever confronted with a knotty problem, Herb turned to the Psalms. He read from Psalm Twenty-five: " 'Turn thou to me, and be gracious to me; for I am lonely and afflicted. Relieve the troubles of my heart, and bring me out of my distresses. Consider my affliction and my trouble, and forgive all my sins.' "

As the service ended, Hy's casket was carried by four men

from Hill and Wood Funeral Parlor, along with Fair Haristeen and Jim Sanburne.

Fiona, supported by Alicia and BoomBoom, followed her husband's casket to the shining black hearse. Aware that eyes were upon her, she held her head up.

Eight people attended the burial apart from the pallbearers: Harry, BoomBoom, Alicia, Susan, Miranda, Tracy, Little Mim, and Aunt Tally.

As they repaired to Fiona's house for the traditional gathering, Aunt Tally waited for Harry to walk next to her.

"Aunt Tally." Harry slipped her arm through the old lady's free arm as Tally used her cane with the other one.

"We could have done better," the nonagenarian muttered under her breath.

"Beg pardon?" Harry inclined her ear toward Aunt Tally.

"Crozet should have done better by Fiona. Whatever Hy did is buried with him. No need to punish his widow."

"You're right." Harry shortened her steps.

"I have a terrible feeling, Aunt Tally."

"We all do, dear."

"It's not just about Hy's death. It's about all of this. Usually I can piece things together. Even if I don't put all the puzzle together, I'm close and I eventually figure it all out. But I'm blind this time."

"Malaise." Aunt Tally nodded. "I think we all feel that, Harry. It's not just the shock of this death or the visceral impact of the others, it's that we can't see why." She stopped, withdrawing her arm from Harry's to put both hands on the silver hound's head of her ebony cane. "Mark me, Harry, I am near one hundred and I tell you with the fullness of my years: there is nothing new under the sun. There are new technologies, but there is nothing new in the nature of the human animal."

"I believe that," Harry interjected while Aunt Tally took a deep breath.

"You do have a puzzling mind—I mean, you can often figure things out because you aren't hampered by seeing things as you wish to see them. That's a great gift. Your grandfather certainly had it, which is one of the reasons I fell in love with him. Your mother possessed it, too, and people with this gift can often run afoul of those who wish to view the world through rose-colored glasses. Use your sharp mind to ask, 'Why do people kill?' "

"Love, money, power."

"Exactly. To that I add revenge and to protect one's self."

As they started walking toward the gracious house, Harry whispered as if to herself, "The vineyards. How do the vineyards tie in to love or revenge?"

Aunt Tally, ears good even if her joints weren't, replied, "Money. There's a great deal of money once one is established."

"Enough to kill for?" Harry lifted her shoulders.

"People kill one another in cities for an expensive pair of sneakers, for drugs, for the damnedest, most inconsequential things."

"True," Harry softly answered.

"One of the great virtues of becoming ancient is I have ample time to cogitate and to continue my study of human nature. They call economics the dismal science. I think not. It's the study of human nature. Thousands of years of recorded history and we've learned nothing. Dismal."

That, too, applied to the small gathering at White Vineyards. One by one the people left, until only Fiona, Alicia, and BoomBoom remained to look over the rolling hills festooned with vines climbing on the wires. In other circumstances this would presage hope. Today it represented loss.

Harry drove her old F-150 back to the farm; since Fair needed to visit his patients, he had attended the funeral driving his own truck. He called the horses his patients. He had a good bedside manner.

Harry resolved to keep tabs on Fiona—she would have, anyway. She also wanted to find out who was calling with checkbook in hand, how long it would take people to show up at the door. Could someone be trying to create a monopoly of local vineyards? But to kill for it—well, that upset her. Just thinking about it made her mad, gave her energy. And she kept thinking, "Could anyone be that greedy? That stupid?"

And she determined to visit local vineyards.

That was a mistake.

35

"Costs twenty-five dollars a plant. That's a hell of a lot better than one thousand five hundred dollars a plant." Dinny Ostermann pushed back his sweat-stained ball cap as he explained a new technique for identifying six common virus infections. "The worm is turning."

"How do you mean?" Harry had dropped by Dinny's small vineyard in Crozet.

Dinny bottled no wine. He picked his grapes and sent them on to whoever gave him the best price each year. As he grew an outstanding Cabernet Sauvignon, the Bordeaux variety of red grape, he enjoyed visits from various vintners' representatives during harvest time.

Mrs. Murphy, Pewter, and Tucker nosed around. Dinny loved animals, so he laughed as Mrs. Murphy leapt straight up to try and snatch a yellow swallowtail from midair. The gorgeous insect fluttered away, her compound eyes seeing the tiniest movement.

"From Canada to Chile, people are waking up to the profit from wine. Wine consumption will finally overtake beer in our country." He hooked his thumbs in his muddy jeans.

"You really believe that wine will overtake beer?"

"More health benefits, and who gets a wine gut?" He laughed.

"Thought you might come to Hy's funeral."

"No. Hy and I didn't much get on."

"You think he killed Toby?"

"Yeah. They hated each other."

"I've been swinging by as many vineyards as I can in Albemarle and Nelson Counties. Trying to find out if anyone has seen the sharpshooters. So far no one has. What about you?"

He shook his head. "No. Heard you found them on strips in your peach orchard, but you haven't seen any on your grape leaves, have you?"

"No. But I've been thinking that it's kind of cool, rain off and on, and pretty good breeze, too. Maybe they'll show up when it's calm and warmer."

"Let's hope not." Dinny's black hair curled out from under his cap. "Damned queer, though."

"I'm furious that someone used my peach orchard for their experiment."

"I would be, too." He removed his cap, holding it over his eyes as he looked toward the sun. "Should dry out by tomorrow." He laughed. "Boots get heavy with all that mud caked in the treads."

"Don't I know it."

"Hey, gives us good legs. We'll both look good in bathing suits." He smiled.

"What a happy thought." She lifted Tucker up, putting the heavy corgi in the cab. "Dinny, I had an odd thought."

"Only one?"

"Only one that I can share." Mrs. Murphy and Pewter jumped in the cab while Harry closed the door and leaned against it. "You know most all the growers and vintners. Apart from Hy and Toby, is there bad blood between any of them?"

He considered this. "I don't know as I'd call it bad blood, but if this were a frog-jumping contest, I'd keep my eyes on my frog, 'cause I expect someone would pour BBs down its throat."

"You think anyone is competitive enough to destroy the other guy's crop? Like with black rot or one of those mildews or the sharpshooter?"

He rubbed his chin, dark underneath the shaved skin. "Seems like it would come back on them."

"What if they unleashed something for which they were prepared? I mean, like downy mildew. Forgive me, Dinny, I don't know these diseases and pests like you do, but if spores were wafted over someone else's grapes, the criminal could have sprayed his own grapes."

"You'd have to be rich."

"Why?"

"Because you'd have to have all those sprayers and booms right there to use before you let loose the spores or the bugs. Couldn't be renting them. Too obvious."

"Don't all the big vineyards have them?"

He nodded yes, but added, "There're plenty of little guys out there with maybe an acre or two in cultivation. They rent the equipment."

"You don't seem surprised by my questions."

"Harry, you belong with those two cats. Curious."

"Guess so. My fear is that I'm trying to find who hates whom. I'm wondering if the killings are over."

"I expect the people who hated one another are dead." His eyebrows lifted. He stepped back up on his small tractor. "Guess you heard that Tabitha Martin donated Toby's body—I should say body *parts*—to the medical school for anatomy."

"Some sister."

"Yeah. I look on the bright side. Toby's helping science. He liked science."

"He was on to something, Dinny."

Harry drove by Rockland Vineyards, spied Rollie Barnes's truck and a farm truck next to it. She pulled down the drive onto Toby's farm, came up alongside the two trucks, and cut the motor.

"Hello, Harry." Both Rollie Barnes and Arch Saunders greeted her.

"How's it going?" she asked. The cats put their paws on the windowsill, since Harry had rolled down the truck windows. Tucker stuck her head out.

"If the weather cooperates, this is going to be Toby's best yield yet. A real tribute to him." Rollie swept over the vineyards with his right hand.

"I dropped by Dinny Ostermann's and things look good there, too. You know, he was telling me about a new technology called RT-PCR that can pin down six different viruses that infect grapevines."

Arch spoke up. "Reverse transcription polymerase chain reaction."

"That's a mouthful." Harry smiled.

"Pretty close to a miracle. Cheap and fast. The old way to

identify corky bark and leafroll virus could take up to three years." Arch liked showing off his knowledge in front of his boss. "Costs a fortune, though. RT-PCR costs twenty-five dollars a pop."

"Yeah, that's what Dinny said. Didn't see you two at Hy's funeral—"

Arch interrupted, "Harry, I'm not that big a hypocrite."

"Didn't think you were, but we all were wondering what Fiona will do. Maybe she can carry it by herself. A lot of work." Harry's voice was without any accusatory trace.

"I offered her a very good price for the place." Rollie sounded like a charitable man.

"After the funeral?" This time Harry's voice betrayed her surprise.

"Someone has to be first in line, and that's going to be me," Rollie explained himself.

"I suppose. I figured the Belgians would hurry back to Dulles Airport after finding Hy at Tinsley Crossroads," Harry replied. "Called Bo to see how he was doing after finding Hy. He told me they're still in the hunt and that he's fine."

"Probably a lot more exciting than what happens in Belgium." Rollie couldn't help but smile. "Bo will be telling that story for the rest of his life."

"It will be a long life. Only the good die young." Harry adored Bo, as did many women. She liked teasing him. Harry then inquired, "Is there a grape resistant to the sharp-shooter?"

"Lake Emerald grape. They developed it in Florida. It's used as a rootstock mostly. Used a lot around Leesburg, Florida."

"We're too far north?" Harry asked.

"Yeah, but it's not the kind of grape we want to grow." Arch left it at that.

"You two need to get back to work and so do I, but I saw your trucks and thought I'd say hello."

"Hey, where's the donkey?" Arch asked.

"BoomBoom took him."

"Place is kind of lonesome without Jed," Arch said.

"Do you mind if I stop by the barn? Think I dropped my penknife in there when I was searching for Jed."

Rollie answered, "Go ahead. I don't think there's much in there."

"I didn't see a knife," Arch offered.

When Harry walked into the barn, she headed straight to the supply room. The boxes of flypaper were still there. She thought maybe Toby had put those sharpshooters in her peach orchard. It would have made more sense to put them in her grapes or someone else's grapes if he had hoped to destroy their business. But Toby could be sly. Maybe he was testing to see if they would survive. She was the only person who went to the peach orchard regularly, and most Crozet friends and neighbors roughly knew her habits and schedule.

She looked around for jars, for any evidence how he might have kept the insects alive. Nothing turned up.

As to the quantities of flypaper, all she could figure out was maybe he got a deal. That wasn't so unusual. She left as ignorant as when she arrived.

36

"I told Coop I snooped around at Toby's barn." Harry and Fair played with the foals when Fair came home from his calls. Although it was Saturday, horses pay no attention to weekends.

The more they were handled, the better the babies would be when they grew up.

"They might be small, but those little buggers can still hurt you," Mrs. Murphy remarked as she sat on a fence post.

"It's the biting." Pewter steered clear of the foals.

"They're smart. They'll learn, and Harry and Fair make it fun." Tucker watched.

"And the mothers like the humans, so that helps." Mrs. Murphy noticed hundreds of tiny green praying mantises who had popped out of their pod. *"Wow, glad I don't have to feed that family."*

Tucker squinted, for the newborns crawled on wisteria

wrapping up and over a small pergola Harry had put at the entrance to her flower garden. *"I can't see that far."*

"You can't see much anyway." Pewter felt ever so superior.

"I can see better than you think. I can see colors, too, even though humans used to think dogs couldn't, and furthermore, Miss Snot, I see better than humans in the dark."

"But not as well as I do," Pewter cattily said.

"I didn't make that claim." Tucker smiled as the light bay foal nuzzled Harry's cheek.

"Funny how humans get things wrong," Mrs. Murphy mused. *"All that business about dogs seeing black and white, and now they have research to prove otherwise. Research can be a good thing, but why don't they trust their own senses?"*

"The sixth sense is the important one." Pewter shifted her weight on her fence post, a bit small for her large behind.

"Knowing without knowing. Yes, they should listen," Tucker agreed.

Fair dug in his pocket for dried-apple treats for the patient mothers. "Coop say anything?"

"Not much. I told her I was researching diseases of grapes. She's been doing it, too. Do you know, when I ran off the names, names only of stuff that can attack grapes, I had four pages, two columns each, single spaced? Now I wonder how any grape ripens."

"The same could be said about any crop." He felt a soft muzzle fill his hand. "Back in the office today I was reading where Asian soybean rust is in Georgia. And it's one of those diseases carried by the air. After all that's happened I'm paying more attention."

"Spores?"

"Yep. Fungal, and it's so virulent that it can destroy plants in one month if untreated."

"Damn, that is a hateful one." Harry pondered. "What can the farmers do?"

"Spray, but that's expensive. The chemicals to kill Asian rust cost eighteen dollars an acre. Not cheap."

"Did it get here on a plane—you know, spores on someone's pants?" Harry was curious.

"No. It's the damnedest thing. Hurricane Ivan carried it here in a matter of weeks. It's been moving slowly through Asia, then Africa, and then South America—slowly as in decades—and all it took was one big hurricane to carry the spores across the ocean."

"But Hurricane Ivan was two years ago."

"Hit Florida bad, and that's where they first found the fungus, on kudzu."

"God, kudzu will take over the universe." Harry gasped.

"I don't know about the universe, but the spores sure managed to get from the kudzu in Florida to the soybeans in Georgia with unseemly haste." He handed out the rest of the apple treats. "I e-mailed Ned and he e-mailed back. I didn't know that soybeans account for sixteen percent of our country's agriculture production. Soybeans are twelve percent of U.S. export. Tell you what—first, that impressed me, and then second, Ned is up to speed."

As they walked back to the house Harry quietly said, "You're as caught up in this murder stuff as I am."

"I'm the one telling you to butt out, keep your nose out of other people's business." He brushed his boots on the hedgehog scraper outside the screen door. "But I keep coming back to vineyards and revenge of some sort."

"And to the fact that growing grapes and making wine are becoming big business. There's millions to be made."

"But first you have to spend millions. It's a rich person's

game. People like Dinny Ostermann benefit, and I hope we do, too, but we won't make the millions."

"What else have you been doing at your computer?" She felt Pewter brush against her leg as she walked into the kitchen.

"Tuna!"

"Pewter, let me make tea. I need a pick-me-up. You'll get your tuna soon enough."

Fair smiled. "How do we know she isn't saying, 'rib eye rare'?"

"Yes!" Pewter stood on her hind legs.

Mrs. Murphy along with Tucker padded into the kitchen. *"A ballerina. Our very own toe dancer."*

"If we get steak it will be because of me," Pewter bragged.

"Steak!" Tucker's ears stood straight up and forward.

As it happened, Fair decided to grill steak. Harry knew not to interfere with his cooking, but she had to laugh behind his back at how "the boys," as she thought of them, ruthlessly competed about their grilling techniques. Ned, Jim, Blair, Tracy, even Paul de Silva had outdoor grills. She didn't know what he was doing out there with his apron around his waist as he wielded a dangerously sharp long fork and knife.

When Fair brought in the steaks, the aroma filled the kitchen.

As they ate their supper, giving the animals small steak tidbits, they kept going over events.

Harry rose to shut the kitchen window. "When the sun sets, the chill comes up fast. This is the coolest May I remember."

"It is."

"Hope you don't have any emergencies tomorrow."

"Me, too. What did you have in mind?"

She put on her sweetest smile. "Herb said Coop could move in when she was ready, so why don't we take the horse trailer and load up her stuff? One haul will do it. She doesn't have much."

This wasn't the Sunday he'd hoped for, but he figured silently that with his muscle power and Harry's organizing abilities they should be able to pull this off in three compressed hours. "Sure. She'll make a good neighbor."

"I'll make it worth your while." Harry smiled.

"Even if you don't, it's hard for a man to win when two women gang up on him, and one is his beautiful wife."

"You are such a flatterer." But she loved it.

37

Maps spread over the hood of her truck, Harry pointed to acres she had shaded with different-colored pencils. Susan peered down as traffic pulled in and out at the post office parking lot, a big parking lot for Crozet.

"Here's Carter's Mountain," Harry said as the two cats and dog watched people, arms laden with mail, bills, and magazines, come and go.

"Harry." Susan put her hand on Harry's shoulder. "I can read a map."

"Sorry. Well, anyway, this is what Patricia and Bill own. Down here is what Hy and Fiona own—I should just say Fiona. White Vineyards, about three hundred acres. Over here is Toby's, and Toby is just under two hundred acres, and here is Rollie. Arch and Rollie's Spring Hill, the main part, is also two hundred acres—well, two twenty. These days that's a lot for Crozet. Okay, shaded in apple green are small growers who sell to the large ones."

"What's the pink?"

"Those are small farms Rollie and Arch have bought up. When you add Rockland—Toby's—to it, Spring Hill controls just under five hundred acres."

Just then Arch pulled into the post office. He emerged from his truck. "Are you coming back to work here?"

"No." Harry smiled.

"It's not the same without you and Miranda. Yeah, the big building and the extra post boxes are good, but we've lost something." He walked over. "Now, what are you up to?"

"Vineyards. Who owns what, who controls what, and you're coming out on top."

He smiled broadly. "Good for Spring Hill. Harry, any more sharpshooters?"

"No. Not yet anyway."

"You just never know. I sure hope they aren't adjusting to the latitude and the warmer winters. If they do, we're in big trouble. Well, let me go pick up the mail. Nice to see you." He turned, then stopped. "Are you two going to put more acres in grapes?"

"Not yet," Harry answered.

"Buy land while you can. There will be a point in Albemarle County where it will be only the very rich and the very poor."

"I don't think I'm going to ever qualify as the very rich." Harry laughed.

"Me, either," Susan agreed.

"Not true. If either of you ladies ever sell the land you've inherited, you'll be worth millions. Let me know. Rollie has a big bankroll."

"Arch, if I sell my land, I sell my birthright," Harry said.

"Me, too. The Bland Wade tract has been in our family since right after the Revolutionary War."

"That's well and good, but if property taxes keep going up, and you know they will, and if, for some reason, your nursery business doesn't bring in enough cash, you'll be land poor, sure as shooting."

"Somehow, Arch, we'll hang on. The land is who we are." Harry spoke for herself and Susan.

"Well, keep it in mind. You never know. And you're both very smart ladies." He smiled and left.

"I guess on paper we're already millionaires based on the value of the land." Susan thought it out.

"We are?" Harry hadn't given it a thought.

"Pretty sure. It was our good fortune to be born into families that never sold off their land no matter how bad the times were. How they kept it together through the booms and busts of the nineteenth century, the war, the horrible aftermath, and then the crash in the 1930s—it's a testimony to how much they loved this place and how much they believed in the future."

"It really is," Harry solemnly replied. "We'll do our part, no matter what."

Arch walked back out of the post office, cell phone to his ear, and waved to the ladies. As he drove by, he slowed and said, "Rollie will pay twenty percent over current market value. He's on a roll."

"A lot of land has opened up in the last month," Harry blurted out. "Seems like you two have come out ahead."

Arch stopped the truck for a minute. "Can't let established vines go to ruin. The wine industry has come too far in Virginia, know what I mean?"

"Fiona is going forward," Susan said.

Arch frowned for a second, then said "More power to

her, but she's another one who could cash in and walk away a rich woman."

"She's already rich, plus she gets back the million dollars of Hy's bail. Just think of all that money at one time. It's overwhelming." Harry's eyes lit up.

"See you, ladies." Arch waved and drove on.

"What're you doin' now?" Harry asked Susan.

"Thought I'd go home and see if I can't find southern hawthorne saplings, little guys for us to plant come fall. I ordered the sugar maples, did I tell you?" Susan found that she enjoyed researching tree varieties, then finding them.

"No."

"They'll come in late September. Boy, I'm not used to thinking ahead like this. I'm used to school calendars." She sighed. "Where does the time go? Danny is a junior at Cornell and Brooks goes to Duke next fall."

"Sure goes fast," Harry agreed. "All right, I'm going back to the farm. Have to see if I can work the boom on the tractor. Never used one before. I might wait and cut hay instead. I'll ask Fair to help with the boom."

"Good luck with the boom." Susan kissed Harry on the cheek, then hopped into her Audi and drove off.

Two hours later Harry happily perched on the cushioned tractor seat as she cut the back acres; this was her orchard grass with regular alfalfa. The mix was popular with horsemen. She'd cut the quadrant with drought-resistant alfalfa later. She had to time it just right and allow the rows to dry out completely. Small wonder farmers obsessively watched the weather. But if she didn't give the blister bugs time to get out of the drying hay, nothing good would come of it.

She made the animals stay back in the barn when she cut hay.

The cats dozed on the tack trunk in the center aisle, the

day was so pleasant. Tucker was sprawled in the middle of the barn aisle.

Riding on a tractor always got Harry to thinking. As the diesel engine rumbled, the newly mown hay exerted a hypnotic quality. The symmetry pleased her. The aroma intoxicated her. She hummed to herself, jouncing along. When she cut the last row, she disengaged the blades and slowly bumped back to the shed. As she washed down the equipment, the tiny beads of water caught the sun, thousands of moving rainbows then shattered on the John Deere green paint. Satisfied that she'd done a good job, she strode into her small vineyard, walking down the short rows filling the quarter acre. Not a glassy-winged sharpshooter in sight.

She whistled on her way to the tack room, sat down at the heavy old schoolteacher's desk, and dialed Rollie Barnes. Luckily he was in his office.

"Rollie, this is Harry Haristeen. I was wondering if you'd give me a minute of your time."

"What can I do for you?" Rollie liked women asking him for advice.

"Well, as you know, I have this piddling quarter of an acre in Petit Manseng. I haven't followed this case going before the Supreme Court about shipping wine out of state. What really is this about?"

"First, let me say that for the most part I favor states' rights, but when they interfere with the free movement of goods and services, I believe there has to be a uniform federal law." He sounded like a politician.

"I'm with you." She was, too.

"Many states ban direct shipment of wine to consumers. Obviously, this puts a huge dent in profits."

"So if a person from Missouri calls Kluge Vineyard for a

case of wine, Kluge Vineyard can't send it to a private customer?" Harry asked.

"Right. It's outrageous." His voice rose. "Of course, we have no way of knowing how the court will rule, but the case is about to come up. If it rules that banning direct shipment is unconstitutional, that will be a huge victory for everyone in this country who makes wine. It's a victory for the consumer, too. Instead of going through a middleman with their markup, we can ship directly to the customer."

"Any idea how the court will rule?"

"No." His voice deepened, the register became less emotional. "The Supreme Court is erratic. Then again, I'm not a lawyer, thank God. I have to be rational or I lose business."

Harry laughed. "Thank you, Rollie. I knew you'd know. I guess a ruling in favor of direct shipment means business will boom and land prices will shoot up higher."

Pleasure purred in his voice. "Oh, yes."

"You're sitting in the catbird seat."

"Is that a good thing?"

She laughed. "Sure is. Ever look up in a tree and see where the catbird sits? Best place, and no one can get him."

"Well, then, you're right."

After a few more pleasantries, Harry hung up, then called Cooper. "Hey."

"Hey back at you," Cooper, in the squad car, answered.

"Need any more help over at the house? I can come over tonight and tomorrow, too. Fair's going to be making late calls tonight."

"He needs to take in a partner or even two."

"Yes, he and I will have that discussion when we go on our vacation end of July."

"I'll believe it when I see it."

"No, we're really going. BoomBoom will take care of the

horses and Paul de Silva said he'd help, too. Of course, Mrs. Murphy, Pewter, and Tucker will go along with us."

At the sound of their names the two cats opened their eyes.

"Vacation?" Pewter murmured. *"Where?"*

The tiger rolled on her side. *"Kentucky. They're going to a horse show and to look at horses."*

"That will be nice." Pewter noticed another little bit of peppermint candy by the tack trunk. *"Think they have good tuna in Kentucky?"*

"Pewter, there's good cat food all over the country." Mrs. Murphy lifted her head to listen to Harry.

"Coop, I've been thinking about the two murders and Hy's suicide. I know Rick thinks I get in the way—"

Coop interrupted. "Let's just say that since you don't have to follow police procedures, you can find things that are critical to us, but you can also put yourself in harm's way. Furthermore, Harry, you can compromise evidence."

"I know, I know. Well, I haven't been in the way about the grape murders—that's how I think of them."

"Because you're still recovering from getting remarried. Obviously, you're returning to reality." Coop laughed. "Not that being married to Fair isn't wonderful."

Harry laughed at herself. "God, am I that obvious?"

"Yes." Coop pulled off the road behind White Vineyards. "What's up?"

"Toby's storage room in his barn contains an unusually large amount of flypaper."

"It did seem like a lot, but he must have been someone who buys in bulk. He had enough paper tablets, toilet paper, pencils, and aspirin for the next year." Coop and Rick had combed Toby's property.

"What about Hy Maudant's place? Did you find boxes of flypaper there?"

"No. In fact, I'm on the dirt road behind White Vineyards now. Harry, most people who keep horses or cattle in a barn resort to flypaper." Cooper was amused.

"You're going to walk up in the back of the grape rows, right?"

A pause followed. "I am. You're really waking up, aren't you?"

"Looking for sharpshooters?"

"Yes." Cooper knew there was no point lying to Harry.

"Anything else? Like black rot?"

"I'm not too well versed on these things, but if the vines are diseased or the young leaves spotted, I'll find out what's wrong."

"But if there is something wrong, Arch and Rollie would know."

"And they'll take measures. They're over there a lot."

"When you went through Toby's and Hy's files, was there material about the sharpshooter?"

"Not in Hy's files. All he had was one sheet of laminated paper with photos. Toby's computer was bursting with information on every possible enemy to his grapes."

"Hmm, was there an extra large amount about the bugs?"

"The problem is, I don't know what an extra large amount is, given the sheer volume of information he had on everything, and I mean everything."

"What about Professor Forland's files?"

"We've been working with the Blacksburg authorities. Professor Forland had the latest research, like Toby, on everything."

"What I was wondering is, was Professor Forland secretly

working on a mutation? Not to harm our crops but if our government wanted to use biological warfare against someone else?"

"No." Coop's voice was firm. "He didn't work for our government. He was called in as an expert by the wine lobby to testify before House and Senate subcommittees."

"Ah."

"Harry?"

"I think this is about revenge. I don't know who was trying to destroy whom first, Hy or Toby. It escalated. Maybe Professor Forland found out Toby's intentions, which would have hurt everyone, and Toby killed him. Hy caught Toby later or figured it out. Hy knew his stuff. He made the big mistake of confronting Toby."

"And then finally overwhelmed with what he'd done, Hy shoots himself? It's all plausible, Harry, but it's not proven."

"But you've thought of this, too?"

"We have."

"Have you thought of why the sharpshooters were in my peach orchard?"

"Yes."

"And?"

"The intention was for you to find them and sound a warning—I think. Again, this is conjecture."

"Didn't work. The scare tactic. No one sold their vineyards because of it, although it's early in the game."

"Yeah, but, Harry, it was a red herring. At least that's what I think. Once you do the research, you find out there's no way that sharpshooters, those little stealth bombers, can live here. So a true vintner wouldn't panic and sell out, but latecomers to making wine might."

"The sharpshooters were brought up from farther down

South." Harry paused. "There's no other way they could have gotten here."

"Clever."

"Somehow this gets back to me. I don't know why." Harry's frustration mounted.

"What do you know that I don't? Why would you be a target with three men dead, one apparently by his own hand?"

"I don't know. You said 'apparently.'"

"Forensics has a small question mark because of the nature of the powder burns. It was Hy's gun. Registered in his name. Like I said, it's a small question mark. We aren't yet treating it as a suspicious death, but the coroner sent his photographs to Richmond for a second opinion." Coop, with her window down, inhaled the fragrance of the earth.

"I keep coming back to those darned sharpshooters."

"Okay, listen to me. There is a very good chance that in some tangential way, you are ... involved is the wrong word, but you know what I mean. If the tactic was simply to scare another grower, it seems putting the bugs in their vineyards would make more sense. But again, you would make sure to find out what the sharpshooters were and you'd go to the right people. It's a little more sophisticated than dumping bugs in White Vineyards, for example."

"Maybe my peach orchard was the experiment. They didn't want to use their vineyard or peach grove if they have one. And maybe I stumbled on it a day early. I don't know. I'm trying to think of everything."

"I found the stealth bomber." Pewter sat upright.

"You did." Mrs. Murphy supported Pewter, which gave the gray cat great satisfaction.

Harry and Coop batted ideas around. All it did was make them dizzy with implication. Ideas aren't hard evidence.

After their discussion, Harry walked out into the center aisle. Movement caught her eye and she looked up to see Matilda dangling from a rafter; blacksnakes enjoy a good climb.

Matilda startled Harry for an instant. "I wish she wouldn't do that."

38

The heavy aroma of coffee from Shenandoah Joe's curled into Fair's nostrils. He sighed, inhaled deeply, then opened his eyes. He'd fallen asleep on the couch, but his boots were neatly lined up on the floor, a pillow was under his thick blond hair, and a blanket covered him.

Pewter, resting on his chest, opened her eyes when he did. *"Good morning. Breakfast!"*

"Pewter, you must weigh twenty pounds."

The gray cannonball on his chest shifted her weight. *"I do not. I have big bones."*

From the kitchen Mrs. Murphy called out, *"Ha!"*

"Oh, shut up. You're no beauty basket, either."

"Maybe not, but at least I'm in shape."

Tucker, patiently waiting by her ceramic food bowl, groaned. *"Not a fight before breakfast."*

"Come on, Pewts, I need to get up."

Grumbling, switching her tail furiously, Pewter vacated her spot.

Fair sat up, rubbed his eyes, then headed for the bathroom.

By the time he walked into the kitchen, Harry had made a cheese omelette, lots of capers in it, with fresh tomato slices on the side sprinkled with olive oil and fresh parsley ground like green confetti.

"Good morning." She smiled as she put the plate on the table along with an English muffin.

"Thanks. When did you get in?"

"Nine-thirty. You were out like a light." She sat down to join him.

Harry wore a cotton undershirt—the kind kids called wife beaters—and thin cotton boxer undershorts. Once the worst of the winter passed, she hated to wrap up in a robe.

"I don't remember. God, I must have been tired. I read your note on the blackboard, drank a tonic water, and sat down to read the newspaper." He watched the cream swirl in his coffee. "How's it going at Coop's?"

"She was smart. She unpacked the kitchen first. Since that's the worst job, anything after that is easy. I've got to remember to bring some flowers, something to make it like home." She rose, grabbed a little notebook on the counter under the phone, and scribbled "flowers" on the page. "Can you think of a good housewarming gift?"

"Does she have a coffee grinder?"

"No. Perfect." Triumphantly, she wrote, "Coffee grinder."

"See how smart I am?"

"I know. You married me." She demolished her omelette. "Horse okay?"

"Yeah. He'll make it. I'd hoped we could haul him down to Virginia Tech, but I don't think he would have made it;

he was losing blood. We put down plastic tarps, clean, tran-qed him, and he dropped on the tarp. Operated there. I don't know if he'll ever hunt again, but he might be able to amble on trails. He just shredded his suspensory, deep lacer-ations in his right shoulder. Had to stitch that up, but it's the suspensory that's the real issue." He cited a ligament in the foreleg.

"Mandy will give him good care, and she'll never part with him." Harry named the owner, a kind woman in her fifties.

"All comes down to the owner."

"I've been thinking about Jed."

"Cuts make you think of him? He's finally happy. He's made friends at BoomBoom's with the other horses."

"Actually, I've been thinking about Jed ever since I talked to Coop yesterday, and then as we were organizing the house we talked some more."

"I'll bet." Fair grinned, then rose to pour more coffee. "Want more hot water for your tea?"

"No thanks."

"Well, what about Jed?"

"He was sound."

"Right."

"Why did Toby call you there?"

"I thought we talked about this."

"We did, sort of, and you mentioned that when you had that impromptu lunch with Arch and Bo that Arch thought Toby had lost his mind."

"Right. You said when you saw Toby at Alicia's he was ir-rational," Fair replied.

"He was. Alicia, Arch, and myself were witness to it. He wasn't a pretty picture. But Coop says that there is a slight question mark about Hy's suicide. The coroner sent the photos to Richmond."

"What does that have to do with Toby?"

"Just this: what if you were set up to look like Toby's killer? What if Hy really told the truth? He didn't kill Toby. He panicked when he saw the body and fled. One of those things—the killer has it all planned out and something unexpected happens. Pretty much life, isn't it? One unexpected thing after another."

"True." Holding his coffee cup in his hands, Fair thought. "Why me? I can't think of anyone that mad at me."

"I can't, either."

"And I don't have anything to do with vineyards. I figure that's the tie, the vineyards."

"I have a quarter of an acre."

"You do, but that's not my business. I'll put my back into it, but no one will ever accuse me of being a vintner."

"Think hard."

He did, but he couldn't think of an enemy. He could think of people who didn't put him high on their list but not a violent enemy.

Two hours after Fair left for the clinic, Harry worked with the babies. She'd gotten them used to halters; now she was getting them accustomed to the lead rope, with their mother's help.

Tucker watched from the middle of the paddock, and each cat sat on a fence post.

Harry trotted with a little fellow.

She suddenly stopped. "Oh, my God, I've been blind as a bat!"

39

It's funny how when one person realizes something, so often another person thinks of this at the same time.

Harry took the lead rope off the foal, patted the little guy, then quietly walked to the barn. Rushing about, being emotional around horses, particularly foals, upsets them. No matter what her realization, Harry was a horsewoman first.

Her cell phone, sticking out from her back pocket, irritated her. She plucked it out, holding the small device, as she opened and closed the wooden gate to the paddock. Then she sprinted for the barn, Tucker at her heels.

As they ran, they heard a big diesel engine throbbing in the driveway.

"Intruder!" Tucker alerted Harry, who heard it, too.

"I'm not taking any chances, Tucker. We don't know whose diesel that is. You stay in the tack room."

Harry skidded into the center aisle, grabbed the fixed

ladder to the hayloft, climbing the steps two at a time. She'd stuck the cell in her back pocket again. When she reached the top step she held the rails of the ladder, which extended three feet beyond the top foot rail. She swung onto the loft floor with such force that her cell dropped from her back pocket. She didn't notice as she ran for the open loft doors.

Mrs. Murphy, dozing with Pewter in the tack room, awakened with a start. She leapt off the saddle blanket over the saddle, dashed out the open tack-room door, and climbed up after Harry.

Tucker sat in the center aisle, looking up.

Pewter opened one eye as she reposed on a second saddle—Fair's, since it had a larger seat. She closed it, only to open it again as she heard the truck door slam, motor still thrumming.

Harry ran past Simon, who was playing with his curb chain, and hid behind the highest stack of hay bales as she thought about what to do. She was three hay bales down from Matilda, who did not like the thumping on the loft floor. Why couldn't Harry walk? In the cubbyhole next to her, Matilda's eggs jostled slightly.

Simon put down the curb chain. The cell phone captured his attention. What a wonderful toy. He scurried to fetch it, carting it back to his nest. He pulled out the antenna and inadvertently pressed buttons until the small unit glowed. This was his best-ever find.

Harry flipped open her pocketknife. She always carried one, as do most country people. The blade, at four-and-a-half inches, was sharp. She was confident it was better than nothing. That was all she was confident about.

"Harry," Arch called. When he received no answer he cut the loud motor. He noticed her truck. He walked to the

back porch door and knocked. No answer. He gave the
fields a cursory look, since she was usually out working or in
the barn. The next stop was the barn.

When he saw Tucker he knew Harry had to be there. He
checked the tack room. Checked each stall and the feed
room. He wasted no energy calling for her. He now knew
she knew and he knew she was hiding. Didn't take a genius
to figure that out. Arch was no genius, but he possessed ample cunning.

A call came on the cell phone. Scared Simon so bad he
flipped the phone right up in the air and it hit the floor with
a thud. The ringing reverberated on the wooden floor,
which made Flatface open her eyes. She was even more dis-
pleased than Matilda.

Mrs. Murphy flattened herself on a hay bale to the left of
Harry, who was crouching behind hay bales. Harry wished
she hadn't dropped her phone, because she would have
called Coop. Too late.

Harry knew her only hope was surprise. Her heart beat
so hard she thought Arch could hear it.

He swung through the top of the ladder, his work boots
hitting the floor. He scanned the hayloft, then walked over
and picked up the flashing cell phone. He tossed it on the
floor and it skidded toward Simon, who watched with his
black shining eyes. His nest faced away from Arch, but the
big man walked over, his boots hitting the boards hard.

Flatface's anger rose accordingly.

Simon, terrified, flopped on his side and played dead.
Arch kicked the cell phone again as he walked past Simon
toward higher stakes. Simon, still as a corpse, nevertheless
opened his eyes, then twitched his nose. Relief flooded over
him, since Arch couldn't have cared less about one slightly
overweight possum.

"I forgot how smart you are." Arch walked with deliberation now. "Of course, Harry, you can't be all that smart. You married that two-timing bastard again."

Mrs. Murphy flattened herself as much as she could. She scarcely breathed.

Tucker frantically ran back and forth under the ladder. *"Pewter, do something! Climb the ladder."*

For all her carping and diva ways, Pewter came through in a crisis. She shot off the saddle, brushed past Tucker, and then stopped quickly. *"Stay to the side of the ladder. If he comes down, bite hard. Run circles around him and keep biting. Maximum pain."* As Pewter hauled herself up the ladder she called over her shoulder, *"Shut up. You don't want him to know where you are when he comes down."*

Tucker immediately stopped barking to crouch by the ladder.

Pewter just reached the top as Arch found Harry, who sprang out like a jack-in-the-box. She hit him with her shoulder low, a decent enough block. Arch reeled back two big steps, his heel squishing into Matilda's eggs. She struck with such speed that all Harry saw was a black blur.

Matilda caught him above the right ankle, sinking her fangs in full length, then she disengaged and slithered with amazing speed to the back of the hay bales. Mrs. Murphy launched off the top of her hay bale as Arch screamed in pain. She hit his head hard, nearly slipped off, and dug her claws into his face to hang on.

Arch bent his head. Harry saw her chance and rammed her knife up under his chin as hard as she could. She stabbed him at an angle. She'd used so much force that the blade stuck in his jawbone. She couldn't dislodge it. She stayed too close. Arch could use his long reach even with the tiger valiantly biting and scratching. He grasped Harry's right wrist, twisting her arm. She hollered in pain.

Pewter, frantic at the sight, climbed up Arch's leg. He didn't bother to shake her off. Arch was fixated on killing Harry. Pewter climbed up his torso, reached his shoulder, perilously dug her claws in, and hung on as she inched down his right arm. Finally she reached his hand and bit for all she was worth. Howling, he released his grasp.

Maybe Harry should have run, but white-hot rage flooded her. She lowered her shoulder again and slammed his gut as hard as she could. This time, his leg throbbing from Matilda's deep wound, struggling to see because of the blood running into his eyes, he hit the floor hard with his knees. But he lunged forward, closing his left hand over Harry's ankle like a vise.

The cats leapt off as Arch went down.

Simon watched in horror. A bit of a coward, Simon's first instinct was to withdraw deeper into his little nest. All creatures recognize their own, who cares for them, and this won over his natural timidity. Simon waddled forth as Harry slugged Arch over and over again, aiming for the exposed handle of the pocketknife so each blow caused searing pain. But he dragged her down. As he wrapped both hands around her throat, blood now pouring out of his right hand and from under his chin, she hit again, so hard that the knife snapped off at the hilt.

The cats, knowing he was strong enough to choke Harry to death despite everything, went for the eyes. When Pewter sunk her claws into his left eyeball, clear gel oozed out. She knew she'd succeeded. He'd never see out of that eye again. The pain seared. Arch had never felt such pain in his life. He let go. Harry scrambled to her feet. Four big strides and she reached her cell phone. Arch, screaming, covered his face with his hands. She prayed her cell worked, and it did. She punched the preprogrammed button to call Coop. As she did, Arch again struggled to his feet.

Wily, Harry knew she couldn't reach the ladder, since he was between her and that escape route.

"Hello."

"Coop. Help. I'm home."

She said no more as he stumbled after her again with the power of someone who no longer cares whether he lives or dies.

Harry stepped back slowly, throwing the cell phone at him. The cats stepped back with her. Simon stealthily crept up behind Arch.

"Hoo hoo, hoo hoo." Flatface had seen enough. She stood poised at the edge of her nest, opened wide her large wings, pushing off without a sound.

By superhuman effort, Arch overcame his pain and ran for Harry again. She took two hurried steps backward, then cut left. His forward momentum and the swelling in his leg prevented him from turning as quickly as Harry. The opened doors of the loft yawned ahead, but he stopped himself just at the edge to keep from falling out.

His full stop allowed Simon to scurry up behind him and bite above his ankle. His little sharp teeth were not capable of as much damage as Matilda's or the cats', but those teeth still hurt. Arch gasped, then he felt a tremendous blow to the head. Flatface blasted him, talons balled tight. He tipped over, flailing to right himself, but fell out of the loft, breaking both legs as he crashed.

Harry ran to the open doors just in time to see Tucker fly out of the barn and grab Arch by the throat.

"Leave him, Tucker. Leave him." Drenched in sweat, her

wrist hurting like hell where he'd twisted her arm, Harry fought for large gulps of air.

"I'll rip his throat out." The mighty little dog had felt so helpless hearing the terrible struggle in the loft.

"Tucker, no, no." Harry fought off a moment of dizziness.

"We need a confession!" Mrs. Murphy yelled.

The infuriated dog understood. She released his throat, but not before leaving some puncture wounds. She guarded him, ready to bite again.

"Thank the Lord, Tucker's a corgi," Pewter, upset herself, blurted out. *"Smart as a cat."*

Harry sat down, putting her head between her legs. Flatface, who'd flown out of the loft doors when Arch sailed out, flew back in. She swooped low over Harry, the air from her wings refreshing, then she soared up to her perch.

"Thanks," Mrs. Murphy called up to her.

"My pleasure," she called down. *"He deserved it."*

Mrs. Murphy, Pewter, and Simon wedged themselves next to Harry. All three licked her hands. Mrs. Murphy then stood on her hind legs to lick her face.

Arch was screaming and sobbing. The worst pain was his eye. The broken legs, the snakebite, the dog, cat, and possum bites hurt, but the blinded eye felt excruciating.

The animals heard Cooper before Harry did, but soon enough she heard the siren, then the stones flying off the squad-car tires as her friend careened down the driveway. More sirens followed.

Harry took a deep breath, wiping away her quiet tears. She wasn't crying from fear but from gratitude. She owed her life to these little friends and to her own fierce desire to fight.

She stood up, shook her head, then knelt back down. She

kissed Mrs. Murphy and Pewter. Simon couldn't bear a human kiss, so she ran her forefinger over his head. Then she headed for the ladder. Stooping to pick up the cell phone, she thought again and put it on the floor.

"My gift, Simon. Thank you."

40

Friendship distills the sweetness of life.

Mrs. Murphy listened as the friends below learned more of what had happened. She lay with her belly flat on the wide, low walnut branch, her legs dangling over each side. Nearby, artfully wedged on the picnic-table, Pewter posed, preened, and was so full of the milk of kindness she almost mooed. No one believed her, but they still fed her bits of fried chicken, little clumps of broccoli heads drenched in butter, and succulent bits of honey-cured ham. Tucker, not quite the dramatist, cast soulful eyes as she walked behind BoomBoom, Alicia, Big Mim, Miranda, Cooper, Susan, Fair, and Harry in turn.

"You're going to wear yourself out going from person to person like that," Mrs. Murphy called down to her.

"I burn the calories off moving."

"O la!" The tiger laughed as the dog gobbled a large chicken morsel from Big Mim's fingers.

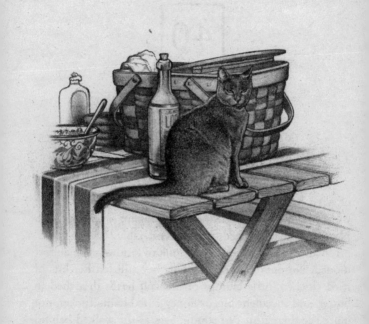

Simon sat at the open loft doors, half-listening to the chatter in Harry's front yard across from him. Mostly he chewed a long raspberry penny-candy stick that Harry had given him. Sweets were Simon's downfall.

Two days had passed since Harry's battle with Arch. Her wrist, wrapped in a bandage, hurt but not enough to stop her.

"So it wasn't a full confession, after all?" Big Mim, who liked to be first to hear any news, had only gotten parts.

When Cooper reached Harry, the first thing she had to do after ascertaining Harry was all right was call for an ambulance. Took another day for Arch to be able and willing to talk.

"He says it is." Cooper passed a plate of corn bread.

"Revenge. A broken heart. I don't buy the broken-heart bit." Susan swept back her sleek pageboy with her right hand. "He'd been without Harry for four years, and it's not like she ever said it would be more than it was."

"Men hear what they want to hear," Alicia simply said. "Sorry, Fair."

"Some truth to it, I expect." He'd been badly shaken by Harry's close call and sick with himself for not seeing the true threat.

"He was so likable." Miranda sought the best in people. She sighed. " 'Be sure your sin will find you out.' " Quoting Numbers, Chapter 32, Verse 23, she then added, "You can't outrun the Lord. Most times you can't outrun the law, either."

"Did you have any idea it was Arch, you and Rick?" BoomBoom put it straight to Cooper.

"Our main suspects were Toby, Rollie, Hy, and Arch bringing up the rear. Toby was the front-runner initially because of his unremitting hostility to the others, his crazed competitiveness. I emphasize crazed. Arch confessed to killing Toby and Hy, but he swears he did not kill Professor Forland."

"It was Toby, then?" Susan asked.

"Yes, I think so. The bullet was from Toby's gun," Cooper replied.

"He rode around town showing off that new gun. He must have been nuts," BoomBoom said, because she'd heard from Alicia how Toby found his misplaced gun in his truck.

"He never thought we'd find the body." Cooper sipped the best lemonade she'd ever drunk. "By the time we did, well, we're eating. Anyway, the coroner did retrieve the bullet. Then it took a little time to trace it."

"He used a brand-new registered gun," Fair remarked, "a beautiful gun, really. He was either crazy or arrogant. He disguised the grave up in the peach orchard, but earth has a way of rising up or sinking down sooner or later."

"What about Toby losing his gun?" Alicia had witnessed his surprise at finding it.

"Who knows? He probably did, or forgot where he'd put it. Toby had a motive to kill Professor Forland. He didn't find out until Arch sort of told him why he wasn't hired to lecture at Virginia Tech. That's what Arch says. He said he knew Toby would figure it out from their conversation at Patricia and Bill's party. So Toby, precarious as he was, went off his rocker. We'll never know, but he probably asked Professor Forland to swing by on his way out of town or he met him somewhere. We don't know why he buried Forland in your peach orchard. I suspect he killed him near here and went up to the orchard when he checked to see if you were around. Again, we'll never know. He was smart enough not to kill him at Rockland Vineyards. The other two murders we do know about."

"But it does come back to Toby again." Fair would never erase the sight of the murdered man from his mind. It wasn't so horrible as it was unexpected, and sad, too, given Toby's deranged state.

"Yes, it does. Toby, toiling away at his computer, realized quickly that the sharpshooters had been deliberately placed in Harry's peach orchard. His first response was that this was a plot to ruin his grapes. Always his grapes. Then he thought about other vineyards. The more he worked on it, the more he realized, no matter that the sharpshooter had been planted, it couldn't do enough damage in a summer to be a problem to the grapes." Cooper poured herself more lemonade.

"Why would that get him killed?" BoomBoom was very curious.

"He approached Arch. Not on the best of terms. However, they were on better terms than Toby and Hy. Toby accused Arch of bringing up the sharpshooters from North Carolina to scare people, hoping some would bail out. He thought Arch and Rollie were going to corner the market and then price-fix. Rollie, before he retired here, and I use 'retire' loosely, engaged in ruthless business practices. He made his fortune crawling over other people. Arch denied this to Toby. But that was the truth."

"Why didn't Arch leave well enough alone?" Big Mim inquired.

"He knew how highly intelligent Toby was. Toby, sooner or later, would figure out the sharpshooters were intended for the Alverta peaches. No, they couldn't destroy the orchard, but they could do some small damage this season, then die in the frost. He knew how much keeping the old variety alive meant to Harry. He would have done more damage to other crops by other means as time went by."

"So he killed Toby with his own gun?" Fair said.

"Yes, but he had the gun at Toby's head and forced him to call you. Arch's anger had escalated from harming peaches to harming you. He said each time he saw you, he hated you more. You don't deserve Harry."

Fair put his arm around his wife's waist. "He might be right there."

"Honey, don't be a flatterer." Harry blushed.

"Sweetheart, you're the best thing that's ever happened to me, and I let you down once in the past and I let you down again. I never saw it coming with Arch."

"Fair, none of us did." BoomBoom cared for Fair, always would.

"She's right. Arch could have won an Oscar for his performance." Alicia's bracelet slid down her arm as she lifted her hand for emphasis.

"You would know." Big Mim smiled.

"Everyone was on the wrong track. Fixed on the vineyards and those who own them." Susan found each detail more riveting and dismal simultaneously.

"Then why did he kill Hy? He confessed to that, didn't he?" BoomBoom felt some relief in that Fiona no longer had to bear the stigma of her husband's supposed suicide.

Such things shouldn't stick to family and friends, but people were harsh about suicide, it seemed.

"Hy, no slouch either when it came to protecting against parasites and fungi, had been studying the sharpshooter as soon as the news hit. His worry, according to Arch, was that global warming was allowing these things to move ever northward."

"Boll weevil." Miranda knew her bugs.

"How about the parasite that kills honeybees that finally made it this far north in 1980 and is wreaking havoc? There sure might be something to this warming stuff." Harry worried, as did every farmer.

"Hy drove out to your peach orchard to see for himself." Cooper continued with Arch's confession. "He determined as did Toby that the sharpshooter had been planted there. Hy thought they hadn't flown up here, because they would have alighted in other orchards and vineyards between here and North Carolina. He definitely knew the sharpshooters were planted. He tried to find out why. Obviously, there was no way Hy would communicate with Toby over anything. The natural person to discuss this with was Arch, thanks to his extensive knowledge. That turned out to be a fatal mistake."

"Hy wouldn't have made the connection to revenge against Fair and Harry, would he?" Susan thought of three lives needlessly cast away.

"Arch wasn't taking any chances. Hy was piecing things together about the sharpshooters. And Arch was shaken that Hy had driven up before Fair when he'd just shot Toby. Arch's plan backfired, and that was just dumb luck. He drove out the back way when he heard Hy's truck coming in the front. He couldn't see because of the hill there, but he assumed it was Fair. Fair would have been parked in the penitentiary for a good long time or bankrupted by the legal fees regardless of outcome. Arch said he couldn't believe it when he found out we apprehended Hy. He thought if Fair were put in jail he could win back Harry. If Fair got off and they were bankrupted, well, he'd have some pleasure in seeing her suffer by staying with Fair."

"Flatface flew over Hy when he drove into the peach orchard," Mrs. Murphy casually reminded Pewter and Tucker.

"No way to tell Harry." Pewter belched.

"Pewter. Mind your manners," Harry said.

"You never burp," Pewter sassed.

"Could be worse. Could have come out the other end." Tucker giggled.

"I'm leaving." Pewter, miffed, jumped off the bench seat. She jumped back up, though.

"Ha! The day you walk away from food, the sun will rise in the west." Mrs. Murphy swung her tail with vigor.

"The next thing Arch realized, obvious now, is that Harry would figure it out, too. It might take her a little longer; she'd have more resistance to the thought. Dominos." Cooper finished off her ham sandwich and longingly stared at the cherry cobbler. She'd wait until everyone else finished their meal before grabbing dessert.

"If it weren't for Mrs. Murphy, Pewter, and Tucker, Arch might have gotten away with it." Harry glanced up at Mrs. Murphy, who was glowing with the praise.

"He wouldn't have gotten away with it, Harry. He might have killed you, God forbid, but we would have nailed him, because I think he would have run," Cooper said forcefully.

"Where's Rollie in all this?" Fair wondered.

"Shocked. Chauntal, too. I had to tell Rollie he had been a suspect and why. Didn't much like that, either, but he admitted he had been, in his words, 'extremely aggressive in business.' His next concern was if he might be sued. Arch is his business partner. I told him he wouldn't be the first person to have a business partner in jail. I also told him," Cooper looked to Harry, then Fair, "that you weren't the kind of people to do that."

"Thank you," Fair simply replied.

"Guess I should thank Matilda, Flatface, and little Simon, too. I told you all what happened earlier." Harry smiled.

"Matilda didn't do it because she cares about you. She was pissed that Arch squished her eggs."

"You don't know that." Tucker used her paw to wipe her whiskers.

"They lay their eggs and forget them. Snakes don't take care of their babies," Pewter announced with authority.

"Could be that Matilda is different." Tucker defended the blacksnake, although she didn't much like her.

"She's different, all right. She's working on being the largest blacksnake in America." Mrs. Murphy inhaled the clean air, a light current swirling down from the eastern side of the Blue Ridge Mountains.

"Isn't that the truth!" Pewter said in a burst of animation. *"Bet her bite hurt so bad, Arch saw an hour's worth of fireworks in a minute."*

"Flatface came through." Tucker smiled.

"She complains about us, calls us groundlings, but she does come through. She can't admit we're all together." Pewter puffed out her chest.

Mrs. Murphy, noticing the expansion, said, *"Are you going to burp again?"*

"No," came the swift, indignant reply.

Mrs. Murphy lowered her voice. *"Is it going to be worse?"*

"I am not going to hurl. I didn't eat that much. I was actually sensible."

This barefaced lie struck both Mrs. Murphy and Tucker speechless.

Mrs. Murphy sat up, stretched, and looked at Simon. *"He ate his raspberry penny candy. Now he's playing with the cell phone."*

"Wait until she gets billed from Rio de Janiero." Pewter's good humor was restored by imagining another's distress.

"He can't use the phone. Simon's not bright enough to figure

it out," Tucker said. *"I don't mean to be ugly, but really, he's not the sharpest tool in the shed."*

"He'll push buttons. He may not know what he's doing, but he'll get something going. He's pulled out the antenna." Pewter was loving this.

"Harry will cut off the service to the phone. Might take her a day to think of it, but she'll go get another phone and transfer the numbers. Of course, who knows? By that time maybe he will have made a call." Mrs. Murphy entered into the spirit of this.

"And when that music plays he'll throw the cell phone in the air, squeal, and run for his nest." Pewter laughed loudly.

The humans, not privy to the animals' conversation, had been talking about why anyone would kill, but especially someone like Arch, as it was hopeless. How could he dream of winning Harry back by harming Fair?

Of course, Arch didn't think she'd know he set Fair up.

"Finally, he snapped and figured if he couldn't have Harry, no one could have her." BoomBoom felt she'd settled the issue.

" 'Beloved, never avenge yourselves, but leave it to the wrath of God.' " Miranda quoted Romans, Chapter 12, Verse 19.

"The grapes of wrath!" Pewter piped up.

"Oh, Pewter." Mrs. Murphy wrinkled her nose.

"You're just jealous that you didn't think of it." Pewter again puffed out her fluffy chest. *"Sour puss."*

Dear Reader,

All this study of grapes interested me because birds come to grapes. But really, I would have rather written a book about cultivating catnip. Mother declared that would have limited application.

Maybe. Maybe not. I'm not giving up on my catnip idea. Sooner or later, I'll get my way. For one thing, I hid her favorite pair of socks. Small revenge, you say. Ha. Imelda Marcos has shoes. Mother has socks. For one thing they are more affordable than a closet full of shoes. So if she sees things my way, I will retrieve the socks.

On May 16, 2005, the U.S. Supreme Court voted 5–4 that laws banning direct shipment of wine to consumers in other states are unconstitutional. Impromptu celebrations filled Virginia. I note here that a Virginian will use any excuse for a party; they are excessively convivial.

All's well here. Hope your life is full of mice, moles, voles, butterflies, and the occasional inattentive bird.

In Catitude,

Sneaky Pie

Dear Reader,

I just proofread the Cast of Characters and note that my coauthor rearranged things, citing the animals as the most important characters.

Her ego is in a gaseous state, ever-expanding. However, I must get up the second cutting of hay, since a thunderstorm seems more than likely this afternoon. It really is true, you make hay while the sun shines. There's no time to fix this and off it goes to my wonderful, wry editor, Danielle Perez.

If Sneaky's done anything else, I won't know about it until I receive the bound galleys. Too late then.

You know, it's hell to work with a cat. They really are smarter than we are. Have you ever gotten anyone to feed you, pay your bills, give you the best chair in the house, tell you how beautiful you are, and groom you daily? Me, neither.

Yours,

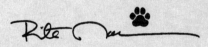

About the Authors

RITA MAE BROWN is the bestselling author of several books. An Emmy-nominated screenwriter and a poet, she lives in Afton, Virginia. Her website is www.ritamaebrown. com.

SNEAKY PIE BROWN, a tiger cat born somewhere in Albemarle County, Virginia, was discovered by Rita Mae Brown at her local SPCA. They have collaborated on fourteen previous Mrs. Murphy mysteries: *Sour Puss; Wish You Were Here; Rest in Pieces; Murder at Monticello; Pay Dirt; Murder, She Meowed; Murder on the Prowl; Cat on the Scent; Pawing Through the Past; Claws and Effect; Catch as Cat Can; The Tail of the Tip-Off; Whisker of Evil;* and *Cat's Eyewitness,* in addition to *Sneaky Pie's Cookbook for Mystery Lovers.*

Please read on for a preview of the next
Mrs. Murphy adventure

Puss 'n Cahoots

RITA MAE BROWN
&
SNEAKY PIE BROWN

Available now in hardcover from Bantam

RITA MAE BROWN
& SNEAKY PIE BROWN

Puss 'n Cahoots

A MRS. MURPHY MYSTERY

Puss 'n Cahoots
ON SALE NOW

1

*L*ong, golden rays raked the rolling hills surrounding Shelbyville, Kentucky, on Wednesday, August 2. At six P.M., the grassy parking lot of the famous fairgrounds accepted a steady stream of spectators. By seven P.M. the lot would be overflowing and the shift to backup parking would begin. A soft breeze carried a hint of moisture from the Ohio River about twenty-five miles west, which separated the state of Kentucky from Indiana. Barn swallows swooped through the air to snare abundant insects, as crows, perched on overhead lines, watched, commenting on everything. Cattle dotted pastures. Butterflies swarmed the horse droppings at the fairgrounds. While butterflies liked flowers and flowering bushes, they also evidenced a strong fondness for manure. Each time a maintenance man dutifully picked up the manure, a cloud of yellow swallowtails, black swallowtails, milk butterflies, and small bright blue butterflies swirled up from their prize. No matter how lowly their feeding habits, it was a beautiful sight.

"*If I weren't in this blasted collar, I'd snatch one,*" Pewter bragged. "*Maybe two.*"

"*They are tempting,*" Mrs. Murphy agreed with the fat gray cat. Mrs. Murphy, a sleek tiger cat, was carried by Harry Haristeen. Pewter was carted by Fair Haristeen, DVM. The cats eagerly awaited the beginning of the first night's competition.

Shelbyville, the second glittering jewel in the Saddlebred world, attracted the best horses in the country. The show commenced a full two weeks before the Kentucky State Fair, the blowout of Saddlebred shows.

The four jewels in the crown were the Lexington Junior League, Shelbyville, the Kentucky State Fair at Louisville, and the Kansas City Royal, the only big show held in late fall, November. All the others were summer shows.

Throughout America, but most especially in Kentucky, Indiana, and Missouri, the Saddlebred shows added sparkle to the season and coins to the coffers. Every town bigger than a minute hosted one, no matter how humble. No one ever accused the Shelbyville show of being humble. A grandstand encircled the immaculate show ring oval. Most of the seating area was covered. The south of the lighted ring was anchored by an imposing two-story grandstand, where food was served if one had a ticket for the feast.

The aroma of the ribs tortured Tucker, the corgi, walking between her two humans. She drooled with anticipation. "*How long before we eat?*"

"*I don't know, but I could faint with hunger.*" Pewter sighed.

"*Oh la.*" Mrs. Murphy thought to say more but realized

if she started a fight she would unceremoniously be taken back to their suite at the Best Western hotel.

Harry and Fair paused to watch horses being worked in the practice ring on the east side of the fairgrounds. Booty Pollard, a famous forty-one-year-old trainer with a fully dressed monkey perching on his shoulder, walked next to a junior riding a three-gaited country pleasure horse. The walk, trot, canter horse was one of those wonderful creatures that take care of their young riders. Fortunately for the junior, this mare's three gaits were smooth. They were leaving the ring. Booty turned his head upon hearing another trainer raise his voice.

Charles "Charly" Trackwell, a big-money trainer and a peacock, shouted at a stunning young woman on an equally stunning chestnut three-gaited horse, Queen Esther. Queen Esther was much fancier than the country pleasure horse Booty's junior was riding. Queen Esther's trot just threw the beautiful woman up out of the saddle. Renata DeCarlo had paid two hundred fifty thousand dollars for the mare. Renata meant to win. She had to work harder than other competitors for the judges to take her seriously; but she liked hard work as much as she liked winning. At thirty-eight—although her "official" bio shaved six years off this age saying she was thirty-two—she was a movie star and there weren't many stars bred in Lincoln County, Kentucky. While everyone wanted to look at her, spectators and judges could be prejudiced. Envy from others found odd ways of expressing itself. Renata often received a ribbon lower than she should have earned. Her gorgeous mare merited being pinned first, the blue ribbon, more often than not. Shortro, her young gray stalwart three-gaited gelding, also endured lower pinnings than was fair.

But Shortro, unlike Queen Esther, was happy if he won a

blue, red, yellow, green, white, pink ribbon. Queen Esther always wanted the huge best-in-class ribbon, as did Renata.

Horses, like people, are fully fledged personalities.

"Relax your shoulders, Renata," Charly growled.

"Beautiful," Harry commented.

"Fabulous mare." Fair prudently focused on the chestnut mare, which made Harry laugh.

They passed the white barn closest to the practice ring, the silver tin roof showing some wear and tear. The old barns might need a coat of paint, unlike the grandstand, but they were airy and quite pleasant. The number of competitors was so great that tent barns had been thrown up to handle the overflow. Each day hundreds of horses competed, some being driven in, vanned, for that day only. Keeping track of what horses were on the grounds proved overwhelming sometimes, because not every horse was competing. Some were companion horses to keep the star horse company. The temporary stalls, bisected by two aisles, were also completely full. The great stables marked off one or even two stalls for a hospitality suite, which would be outfitted with canvas panels and drapes in the stables colors. Many boasted a tented ceiling inside to further enhance the welcoming atmosphere. An open bar and refreshments added to the festival atmosphere. Directors' chairs—again in the stable colors—tack trunks, bridle cases, ribbons hanging on the "walls," as well as lovely photographs of clients and horses completed the setting. The labor that it took to create these oases of cheer, along with another stall made into a special changing room for the riders, often behind the hospitality room, amazed Harry each time she visited one of the big Saddlebred shows, which she did once a year. Although a passionate Thoroughbred woman, she loved the Saddlebred. She'd trained a few from Kalarama Farm to be foxhunters. Saddlebreds could jump, really jump, which delighted Harry. The Thoroughbred, with its sloping shoulder and lower head carriage, ideally has a long, fluid stride. The Saddlebred's energy is expended upward, high stepping with some reach, and the head is held high. Go back one hundred fifty years and the two different breeds share some common ancestors.

Joan Hamilton, one of Harry's best friends, was the driving force behind the breeding program at Kalarama Farm. Her husband, Larry Hodge, trained and also rode many of the horses. As often happens in the horse world, when the right two people find each other, a magic glow shines on everything they touch.

On the way to the Kalarama ringside box, Harry and Fair strolled the midway crammed with a lot of stuff you'd like to buy and a lot of stuff you wouldn't. The jewelry shop tempted Harry. She stopped to admire a ring with square-cut rubies and diamonds set in a horseshoe. It was the most beautiful horseshoe ring she'd ever seen.

The ubiquitous funnel cakes cast their special doughy scent over the area, as did hot dogs, ribs, slabs of beef, and delicious chicken turning on a spit. The food shops, jewelry shop, and clothing shops were interspersed with people from the local farm bureau, various civic organizations running the booths, all having a good time. Most of the civic booths were under the grandstand facing the midway. A gleaming SL55 Mercedes lured folks to buy raffle tickets, one hundred bucks a pop, proceeds going to charity. Flattening your wallet proved all too easy walking along this small, seductive thoroughfare.

The uncovered western grandstand loomed over one side of the midway, and there were booths under it, as well. Everywhere you looked, right or left of the short midway, there was a booth. Right in front of the western grandstand, smack on the rail, were boxes, with six or eight folding chairs inside. These, rented by the great stables, were magnets for the spectators. Riders, breeders, and owners usually repaired to their box, which unlike the rented stalls did not bear the stable colors but sported a chaste white rectangular sign with the name of the box owner in simple black Roman letters.

Joan leaned forward to talk to her mother, the diminutive, lively Frances, and her father, Paul, as they checked their programs. Paul was one of those people who exerted a warm charisma, drawing people to him. Neither of the elder Hamiltons ever met a stranger.

Harry stepped into the box, Mrs. Murphy in her arms. Fair, Pewter, and Tucker immediately followed.

After hugs and kisses all around, everyone settled in their seats. Cookie, Joan's brown and white Jack Russell, squeezed with Tucker on a seat.

When Harry and Fair had arrived yesterday, they viewed Joan's yearlings, mares and colts, and watched Larry work the horses. Harry learned from watching Larry, who knew exactly when to stop the lesson. So many trainers overtrained, the result being the horse grew sour or flat. Since a Saddlebred must show with brio, overtraining proved a costly mistake.

Frances, wearing a peach linen and silk dress with a corsage, turned to her daughter and said, "Joan, did you show the newlyweds Harlem's Dreamgirl?"

"Yes, I did."

Paul, a twinkle in his eye, twisted in his seat to wink at Fair. "You got the dreamgirl."

Fair slapped the older but still powerfully built World War II Navy vet on the shoulder. "I think we both married our dreamgirls."

"Paul and I married in the Dark Ages." Frances laughed.

"Still a honeymoon," Paul gallantly said.

Joan took off her beige silk jacket as the heat bore down. A gorgeous pin, a ruby and sapphire riding crop intertwined through a sparkling horseshoe, graced the left lapel.

"Joan, did you fix the clasp on that pin?" Frances asked.

"Yes, I did, and it's tight as a tick."

"Good. You know I think that's the prettiest piece of my mother's jewelry."

Joan, knowing her mother wouldn't be satisfied until she had examined the pin, slipped her coat off the chair, handing it to her mother.

Turning the lapel back, Frances fingered the pin. "Well, that should hold it." Before handing it back to Joan, she noted the careful work the jeweler had performed. "You know that's our lucky pin. You wear it when it counts, but always on the last night of the show."

Everyone studied their programs.

"Third class has that movie star in it." Paul read down the list.

The third class was the adult three-gaited show pleasure.

"She's going to have a tough time beating Melinda Falwell." Joan folded back her program.

"Booty's client." Paul named Melinda's trainer, a gregarious man still recovering from a sulfurous divorce last year. The recovery was financial as well as emotional. It was Booty whom Harry and Fair had seen walking out of the practice ring.

Five years ago an intense rivalry set off fireworks in the Saddlebred world as the old guard began to retire or die off, leaving the younger men and a few women in their middle years to come forward in a big way. Larry Hodge, Booty Pollard, and Charly Trackwell had taken up where Tom Moore, Earl Teater, and the late Bradshaw brothers had left off. Pushing behind Larry, Booty, and Charly were men and more women than in previous generations, in their late twenties and early thirties, one of whom, Ward Findley, evidenced special talent.

Saddlebred trainers rode the difficult horses or the horses in the big classes, which would add thousands of dollars to the horse's worth if the animal showed well. In the Thoroughbred world, trainers did not ride in the races. Here they did, which gave the shows an extra dimension. It was as if Bill Parcells played quarterback or Earl Weaver stepped up to the plate.

The amateur riders, coached by the trainers, didn't necessarily ride easy horses, but usually the horses were more tractable and less was at stake. A win at one of the big shows could send a horse's value skyrocketing. Few people are immune to that incentive, hence the enduring appeal of the trainer/rider.

Ward Findley, who was twenty-nine and had close-cropped, jet-black hair and sparkling blue eyes, quickly came up to the Kalarama box, leaned over, and whispered to Joan, "You'd better get to the barn." Right behind Ward came Booty Pollard, his pet monkey on his shoulder. "Trouble," Ward continued. The monkey, Miss Nasty, chattered as she peered at everyone in the box. Miss Nasty loved Booty, but she hated his snake collection, which he kept at home. She, at least, got to travel. Fortunately, the snakes did not. Booty did have peculiar tastes in pets.

Paul, overhearing, stood up.

"Daddy, you stay here. People need to see you and Mom." Joan was already out of the box.

Fair, an equine vet, followed her. Kalarama had their regular vet, but he didn't attend the shows. The organizers kept a vet on the premises so there was no need for each competitor or breeder to tie up their own vet for the four evenings of the show.

Not to be left behind, Harry scooped up both cats, her

progress slowed by the two unhappy kitties squirming in her arms.

"If you'd put me down I could follow just fine," Mrs. Murphy complained.

"She thinks you'll run off," Tucker, excited by the tension in the humans, commented.

"You're a big, fat help," Mrs. Murphy growled.

"I'm a dog. I'm obedient. You're a cat. You're not." Tucker relished the discomfort of her two friends, since they often lorded over her.

The conversation abruptly ended as they reached Barn Five, where three horses were being led into the barn, Charly Trackwell trotting after them, his face grim. They were not Joan's horses.

"Isn't that the chestnut mare from the practice ring?" Pewter studied the gleaming animal, her long neck graceful.

"Yes." Mrs. Murphy was happy when Harry unhitched Pewter's and her leash and quickly deposited them in the hospitality room. Pewter used the opportunity to jump onto the table, snatching a succulent square of ham.

"You're a goddamned diva!" Charly shouted at Renata DeCarlo, who stormed ahead of Charly.

The loss of board and training fees for three horses would hurt Charly a bit, but the real blow was losing his movie-star client.

Joan prudently stood by a stall, since Charly now faced Larry, Renata to Larry's side. Fair stood behind Larry.

"I'm sick of you shouting at me, Charly." Renata, face flushed, was remarkably calm.

Charly turned to Larry. "You're behind this, Hodge. You've been trying to steal Renata away from me since she came to my barn."

"That's not true." Larry kept his voice level.

"You love the glamour. And you'll make a bloody

fortune. You always do." Charly, shaking with rage, stepped toward Larry.

Renata grabbed Charly's arm, which he threw off. "You've criticized me one time too many. You're an egotistical shit and I'm sick of it."

Much as he wanted to hit her and Larry, too, Charly managed to control himself. He stopped breathing for a second, then gulped air. "Renata, you redefine the word 'ego.'"

"We can all sort this out tomorrow when everybody has calmed down," Larry sensibly suggested.

"The hell with you." Then Charly wheeled on Renata and pointed his finger right in her face. "I know about you." With that he turned on his booted heel and left.

Manuel Almador, Larry's head groom, watched along with Jorge Gravina, second in command to Manuel. Their distaste for Charly flickered across their faces.

Renata, floodgates now bursting, allowed Joan to shepherd her to the hospitality room. The people who gathered at the barn's entrance dispersed, a few to follow Charly. They had to trot, since his long legs covered the ground.

As Renata's sobs subsided, Larry, Fair, Manuel, and Jorge consulted one another in the aisle.

"Manuel, you and the boys will need to sleep here all week. Take four-hour shifts. Charly will have his revenge, and I don't want it to be on Renata's horses or ours, either."

Manuel nodded; he knew Charly's reputation.

Handsome Charly, an explosives expert and captain in the first Iraq war, was explosive himself.

"I can check, too. We're just down the road," Fair offered.

"Thanks. The men can handle it." Larry appreciated Fair's offer. He glanced at his watch. "Olive." He named a client riding in the next class. Larry needed to walk with her to the arena, then stand alongside the rail so she could see him. He smiled. "No charge for the extra entertainment."

Back in the hospitality room, the animals listened as Renata ticked off Charly's list of faults, most notably that he was arrogant, didn't listen to her, and was a man, which seemed to Renata to sum up his original sin.

"Dramatic," Tucker succinctly observed.

"It takes a while for humans to dissipate big emotions." Mrs. Murphy sat on the maroon tack trunk piped in white and black. *"Some of them never do. They're still talking about what happened to them thirty years ago."*

"Key to happiness, a bad memory." Pewter swept her dark-gray whiskers forward. The stolen ham, happily consumed, contributed to her golden glow.

Mrs. Murphy's green eyes studied Renata's perfect face. *"A little too dramatic for my taste."*

The three Virginia animals, along with Cookie, sneezed. Renata's perfume was too strong for their sensitive noses, but Joan didn't respond to it. The animals marveled at the failure of human noses, even one as delicate and pretty as Joan's.

Finally, Joan calmed down Renata, reminding her that she was riding in the third class. She guided Renata to the dressing room. Renata considered the third class a warm-up for the rest of the week. She needed the taste of competition more than the gelding she would be riding, a flashy black-and-white paint named Voodoo. She could have skipped it but wanted to teach Charly a thing or two. He wasn't going to affect her riding. Renata, ready to wail anew when she realized her tack trunk and clothes were at Charly's hospitality room, was short-circuited.

At that moment, Charly's head groom, Carlos, appeared along with Jorge in Kalarama's room, with Renata's trunk, clothes, and tack. Not a speck of dirt besmirched anything.

She liked Carlos and tried to give him a tip, but he refused. Jorge refused also.

As Renata changed, Jorge tacked up Voodoo, while Shortro and Queen Esther watched. Voodoo, the first good Saddlebred Renata had bought, had a special place in her heart. Voodoo taught her a great deal while forgiving her mistakes.

Joan, Harry, Fair, and the animals walked back to their Kalarama box as the crowd clapped for the contestants leaving the second class.

Paul and Frances were now looking down from the top tier of the main grandstand. The odor of the food had enticed them from the box. Joan settled in her chair. The third class, with a full twenty-five entrants, seemed to go on forever, finally being won by a young lady riding a horse bred in Missouri by Callaway Stables, outside the town of Fulton.

Joan reached around to drape her jacket over her shoulders. She gasped. "My pin."

Harry looked at the jacket, then got down on her hands and knees to inspect the ground. "Oh, Joan, it's not here."

Fair stood up, checking the entrance to the box. "How about if I go to lost-and-found in case it fell off and someone picked it up?"

"It didn't fall off. The clasp had a triple lock." Joan's face, mournful, registered this loss. "Someone took it off."

"Maybe your mother did when she left the box." Harry was hopeful.

A flicker of hope illuminated Joan's beautiful features. "Well, maybe." Her voice lowered. "I kind of doubt it. All these years I've been coming here, I never worried about anything being stolen. I can't believe this." She sighed deeply. "Mom is going to be really upset with me." She paused. "I'm upset."

"Not to be crass, but how much do you think the pin is worth?" Harry put her hand on Joan's shoulder.

"I don't know. Twenty-five thousand? Thirty?"

"God!" Harry, mindful of every penny, now turned whiter than Joan.

"We may find it yet," Fair said comfortingly.

Joan's shoulders straightened. "We might. But I don't know if we'll like what we find with it."

"That's a strange thing to say." Harry's eyebrows raised quizzically.

"I have this terrible feeling..." Joan's voice trailed off.

This melancholy premonition vanished as Miss Nasty, Booty's sidekick, free at last, rollicked along the top board of the show-ring rail.

How long she'd escaped her confinement was anybody's guess, because she could be stealthy when she wished. Now her desire to be the center of attention overtook her.

Fortunately, the horses for the fourth class would have a five-minute wait as two tractors with drags fluffed up the footing in the ring.

Pewter observed the young monkey. *"Ugly as a mud fence."*

"Must have slipped her chain." Tucker did think it was funny that Miss Nasty waved her tiny chapeau to the crowd.

Cookie, who knew the monkey only too well, replied, *"Miss Nasty doesn't have anything as common as a chain. She's tied with a silken cord that has a gold lock on the end. She knows how to pick it. And she can pick the lock to her cage, too. Booty should keep her in her cage all the time, but he likes to have her with him. She gets into everything. Once she climbed into a car and started it. I heard she let out his snakes, and some of them are poisonous. No one would go to his house until he found them all."*

"People leave their cars unlocked at shows?" Mrs. Murphy registered surprise.

"No big deal." Cookie nodded.

"If Miss Nasty picks the lock on her silken cord, why doesn't Booty use something stronger?" Pewter wondered.

"Oh, he accuses people of freeing her. He can't face how naughty she is. It's a good thing he can't understand what she says. She should have her mouth washed out with soap." Cookie laid back her ears as Miss Nasty approached, paused to stand up and clap, then waved her hat and put it back on. She dropped to all fours, loping along the top rail again.

"Her dress is fetching." Fair laughed at the pink sundress, which matched her straw hat, a small fake peony attached to the pale green chiffon ribbon.

"She owns an extensive wardrobe." Joan, despite her pin's disappearance, smiled. "When Annie divorced Booty, he acquired the monkey, naming her Miss Nasty in honor of his ex-wife."

"Low blow." Harry giggled.

"Not low enough." Joan's grin widened. "Her dresses and ensembles are copies of Annie's. Annie shopped a lot at Glasscock's, an expensive store in Louisville, so I bet you Booty pays plenty for Miss Nasty's frocks."

"No!" Harry found this delightfully wicked.

"How did he remember what Annie wore?" Fair was puzzled, because he wasn't good at remembering such details.

"Booty is as vain as Charly about clothes. He even remembers things I wore years ago," Joan replied.

"Maybe he's gay." Fair shrugged.

"That is such a stereotype." Harry punched him.

"Booty's not gay, he just likes clothes, fashion. He's got an aesthetic streak. I mean, he wears alligator belts and boots. I expect the belts alone cost three hundred fifty dollars."

"Ex-wife ever see Miss Nasty?" Fair thought that would provoke fireworks.

"She's seen her." Joan's eyes twinkled. "It was not a successful introduction."

"Did they wind up at the same party with the same dress?" Harry laughed.

"In fact, they did. Booty must have called every friend of Annie's he knew to find out what she was wearing. They were in Lexington, and I expect the screams could be heard all the way to Louisville, maybe even down to Memphis. Annie vowed revenge, but only after she'd called Booty every name in the book and some we'd never heard before." Joan paused a beat. "Best party I ever attended."

The laughter drew Miss Nasty to the Kalarama box. She poked her fingers in her various orifices.

"Crude." Pewter wrinkled her black nose.

"Fat." Miss Nasty turned a somersault.

Booty appeared at the in-gate at the other end of the ring from the Kalarama box. Spying his cavorting pet, he hastened toward her. She stopped, stood up as tall as she could. She rubbed her chin.

"Miss Nasty, Daddy's coming," Joan jollied her. "Daddy's wearing a pink shirt to match your pretty dress."

"He'll beat your red ass until your nose bleeds," Pewter, enraged at being called fat, predicted.

Miss Nasty extracted something unpleasant from her nostril, flinging it at Pewter.

The cat lunged forward toward the offending creature, but Miss Nasty leapt off the rail, scurrying toward one of the tractors. Skillfully timing her leap, she landed on the back fender, then reached for the back of the seat and grabbed it to swing onto the driver's shoulders. He swerved but recovered. He knew Miss Nasty, so he made the best of it.

Booty walked inside the ring. He dangled an enticing

piece of orange. At the first pass of the tractor, Miss Nasty was tempted. On the second, Booty turned his back on her to head out of the ring. She succumbed.

Booty swooped her up amid cheers.

"He really is wearing an alligator belt and boots." Harry gasped.

"You can buy me that for my birthday," Fair suggested.

"I think I'd better buy a lottery ticket first." Harry calculated the expense of the boots and belt. Then she saucily said, "My birthday is in five days, but I'll pass on the boots. Pass on the monkey, too."

"I'll kill that monkey," Pewter fumed.

"You say that about everything," the tiger teased.

"I will!"

"You'll have to brave boogers to do it," Mrs. Murphy warned.

"Or worse." Tucker appeared solemn.

"You just wait and see." Pewter ignored the teasing.

Harry dropped back to her hands and knees again, looking on the wooden floor of the box. "I swear I'll find your pin, Joan. You know how I get. Don't despair."